TAKE

by

K.I. Lynn

&

N. Isabelle Blanco

Take

Copyright © K.I. Lynn & N. Isabelle Blanco

This book is a work of fiction. Names, characters, places, and incidents either are products of the author's imagination or are used fictitiously. Any resemblance to actual events or locales or persons, living or dead, is entirely coincidental.

Cover image licensed by shutterstock.com/ © Gabriel Georgescu
Cover design by L.J. Anderson/ Mayhem Cover Creations

Editor
Marti Lynch
Vanessa Bridges - PREMA

Publication Date: January 6, 2016
Genre: FICTION/Romance/New Adult
ISBN-13: 978-0692610312
ISBN-10: 0692610316
Copyright © 2016 K.I. Lynn & N. Isabelle Blanco
All rights reserved

Thank you to all our fans. Your support means so much to us.
As we said in Need, we fucking love all of you.

~K.I. Lynn & N. Isabelle Blanco~

Part 2

"*Heav'n has no Rage, like Love to Hatred turn'd. Nor Hell a Fury, like a Woman scorn'd.*"
- William Congreve

"*And I'm ready to walk through that hell, a thousand times over if necessary. I'll walk through it with no clothes on, let the flames singe every bit of flesh on my body. But I'm fucking getting my girl back, no matter the cost.*" *- Brayden*

-

ONE
BRAYDEN

April 18th, 2015

"Don't you get it? You can make my body come against my will, a thousand times if you want, but that doesn't change anything."

It's only been about an hour since I heard those words, maybe less.

It feels like they've been haunting me a lifetime already.

Or is this merely a taste of what's to come? Is this anger and impotence swirling in my chest just the beginning?

It's funny how a matter of a few minutes can completely change a person's perspective. I was so sure upstairs. Grounded. Cocky, even.

But the words, man. They keep digging deeper and deeper with every minute that passes, burrowing past all of my beliefs. All of my common sense.

That's the power of words, though. Isn't it?

Did she mean them? Was that just her anger talking?

I don't know what would be worse: knowing she meant them, or this sick speculation that twists over and over in my head.

"It's too late, Brayden. Too. Late."

I spent years playing a stupid game, trying to deceive myself. Always convinced that I was ready to let her go. Ready to move on and live without her.

Yet I always knew, didn't I? I always knew I wasn't really letting her go, that I wasn't ready to do so.

That I never would be.

That's why I kept coming back. Living without her isn't a possibility, and subconsciously, in the pit of me where there was actually some truth, I'd known that.

This insane despair crawling up my throat right now, the dark rage that's choking me slowly, one breath at a time at the thought of truly losing her is the final piece of evidence.

I was never going to let her go.

I can't do it, no matter how much she asks me to, especially not now with the certainty infecting every cell in my body.

That's why I'm here, back where I started out the night. Hiding in the shadows at the side of the house, a drink in my hand, my chest in slivers inside my leather jacket. I've probably had four drinks in the last ten minutes alone.

Am I trying to get drunk? Maybe. I shouldn't, but I also can't help but try to chase the feelings away.

I haven't seen Kira again. I'm not sure a part of me wants to just yet. She had every right to slice me up the way she did, every right to continue doing so, but I'm too raw right now to face her.

Too hooked to leave her completely alone.

Even though I'm not staring at her—in fact, I have no clue

where in the house she is right now—this is my way of keeping an eye on her. Making sure this party doesn't get really out of control and she isn't dragged into anything too sordid.

I know what she'd say if she heard my thoughts right now. How she'd throw in my face that, until recently, I was all up in the sordid, partaking like a true hedonist.

The thought actually makes me smile.

She's right. I'm willing to change that now, to be better, for her, but it doesn't change who I've been all these years.

Where I've been and what I've been up to.

That's the real problem, isn't it? Who I've been. It isn't so much a matter of getting Kira to forgive me, it's a matter of getting her to believe I've really changed. For her to believe I don't want anyone but her.

I throw back the rest of my drink and take out my phone. I don't know what I'm hoping for, or why I would even hope for it. After I changed my number for Kira, only she, Ryan, my parents, and a few of my college friends have it.

None of the girls I ever fucked in the past have it. Yeah, I did that shit on purpose. I meant it when I said I was closing that door permanently.

Not seeing a message hits me with disappointment. Especially because, despite all logic, I know what I was hoping for.

Time for another drink.

I retrace the same path I'd taken earlier, heading toward the front of the house. Someone set up a garbage bin right at the end of the path, obviously anticipating that some people would hang out where I'd been.

So far, it's only been me. That I've seen anyway.

I deposit the red Dixie cup in my hand into the bin. One step in the direction of the front door and I see a metallic black BMW peeling down the road. The car turns sharply into the driveway and parks behind another black car.

I'm knotted inside, warped, but even on my best day I wouldn't be able to stand the sight of that car.

The sight of its owner.

How fucking dare he?

I'm down the driveway in the blink of an eye, crossing the distance at top speed.

Austin exits his car, looking all determined and shit.

And what gets to me the most? What has me ready to *undo* him?

It's that determination. The hardcore, no-holds-barred resolve on the guy's face.

I kicked his ass for touching Kira. I made damn sure he knew that was why I was kicking his ass. So he knows why I'm enraged at the sight of him here. Why I'm coming at him the way I am.

The fucker is ready to meet me head on. Ready to take me and all my fury just so he can get close to my girl.

He slams his car door right before I get in his face.

He meets me, and we're nose to nose, chest to chest.

Two men utterly in love with one girl and ready to destroy each other for it.

"What are you doing here?" I ask him slowly, because in the back of my mind I haven't forgotten it's Kira's birthday. I'm giving him a chance to walk the fuck away so I won't have to pummel him into the driveway and ruin Kira's night further.

His jaw hardens. "You really didn't think I'd miss her

eighteenth, did you?"

I read every damn word behind that sentence. I swear to God, the subtext is too clear to ignore. Too blatant for me to stand it.

He came to do the very same thing I came to do now that Kira's eighteen.

Claim her.

Both of my fists curl, tightening so hard I immediately start to lose blood flow.

And I don't care. I don't feel anything but the violent hatred pulsing through my veins. "You need to leave."

He gives me this little sardonic laugh that makes me wonder if he realizes how close to killing him I actually am. "She's eighteen. So what's your excuse now, huh?" He tilts his head, light blue eyes narrowed. "Though that was a weak excuse, man. We both know that doesn't really matter."

Almost as if he's goading me. Pushing my buttons. Looking for a specific response. And, suddenly, I remember something he spat at me the last time we fought, when we'd been rolling around on the ground and going at each other like two wild animals, hit for bloody hit.

"This isn't about her being seventeen and you know it."

I narrow my eyes right back at him, exhaling as slow as I can, trying to keep it together.

But a part of me wants to lay it all out in the open. Make him understand just how I feel about Kira.

How fucking far I'll go to keep any man—especially *him*— away from her.

"I'm never going to forget how you took advantage of her, you fucking piece of shit."

He throws his head back and barks out a laugh, and that's

when I realize his fists are clenched, ready to start breaking bones.

Just like mine fucking are.

"I didn't take advantage of shit, Brayden. She. Came. After. *Me*."

This motherfucking, good-for-nothing, pile of . . .

The image burns straight through my synapses, branding itself, adding to an already overbearing torment. All I see is Kira, searching him out, offering herself to him.

Him happily taking . . .

I don't realize I've begun to pull my fist back until I hear my name being screamed behind me.

"Brayden! No! Stop!"

I jerk to a stop.

So does Austin.

Fucking hell. I won't rest, I won't stop, I don't think I'll even fucking sleep until I've broken every bone on his face.

"Brayden!" Kira's little heels click on the driveway as she gets closer. And then she's right there, maneuvering between us, her hands landing on my chest as she starts to push me back away from Austin.

The man she fucked.

The man she keeps claiming she wants to try and be with.

Her lips are still swollen from my kisses. Her hair remains a mess. The lights illuminate her hazel eyes. Her face.

She's so damn gorgeous. All I want to do is wrap my arms around her. Hug her tight and breathe her in.

"Don't do this," she pleads in a low voice.

I'm letting her push me back, letting her stop me from doing the one thing I want to do more than anything. The one thing that's my right to do considering she's mine.

6

"I'm not." My voice is shot to shit. Low enough so only she hears it. "Look." I hold my arms out away from myself, motioning with my head down my body, drawing her attention to the fact that she's in control right now.

She blinks, surprised, then looks down at where her hands are braced, right above my raging heart. Then she looks at the ground and the distance she's put between me and Austin.

Her head turns in his direction and the apologetic look she gives him annihilates something inside me.

She faces me again, her expression hard, not at all soft like it'd been when she looked at him. "I asked him to come tonight. It's my birthday. Don't ruin it for me anymore than you already have."

If she'd taken a knife and shoved it right in my chest, it would've hurt a lot less than hearing those words from her. "Is that what you want?" I hiss, fists clenched again as I fight the primal beating of every male instinct in my body. Will she ever know how much this is costing me right now? How hard it is not to grab her?

Is she aware that her hands are still on my chest, as if she can't let go, despite what she's saying?

"You want him here instead of me?" The words are nothing more than a whisper, meant only for her to hear, but that doesn't mean I don't hear the hurt behind them.

That she doesn't.

Her eyelashes flutter, and she blinks up at me, surprised, like it's fucking mind blowing that I'm aching over her right now.

Was I really that good all these years? I somehow managed to convince her I didn't care this much?

7

"I . . . I . . ."

"Say it, Kira." I lower my head just an inch, dying to lower it the rest of the way, to feel those pouty lips. To claim them in front of Austin. But I don't. For her, I hold back, forcing myself to keep an appropriate distance, to only stare into her eyes. "Tell me you want him here instead of me."

Her fingers flex on my pecs, and I can sense how hard it is for her not to grab onto me right now. "Will you actually leave without a fight if I do?" Her eyes flash as she waits for my answer.

A challenge.

I swallow back every selfish demand that my mind, heart, and body shout out, and nod at her. "If that's what you want . . ."

We stare each other, and I can't make out what I see in her eyes, but I do see one thing loud and clear.

She's struggling.

Her chest shakes with her next breath, and even after her lips part, it takes her a few seconds to get the words out. "I . . . yeah. Go. I asked him to be here tonight."

Holy fuck, this girl actually has me close to crying. "You asked him. But you didn't say it. Do you want him here instead of me?"

Her stubborn little chin rises. I almost expect her to say it and I brace myself for the impact.

She doesn't.

And in the silence that follows, somehow we end up an inch closer, and I have no clue if I made the move, or if she did.

We're panting, breath for fucking breath, our bodies more in sync than they've ever been. I realize this, and with that realization comes a spark of hope. Hope that what's between us will help her make the right choice.

That right here, right now, in this fucked-up moment, she's feeling *me*, and that she gets the pain eating at my insides.

"I want him here instead of you," she whispers out of nowhere, so low I almost lie to myself and tell myself I didn't hear her. Her eyes won't meet mine.

"W-what?"

Kira swallows, and I think I see tears swimming in her eyes, but then she blinks and they're gone. "You heard me. He stays. I want you to go."

I can't remember anyone ever fucking up my head as much as my parents' fighting had, but this moment right here, if I can't fix it, if there's no bouncing back for us, will be one that I never forget.

The girl I love just chose another man over me.

She wants him here on her eighteenth birthday instead of me.

She gave him her virginity instead of me.

I deserved all of that; it won't matter in the long run. If I can't win her back, this night will fuck with my head for the rest of my life, ruining any chance of me loving any other girl ever again.

She's destroying me.

The fucked-up part? She has every right to do so.

And I love her, so I'll give her that.

I jerk away from her, and her hands drop to her sides. I don't miss seeing her clench them.

I wish that were enough to ease the howling inside me. I really do. It might be hard for her to let me go, but she's still choosing to do so, and she's choosing to do it over him.

9

Will she let him touch her tonight once I'm gone? Make love to her?

I stop that train of thought before I lose it all and say fuck it as I storm around her and head back to destroy Austin.

"Enjoy the rest of your birthday," I tell her. The sad thing is, I really do mean it, and I know she can hear that.

Her mouth falls open and a stricken look crosses her face for a moment.

Then, just like that last beautiful softening of her guard, it's gone with a blink.

Christ. I've done a million hard things when it comes to this girl, but this one takes the cake.

I'm tempted to jog down the driveway because it'll get me out of there faster, but I refuse to look like I'm running away in front of Austin. Stepping up to Kira, I pause long enough to lean down and place a quick kiss on her forehead.

It isn't quick, though. My lips refuse to leave her skin, and my eyes slide closed as I take in the scent of her, like a man starved. She doesn't acknowledge my kiss, nor does she move away. Eventually, common sense returns, and when I open my eyes and move away from her, that bastard Austin is there, staring at us.

His eyes are calculating. Full of conclusions.

I should try to do something to dispel them, shouldn't I?

But I don't. I'm already giving him and Kira more than I can bear tonight. I won't give that up also. It's the only claim I've been able to lay on her, no matter how small or disastrous, and I'm not taking it back.

Quick steps take me down the driveway to where my car's parked. Once in the driver's seat, I catch sight of Kira and Austin standing in the driveway. He's moving closer to her.

Her eyes are still on me.

But she asked me to go, so I'll go.

Turning the ignition, I peel out of the driveway and down the block in less than five seconds, gunning it with all the speed the car has.

Still not enough. I still feel her.

It's always been like that, hasn't it? No matter how far I fucking go, I always feel her.

And now she's with him. Will be with him for the rest of the night.

Goddamn it, what the hell am I going to do? How the hell am I supposed to get through tonight?

On the way back to the hotel, I veer off the road and into the parking lot of a liquor store with the intention of buying every damn bottle they have in stock.

Kira

I watch him leave, and it's the very last thing I expected him to do. I asked him to. He told me he would if I asked, but . . .

"Kira, are you okay?" Austin asks me, coming closer.

I can't take my eyes off Brayden, even as he starts the car and speeds off . . .

"Kira?"

"Huh?" I shake my head, trying to focus on Austin.

My eyes are still locked on the road, even though Brayden turned the corner and is long gone.

"Kira, babe, you wanna go inside and relax for a bit?" Austin's hand lands on my arm.

I can't stop thinking about the look on Brayden's face.
Can't stop thinking about him, period.
He left. He actually left because I asked him to.
So why do I feel so wrong about it?

TWO
BRAYDEN

"What the fuck do you mean you left her with Austin?"

I don't pull the phone away from my ear, even though Ryan's yell is loud enough to pierce my eardrum. Sitting on the loveseat in the hotel room, I stare blankly at the wall, holding my phone with one hand, a bottle of Lagavulin in the other.

There's another two bottles waiting at my feet. Just in case. I threw down more than three hundred dollars on all three bottles, but considering how this specific type of scotch always lays me out on my ass, I consider it money well spent.

Tipping the bottle, I take another swig. "I had no choice, Ryan." Shit. I sound as defeated as I feel.

As drunk as I'm starting to get, too.

"What the hell do you mean you had no choice?" Ryan yells. There's a soft feminine voice in the background, soothing him, telling him to relax.

He's with Dana. Sure, I dropped him off at her place, but

13

it's still a new concept—Ryan with a girlfriend.

I'm here, in this hotel room, with nothing but this rage and agony pulsing through me.

I'm happy for him—he finally got his girl. I really am. Still hurts, though.

He didn't hurt her as much as I've hurt Kira.

Is she busy trying to forget me? Trying to hurt me some more? Is she allowing Austin to do every single goddamned thing I'd kill to do to her?

Another swig.

"Answer me, Brayden."

"She asked me to," I whisper, and another gulp burns its way down my throat. My stomach turns, almost rejecting it. I'm drinking too much, too fast.

Let me get sick. Don't care. It sure as shit can't feel worse than I feel right now.

"And that's enough of a reason for you to just leave him there?"

"She has so many reasons to hate me already . . . she looked so sad. There were tears in her eyes. She asked me not to ruin her birthday any more." I hear myself uttering the words as if from afar, lost in the twisting labyrinth of misery in my head.

I'm so fucked up over this girl. I shouldn't be. I should have never allowed any woman to have this much power over me.

Hah! *Allow*. As if I ever truly had a choice.

Ryan is silent and I hear Dana speaking to him in the background. From the little bits I manage to pick up, I can tell she's now fully in on what's going on. That she's giving him advice.

Sounds like she's telling him to side with me, to understand. That I have a point.

If I wasn't so utterly morbid right now, I might be able to smile at that.

Ryan sighs. "I don't like him near her."

I throw my head back and laugh bitterly at that statement. There's no need for me to even tell him what that laugh means; he knows.

"Shit. My bad, bro. I keep forgetting this is probably harder for you than me."

The bottle is raised to my lips again. I'm halfway through it by now, can feel the alcohol starting to hit. The numbing buzz taking over.

It's not anesthesia. Nowhere near close. Nothing short of that will dull the pain I'm starting to realize.

"Maybe I should just head over to the party," he says.

"She'll end up hating you, too." It's true. We've both gone about this the wrong way, no matter how entitled we are. Kira is a woman, with her own free will. With her own right to decide what's best for her—what's going to help her forget the pain I caused her. Help her be happy again.

Us getting in the way of that only hurts her more.

But, *fuck*, I just wish to high hell it wouldn't have been Austin.

"So what the hell are you going to do?"

"I have no fucking clue," I grit out.

"Are you giving up?"

I stare down at the hazel eyes of the kitty tattoo on my wrist. "I think she wants me to."

"Can you?"

The answer to that is easy. "I don't think so." But that's not where it ends. Suddenly, it's all bursting out of me, like a flood, unstoppable. Destructive. "What does it matter,

15

though? I gave her every reason to hate me—"

"She doesn't hate you, Brayden."

I laugh again at his statement. "You didn't see her eyes tonight. She does. And I don't blame her. I never will. I can't force her to believe that I love her. Won't matter if she does if she can never forget everything I did to her. I'd hate me, too, if I were her."

His frustrated exhale comes over the phone. "Even if she does hate you, you do know what that means, right?"

I fall silent at his question, confused.

"It means she still loves you. You can't hate something you don't care about. Think of your dad."

That is the very *last* person I want to think about right now. That wound needs to remain tightly sealed, thank you very much. I'm already bleeding internally over Kira. I don't need to add whatever sick emotions my father has caused into the mix.

"I know it's hard to think about it right now—"

"Stop psychoanalyzing me."

"*Somebody* has to, because it sounds to me like you're letting yourself get caught up in the pain and you're not thinking clearly."

"What the hell do you want me to say?" I shift in the seat, too worked up, too raw to take this. He's adding to my frustration, poking at an already irritated weakness, and I don't know how long I can hold out without snapping at him. "Your sister told me it's over. Done. She told me there's no hope, pretty much let me know that no matter what I do, I'll never be able to fix it. *Then* she told me to leave and that she wanted Austin there instead of me!" The last part leaves me on a roar, and the still half-full bottle goes flying out of my hand, shattering against the wall.

Immediately, I'm reaching for one of the others at my feet, ready to open it—

"Brayden, are you drinking?"

Sighing, I leave the bottle on the ground.

"Stop for a second and hear me out."

"Your girl's not with another man, doing God knows what with him," I murmur angrily, my fingers twitching listlessly. I need something in them—a bottle back in my hand.

No, what I actually need is Kira, her soft skin beneath my fingertips, her pretty eyes staring up at me like they once used to. Like she adored and admired me.

Like she couldn't imagine a life without me.

"Not right now, no, but it did happen."

I snap to attention at Ryan's comment. "What?"

"What do you think got my ass in gear? She got sick of waiting for me, started moving on with her life."

Man, I realize, there's really so much about what went down between him and Dana that I've been clueless about. That he hasn't told me. In the back of my head, I wonder why he never did, but I also can't fault him for it. It's not like I'd given him a front-row seat to what happened between me and his sister.

Yeah, partially because she is his sister, but it was also too weird to give him the 4-1-1 on how messed up a girl had me.

"How did you deal with it?" It's not like I'd seen him stumbling all over the place, drunk off his ass like I'm getting now.

Wait. I had seen him like that. But we'd been partying together.

"Exactly as you're dealing with it now," he tells me,

17

confirming my suspicions.

Suddenly, I feel like an even bigger piece of shit as I realize what a "great" friend I've been.

I wasn't there for him. Okay, I didn't know, but I could have paid more attention, maybe seen some signs that would have helped me know he wasn't doing so well.

"But Dana forgave you."

"Eventually."

"Didn't take too long from my point of view."

"I also didn't fuck up nearly half as long or half as bad as you have, you stubborn fuck."

I sink lower on the loveseat. The self-hate is a hurricane rolling in my chest. Deadly. Growing deadlier by the second.

In desperate need of an outlet.

Trapped.

"Like I told you. It's hopeless—"

"You're really starting to convince me that you're ready to give up on her."

I do the smart thing and shut the fuck up.

"Hear me out before I also decide that it's time for you to give up."

Lips pressed together, I remain quiet, my hand itching to reach for one of the bottles.

"How far are you willing to go to get her back?"

"It's not a question of how far. It's a question of *if* she'll ever—"

He interrupts me again. "How. Far?"

"Anything." The word leaves me as a whisper, but that doesn't make it any less true.

"So stop being a bitch about it and deal."

"Excuse me?"

"You heard me. You don't need to be getting drunk right now. You need to fucking sleep, formulate a plan. Convince yourself that it's gonna keep hurting and keep freaking going."

This wise motherfucker, I swear to God. The stubborn side of me wants to contradict him, argue some more, but what's the point? He's right.

Sighing, I get off the loveseat.

"Did you hear me?"

"I'm on my way to get some water."

He's silent for a few seconds. Then, "Good boy."

"Fuck you, dude."

Ryan laughs, and my lips twitch despite themselves.

"I know you love her, bro. This right here is convincing me, although it was pretty obvious. Unfortunately, I'm not the one you hurt, and Kira is still more stubborn than I am no matter what she says. She may even be more stubborn than you."

"Hah. If only she heard you."

"It's true."

I pour myself a glass and throw it back, refilling another right away. It's going to take a shitload of water to start negating any possibility of a hangover tomorrow. I don't feel that drunk, but I also know that there's still more alcohol being processed in my system. Not all of it has hit me yet.

On that note, I need to order some room service. Get some food in me.

"What do you suggest I do?" I ask Ryan, because aside from being ready to go for tomorrow, I have no real plan.

He pulls the phone away from his ear, and I hear him talking to Dana again. "Dana says she knows the sister of one of

Kira's friends."

I perk up like a goddamn dog at the sound of that, ears twitching and everything. An in? An honest, serious in? "Which one?"

"Jenna. Dana is going to try to figure out their plans from now on, and I'll be able to let you know."

Swear to God, I feel like fist-pumping the air.

"Just keep taking those hits, Brayden. You're not going to convince my sister any other way. And if she truly is with Austin—"

"I'm fucking taking her from him," I say, my resolve returning on a rush. Hell, yeah, I am. Ryan's right. I let myself sink into the pain of it. Didn't pay attention to the other signs.

There really were tears in her eyes.

She could barely bring herself to say she wanted him instead of me.

She watched me the entire time as I pulled away from the house, even as he walked closer to her.

There's still something there, and I'll be damned if I don't keep pushing. Take advantage.

"Can Dana try to find out what their plans are for tomorrow?"

"She's texting Jenna's sister now."

It's wrong on so many levels. Devious as fuck, too.

Kira's going to kill every single one of us if she ever finds out.

"Tell your girl I said thanks, man. Seriously."

"She says you're welcome but she's really doing this so I don't have to deal with your moody ass all the time."

I laugh at that. I haven't had much time to get to know

Dana, but she's starting to seem real fucking cool. "You too. Thank you."

Ryan sighs. "I'm doing it for her as much as I'm doing it for you. And because if Austin somehow ends up as my brother-in-law in the future, I think I'm going to kill someone."

I almost hiss like a snake at that comment. A straight-up cobra. "Dude, what the fuck is it with you and marriage?" But I'm fixated on that comment. He'd kill someone? I'd torture and skin them alive if something like that were to happen.

"Just stating the obvious."

"Does Dana know you're this obsessed with marriage?"

"Fuck you."

Ah, sweet payback. I laugh again, my chest feeling so freaking light it's almost disgusting. Then again, that's what makes him my best friend, isn't it? The fuck has always been good at picking me up when I fall.

"Dana got a reply. The girls are going shopping tomorrow at Kenwood."

She couldn't get me an exact time without looking too suspicious, but fuck it. I'll wait all day there if I have to. I thank them again and rush to get him off the phone. Almost tripping to the room's phone, I pick up the receiver and order enough food to feed a dozen people.

Gotta make sure I'm good to go bright and fucking early tomorrow.

As I wait for the room service, I sit on the bed and pull up Facebook on my phone. I'm a glutton for punishment, I know, but this is more necessary to me than even the food.

Kira's status reads: *Thank you so much to everyone that wished me a happy birthday and came over to rock it with*

me. Party was effing awesome! So done though.
#DyingToSleep

It's only 1:30am. The party is over already? Did she end it? Kick everyone out?

Is she alone, or is Austin with her?

The thought is like venom flashing through my system. I close my eyes and push all of it to the back of my head.

I'm not going to say it doesn't matter if she's with Austin or not, *because it fucking does.* It matters more than anything.

It won't be the end of us. She can be with him as much as she wants, as many times as she wants. The outcome of all this will still be the same.

I'm going to fucking kill him for it.

But not before I take her back.

THREE

Kira

April 19th, 2015

Challenge. A word with many definitions, most of them meaning the same thing. One of the main definitions? A task or situation that tests someone's abilities. In other words: the kind of dare the human ego cannot refuse.

That's what I've become to Brayden. I'm convinced.

But why? He can't brag to anyone once he sleeps with me. Can't go around town saying that he, too, got a piece of Kira. Unlike Austin, Brayden's my stepbrother, so even if something were to happen between us—more than already has—who the hell would his ego show it off to?

No one, that's who. So why, damn it? Why won't he leave me alone?

"I hate you!"

"And I fucking love you."

I slam my eyes closed and shake my head, as if doing so will actually dispel the memory of those words. I probably look like a crazy person standing here, in the middle of

23

Victoria's Secret, holding one of their huge black shopping bags, eyes shut and head shaking like I'm trying to invoke Jesus himself.

Funny thing is, I *am* a crazy person. Absolutely one step away from a total breakdown. That's how I feel after hearing those words from him.

My heart twists viciously inside my chest.

I ignore it.

Opening my eyes, I focus on the lacy cream and black bra in front of me.

My phone buzzes in my back pocket.

Eyes glued on the lingerie before me, I bring it out and unlock the screen. I read the text before I realize who it's from.

If you're going to buy that, I must BEG you to let me see you in it.

Son of a . . .

I whirl around right as Brayden comes to a stop in front of me.

He slips his hands into his pockets and gives me this wide, blissed-out smile. He stands there in his dark, low-slung jeans and dark blue T-shirt, the material stretched tight across his chest and shoulders.

On his neck, there's this dark purple bruise.

A clear imprint of teeth.

He's not even trying to hide the mark I left on him.

I hate him. "Why the hell are you smiling?"

There's only one iced coffee in my system. Maybe two hours of sleep.

Austin tried to kiss me last night.

What did I do in response?

I turned my head and asked him to leave. *After* he spent almost half an hour hugging me, trying to cheer me up because this asshole over here ruined my birthday.

So yeah, I'm cranky.

And Brayden's still smiling at me like the mere sight of me makes him ecstatic.

He doesn't answer my question.

I raise my eyebrows and shake my head in a *"well?"* gesture.

Brayden steps up to me. He tucks my hair behind my ear and leans down to kiss my cheek. "Hey, baby."

Gah!

My toes curl inside my flats.

Fucking traitors.

I reach behind me for the bra I'd been staring at, fling it in his face, and walk away. Because I'm the queen of maturity today.

My heart races the whole time.

I don't expect a bra to the face to deter him, so when he catches up to me, all I do is roll my eyes and make a sharp left.

Maybe if I ignore him, he'll eventually go off and find another girl to flirt with.

Somewhere beyond my bitterness and cynicism, I know he's not going to do that, and the thought alone is enough to give me pause.

He catches up to me and throws the bra into my shopping bag.

I scowl at him. "How do you even know if it'll fit me, dumbass?"

His eyes drop to my chest. Their emerald shade darkens and flash with a bodily hunger.

Right on cue, my nipples perk up.

Running his thumb along his bottom lip, he murmurs hotly, "Kira, I *know* those tits."

"You've barely seen or touched them," I snap. Oh God, why did I say that?

His eyes darken even more. "Trust me, baby. The sight and feel of them is etched into my mind."

My nipples tighten to the smallest points possible, straining toward him. I can almost hear the little fuckers begging for *him, him, him*!

I take a step back, honest-to-God frightened and too weak to sift through the lust and pain I feel.

"Kira, oh my God look at the size of this thong, girl . . . never mind. Look at the size of all that man meat. Hello, there."

Marilyn.

"Yo, Lyn! Let me see that—Jesus-fucking-Christ." Insert low melodramatic gasp that isn't really that low to begin with. "It's Brayden Hunt."

Ashley.

"Well, hello, big, sexy, and yummy. Kira, introduce us to your hot-as-hell stepbrother," Jenna says.

I want to kill them all. My only friends. Just because they're drooling over Brayden.

"Not now," I tell them, struggling to hide how annoyed I am. Not stopping to analyze the impulse, I walk up to Brayden and tug on his sleeve to get him away from them.

He doesn't budge.

"Besides—" I tug some more "—he'd try to flirt with all three of you at once. Total sleaze like that."

"We wouldn't mind," they answer as one.

The vein in my temple almost pops.

Are they fucking serious right now?

Of course they are. It seems that almost every living, breathing female wants a taste of Brayden Hunt.

I renew my efforts to pull him away from my friends before they get any more ideas.

"Sorry, ladies," Brayden says, finally walking backward as I continue to pull on his sleeve. "I'm a one-woman man now, and that's not going to ever change."

What he just said doesn't register until we're by the dressing rooms.

I let him go as if burned.

My heartbeat's in my throat, choking me . . .

His smile is so wide now—the epitome of cockiness—and I just want to smack him across the face with my shopping bag. "*What*?"

Back into his pockets his hands go, and . . . is he rocking back and forth on his feet like an excited kid?

He is! This motherfucker is downright giddy.

"What?" I ask again.

"Nothing, baby."

"Stop. Calling. Me. That!"

That smile remains fixed firmly on his face.

I shove him away. "You can go now."

Brayden grabs my hand.

Gasping under my breath at the way my entire body heats up, I rip my hand out of his grasp. My mind twists and twists, spiraling into the memories of last night.

Him, on his knees, his mouth on my aching cunt, licking me until I had no choice but to come on his tongue.

Him telling me that he loves me.

"No. We're spending the whole day together." He shrugs like it's no big deal.

"You can't. I'm hanging with my friends today." Must get away. Must get away.

"I'll tag along."

"The hell you will. You can't."

"Sure I can."

Desperate for an escape, I look around.

The dressing rooms. No way dipshit can follow me in there, and even if he waits for me, I'll have a few solid minutes to regain some control. To remind myself why I can't want him the way I do.

Because years of constantly reminding myself have worked out really well for me so far. Right.

Still, I bolt straight into the dressing room. There's no one back here to count how many items I'm trying on.

Fuck it.

I dart behind a curtain all the way at the end, panting.

I'm alone. Thank God. Unfortunately all the privacy in the world can't erase the images in my head.

Or the hungry pounding of my pussy.

Or the fact that there's no way I can try on any of the panties I picked out. I'm fucking soaked, thanks to that asshole.

I grind my teeth, infuriated by the never-ending lack of control—

A head of black hair appears above the curtain.

Then a face.

"Are you fucking kidding me?" I hiss, glaring up at him.

He's so tall that he has no problem looking into the stall and smiling down at me. "You look fucking adorable when you're angry. You know that?" The curtain starts to move.

I snatch it out of his hand. "You've been telling me that since we were kids. It's still not a free pass to piss me off all the damn time!" Too late I realize what I've admitted, the memories it dredges up.

Any wider and that smile is going to burst open his face.

One could only wish.

"You need to get out before someone sees you," I say, holding the curtain in place.

He pulls on it lightly, his eyes dropping to my chest. "A chance I'm willing to take. Let me see you try on that bra."

How can a request like that make my clit literally tremble as if stroked?

"What on earth makes you think I would do that?"

Molten eyes meet mine, focused. Intense. I feel like I'm being eaten alive by that stare. "Because you *want* me to see you in all that lingerie, Kira," he rasps.

My mouth goes dry. "Idiot, you're my stepbrother. What if one of my friends come back here and see you standing there like a psycho?"

"Willing to risk it."

Staring up at the ceiling, I wonder what the fuck I ever did to deserve any of this. Even worse, his obnoxious, demanding way of flirting is getting to me. All I feel is that yawning chasm of hunger for him, the soul-deep ache that wants to connect with his body.

No, not "connect." *Fuck.* It always comes down to the sex with him. I refuse to attach feelings to it any longer. I'm just horny for him and frustrated because I can't have him.

Nothing more.

Annoyed, I yank open the curtain.

And come face to face with that massive chest. "Excuse me."

He doesn't move.

Not surprising.

"Brayden."

His hand shoots up, cupping my jaw. His thumb skims along my bottom lip, parting my mouth open slowly. The look in his eyes makes me tremble harder.

"Fuck, baby. You're practically vibrating for what I'm dying to give you."

I can't help but moan quietly at his statement. Miserable due to my weakness, I jerk my face out of his grasp. "Please move."

With a low sigh, he does.

Another pause on my part, and I'm reminded of last night again. I'm used to Brayden doing what he wants, whenever he wants. Him actually acquiescing to a request of mine is utterly new to me.

I blink up at him, taken aback.

He glowers at me.

I wonder . . . biting the corner of my lip, I decide to give it a shot. "You can go now."

"You're pushing it, baby," he says, eyes on my mouth.

Fuck me. I swallow hard. "I want you to leave."

"I already gave you that last night. Today? I'm sticking around. For a little while, at least."

So much for acquiescence. "Brayden, I can't afford to argue with you about this with my friends around."

"Then don't."

I resist the urge to jam one of the hangers into his eye. Regardless of my feelings toward him, it really is a very pretty eye. "What can I say to get you to leave me alone?"

Brayden gives me a sheepish smile and shrugs. "Absolutely nothing. Short of forgiving me and admitting you're mine, of course."

"I'd be lying if I said any of that." I stomp out of the stall. I'm almost at the entrance to the dressing rooms when it occurs to me. "You can't exit at the same time as I do. What if my friends see you?" There's no plausible way to explain why my stepbrother is in the dressing room with me.

I won't lie; I'm also hoping to use the opportunity to lose him.

"I'll wait, but don't think I won't find you if you try to run out of here."

Turning, I glare at him.

He lifts an eyebrow. "I know you. No running, baby."

"Damn you. Stop calling me baby!"

The other eyebrow joins the first. He stares at me as if he knows why it drives me crazy when he calls me that, what it does to me.

He makes me feel powerless. Like I have no choice in this attraction, and I hate him for it.

But I have no plans of ever fucking him, not any more, and fucking him was the only thing I would've risked discovery for.

That and being his girl.

A discarded, stupid dream.

I will not face an entire town's censure for nothing more than an inconvenient distraction and a few moments of lapsed judgement. That means I've somehow have to convince this stubborn fuck to behave so that no one suspects what's going on between us.

Which also means I'm stuck with him until I can persuade him to leave.

"You're a ruthless bastard," I grumble.

"Only when it comes to the woman I love."

My brittle heart threatens to crack. "Whatever. Just wait here until it's safe to leave." I hightail it out of the dressing room, looking left and right like a guilty bitch.

Which I am. A guilty bitch who had just been entertaining the idea of letting her stepbrother eat her out inside that dressing room.

Ashley spots me from the line and calls me over.

Schooling my facial expression, I join the girls in the line.

"Did everything fit?" Ashley asks me.

I nod. A nonverbal lie.

Great. Looks like I'm buying the bra Brayden picked out for me.

"Where's that hot piece of man meat you have for a stepbrother?" Jenna looks around, clearly trying to spot Brayden.

Unwarranted rage ignites in me. "You do realize he's the biggest whore in town, right? And, hopefully, he broke his leg somewhere and won't be joining us."

Marilyn smiles. "You guys seem to act like you're really brother and sister. It's adorable."

This horrifies me. More than it should. I don't want to be seen as a girl interested in Brayden; the thought of us coming across as brother and sister makes me downright sick.

I'm such a mess.

A warm, muscular arm drapes over my shoulders. I know who it is without looking.

"Kira only pretends to hate me," Brayden says. I can hear the smile in his voice.

"This is a filthy lie." I elbow him in the side. He, of course, doesn't let me go. "I despise you, and you know it."

"Kira's full of it. She loves me." He smiles at my friends.

They melt in unison.

I hate them all.

Especially Brayden for that lie he just said. It's impossible. Who would be foolish enough to love someone who has hurt them so much?

One of the girls at the register calls next. I rush forward, out of his hold, and hand her my items.

Brayden stops next to me and hands her his card.

What the hell?

Is he stupid?

I open my mouth to protest.

His eyes flicker in my direction. "Fight me over this baby, and I'll kiss you. Right here, in front of everyone."

I believe him. I really do.

And I'm absolutely disgusted with myself because I'm getting wetter with each "baby" he throws my way. "You wouldn't," I whisper, calling his bluff.

He licks his bottom lip. "Try me."

The self-disgust expands at the impulse I have to *try* him. Definitely no doubt that he means it. For some reason, he's become even more amoral than before. When it comes to me, a part of him really doesn't care what everyone would think of him. He doesn't care if they judge him for wanting his stepsister.

Silently seething, I watch as the cashier uses his card to ring up my lingerie purchases.

I now own sexy bras and panties that Brayden bought me.

Unfortunately, I'm not the only one watching. The girls are too.

Can they tell why he's buying me these things? That he wants to see me wearing them?

Is it obvious that I'm aching, my clit needy and swollen because *he's* the one paying for my lingerie?

I'm breathless the entire way out of Victoria's Secret, and Brayden watches me, as if he knows why I'm having a hard time breathing.

"Cheesecake Factory, guys. I'm fucking starving." Marilyn walks ahead of us, her blond ponytail bouncing behind her.

My way out. "Well, Brayden. It's been real. Thanks for the—"

That damn arm drapes over my shoulders again. "I'm pretty hungry, too. Cheesecake Factory sounds perfect."

Jenna and Ashley stare at us.

I fight to keep my face from turning red.

Thankfully, Brayden has the common sense to get his arm off me.

"You can't go find somewhere else to eat while I hang out with my friends?"

"Nope. Plus, the girls don't mind. Do you, girls?"

"Of course we don't mind," the trained little monkeys sing.

Of course they don't.

Jenna turns, walking backwards, brown eyes fucking Brayden up and down. "You can tag along whenever you want."

FOUR

Kira

I stew in an unnerving fury as we walk to the restaurant.

Jenna doesn't know I'm attracted to him, what I once felt for him, I remind myself. Yes, I want to freaking kill her, but she's like this with all hot men. Always has been.

All my friends are shameless when it comes to sexy men. It's to be expected that Marilyn and her twin Ashley keep sneaking horny glances at Brayden also.

Doesn't matter that I know all this, how I try to rationalize it. By the time we're in the Cheesecake Factory, my mood is beyond foul. A hostess leads us through the dimly lit restaurant toward a booth.

I stop in my tracks, fully expecting my friends to go at it, battling for the right to sit next to Brayden.

They all cram into one side of the booth, talking and giggling.

They left the other side empty for just me.

And Brayden.

That's when panic hits. *Oh no . . .*

"You have to go," I tell Brayden in a rush. They're going to interrogate me once he leaves, and I'll have to come up with believable lies and do so fast, but the sooner he leaves the better.

The sooner he leaves, the sooner they stop jumping to more conclusions.

Brayden pauses in the middle of reading something on his phone. Scowling, he puts it in his pocket. "Tough luck. I'm not going anywhere."

What is he so mad at? "I'm serious, Brayden. I think my friends suspect something. I *know* them."

"Tough. Luck." He grabs my arm, practically forcing me to the booth, staring all around the restaurant with that expression that promises a beatdown.

Who is he looking for?

I want to bash him over the head for not taking me seriously. Not that I can. All I can do is slide into the booth, guilt and panic suffocating me.

The girls purposely sat together, leaving me no choice but to sit next to Brayden. If any of them had really wanted him the way they'd seemed to, it would've been Battle Royale among them to get to sit next to him. There's no doubt in my mind they suspect who Brayden is to me.

The guy who destroyed me months ago.

He slides in next to me, leaving a foot of space between us. His eyes continue to flicker around the restaurant.

Ashley's twinkling blue eyes focus on me.

I get busy studying the menu, making sure to keep my eyes away from Brayden.

Deja vu hits.

The last time I was in a restaurant with Brayden, in an eerily similar situation, I ended up getting fingered under the table.

Then, I was eaten out inside a bathroom stall.

Right before he rocked his huge cock against my pussy and I felt it coming in my hands.

God help me.

Arousal slaps me, gaining force. I cross my legs, my pussy throbbing between them. I can't have him near me. I just can't.

A waiter comes to take our orders.

When it's my turn, I can't find the strength to speak. Brayden's at least nice enough to order something for me— the same thing he's having, but really, at this point I don't care.

I don't need food. I need distance from him. Space. He's affording me neither. Yes, there's at least a foot between his body and mine, but just having him in the same room drives me nuts.

Brayden's large hand lands on my knee.

I choke back a gasp. No, not again.

Please, don't do this to me . . .

"Move over, I have to go to the bathroom," Jenna tells Ashley and Marilyn.

"Actually, me too." Marilyn stands.

Ashley follows her out of the booth. "I'll go with you guys."

Panicked, I open my mouth—

Brayden's hand slides up, cupping my pussy over the thin, loose genie pants I'm wearing.

Silencing me.

The girls abandon me, without so much as a "we'll be back."

"Let go of me," I say under my breath.

Brayden turns his head in my direction. The way he stares at me heats me up all over.

I look away.

He rubs his fingers into my clit. "Look at me, baby."

I bite down on my lip, trying to shift away. "B-Brayden. Stop. *Please.*"

Sucking on his bottom lip, he rubs my clit again, soft circles that almost make me levitate off my damn seat. "You need to come, Kitty. Let me give it to you. I'm dying for it."

"St-stop. People . . . my friends."

"I'm keeping an eye out. Don't worry about that. Just feel me."

I do. I feel what he's doing to me everywhere, each light stroke driving me crazier. Pressing my legs together does nothing but trap his hand there, right up against my aching core.

The pleasure spikes. My hips rock into his hand. I'm too hungry to fight this. The desperation claws at my soul, ripping my resolve from me.

Brayden grabs my hand and pulls it under his arm, laying it over his lap.

One feel of him, rock-hard, the fleshy tip twitching under dark blue denim—I fall into his side, shaking. My hand clenches around him.

I want it.

Fuck, I haven't had it yet, and it feels like I *live* for that dick.

He groans deep in his chest, the sound pure gravel.

My eyes lock on the side of his neck, on the clear imprint of teeth. My teeth. I bit own on that spot last night, marked him as mine.

I want to give him more.

Want to bite that big, hard body everywhere.

I want to sink my teeth into him while the huge length in my hand pounds into my pussy.

My hand squeezes him, sliding up and down, loving the feel of him.

"Fuck, Kitty. Wait," he whispers in a wild tone; I look at him. He's staring straight ahead, his expression neutral, but his eyes are unfocused with lust. The veins on his thick neck bulge, the skin bright red. "Baby, stop. I'm going to lose control." He tries to pry my hand away from his dick.

I refuse to let him. His fingers are still playing with my clit, making it throb harder. "No. Give this to me."

He hisses at my words. "It's yours. Whenever you want it."

I want it *now*. I want him to drag me off somewhere and slide it into me. Give it to me rough and raw so I can finally fucking forget him.

"Baby, you have to let me go," Brayden pleads quietly.

I love this. Love having him under my control, his sanity shredding apart bit by bit *because* of me.

In other words: I love knowing I can do to him what he does to me.

Hiding my face behind his shoulder, I moan. "Brayden, it's . . . God, I'm going to . . ."

"I will too if you don't let me go, and I won't be able to control it. Kitty, you have to let me go."

All his urgent tone does is turn me on more. "I want this." I don't even know what I'm saying anymore—can't understand the magnitude of what I'm confessing. The consequences it will have. "I want this cock."

"*Fuck.*" He rubs my clit harder. Faster . . . "Tell me to take you somewhere and give it to you. You know you want it, Kira. You want that tight little pussy grabbing onto my cock."

I wish I could refute that.

I want to demand he do exactly as he said.

I'm too weak to do any of that.

Biting into the back of his shoulder with all my strength, I swallow back a scream, falling apart, coming so hard my legs go numb as sensation arcs through me.

And, oh God, I'm coming in a restaurant, in plain view of anyone that could happen to look, and I can't stop fucking coming.

So good. *Yes.* I bite down harder into his skin.

Brayden yanks my hand off him. Tension shoots through his body.

Even half-gone, I know what it means.

Someone's coming.

The fear that my friends might see us jerks me upright. I stare down at my lap, trying to use my hair to hide my most likely flushed face.

I reach for his hand, wrapping my fingers around his wrist to remove it from between my legs.

A giggle.

A sound I know very well. One that makes me sick to my stomach.

My head jerks up at that evil, malicious, almost fucking witchy sound.

"Hi, Brayden!" Jennifer stops at our table, her face glowing at the sight of him.

I can't stop hating her. Can't get over it. I don't think I've ever despised anyone as much as I despise her.

Instead of pushing his hand away, I press it closer. It's instinctual, a bitter impulse I have no control over. I don't want him to forget it was *my* pussy he was just begging for.

His hand snaps around my mound roughly, an utterly possessive grip that steals my breath.

And then I realize why.

Austin stops next to Jennifer, eyeing me and Brayden.

I go weak, my hold on Brayden's hand loosening.

Austin's hanging out with Jennifer?

Nausea rolls inside me.

Austin's eyes meet mine, and guilt flashes in them. That is, until he looks away, locking eyes with Brayden.

Both men size each other up, and if I didn't feel so sick, I might be worried about them attacking each other.

"What are you doing here, Brayden?" Jennifer doesn't even try to distance herself from Austin before she smiles flirtatiously at Brayden.

That fucking bitch. Is she trying to make Brayden jealous?

Oh. My. God.

The lack of space between her and Austin . . .

They slept together again. Recently.

Did he leave my house last night and go straight to her?

Or did he seek her out this morning so he could bust his nut inside her?

I stare straight at him, willing the answer to my silent questions out of him.

Austin's eyes momentarily find mine once more.

More guilt.

I'm going to throw up.

"I'm hanging out with Kira," Brayden says calmly, but his body vibrates with a silent fury that I can't help but sense.

Jennifer barely acknowledges me, but the disdain in her eyes is pretty fucking clear.

Don't worry, bitch. I feel the same way.

"That's so nice of you to make time to hang out with your sister."

I slide my eyes closed and count to ten. It does nothing.

I fucking hope Austin said my name while fucking her.

A petty, vicious thought, but the ugliness in her brings out the worst in me.

When Brayden doesn't respond to her snide little comment, Jennifer sidles up to Austin and links her arm with his.

He lets her.

Any lingering doubt vanishes.

I asked him to leave last night and he ran to her.

He slept with her again.

She and I . . . we really are trading men back and forth.

It's fucking disgusting.

So disgusting that it's making me want to cry.

I don't want to trade men with her.

I don't want Austin now that he's been with her again. When he's also been with her so many times in the past.

Don't want Brayden, either. I don't want any man that has touched, kissed, and been inside that fucking slut.

She was just sucking Craig's dick at a party last week.

"Let me up," I tell Brayden, hearing how small my voice is.

His eyes snap to mine.

That quiet rage in him lances me.

43

I know what he thinks.

I don't care.

I need to get away from them. All of them. This level of dysfunction is more than I can honestly endure.

My friends finally return. They slow down as they get closer.

"Brayden . . . I have to go."

His jaw twitches, but he eases out of the booth anyway.

In my haste, I almost bolt without even saying goodbye to my friends.

Brayden takes care of that for me. "We forgot we have to meet up with our family."

Good enough. I wave and somehow walk away from the table without looking in Austin's direction.

Austin calls out my name.

I speed up.

"Leave her the fuck alone," Brayden snaps at him.

Tears rush to my eyes, but I blink them away. I won't cry for Austin. I've already cried enough for Brayden, and he was once the guy I actually loved.

I know in the back of my mind that Brayden is following me, yet when he catches up with me outside and grabs my arm, I gasp. "Brayden! Let me go. You're hurting me!"

He drops my arm, his breath racing, his eyes almost black in the shadows from the sun. Neither of us says anything, and he refuses to look at me.

He's furious.

So am I. For being an idiot. For believing Austin wanted something real with me.

For entertaining the idea of trying with him even though I feel nothing when he touches me.

44

"Let's go." Brayden's voice is hoarse. There's chaos inside him, contained but potent. I feel it.

"I came with my friends." Shit, how could I forget? I have no way home.

"I'm driving you." He says it in a way that brooks no arguments. He's already pulled his keys out of his pocket.

Logic dictates that I should argue. Going anywhere with Brayden is a bad idea. Being alone anywhere with him always, always leads to a lapse of judgement.

But he's angry. More than that, I can sense that invisible injury in him, the one I picked up on last night when I sent him away in front of Austin.

Brayden's hurting. Just as much as I am.

It's too much to analyze. I'm not ready. I don't know what to do with that. Instead, I find myself nodding.

Truth is, I'd rather get a ride home with him than with my friends. I can't bear to pretend right now. Or worse, have to dodge their questions and come up with believable lies.

"All right. Let's go."

A double take from Brayden. For that one millisecond when his eyes meet mine, all I see is cold despair. A pain he's trying hard to hide.

Even guarded, his green eyes seem to shimmer with so many things.

I ignore the tightness in my chest and follow him to his car.

And that's when I realize what I'm about to do. I'm going to get in that car with over six feet of angry, tumultuous man. A man whose scent alone scrambles my brain.

A man whose presence alone reminds me of years of agony.

A man I still want.

Brayden lays his hand flat on the roof of his car. He still won't look at me. "Kira, get inside."

I don't move, frozen in place by everything I feel. And, fuck, right now I *feel* so much.

He's here, pursuing me, and he seems to be willing to take hit after hit for me.

And none of that can erase an ounce of the resentment I feel when I look at his beautiful face. I'm fucking choking with it.

"Kira, let's go. Please."

It's that softly muttered please that does me in.

I can never forgive him, but I have no interest in hurting him any more right now.

I'm hurting enough for the both of us.

Silent, I get into the car. Brayden doesn't say anything either. My body trembles with awareness. The silence on his end is so intense he might as well shout and rage at me.

He doesn't. Whatever he's feeling, he swallows it, keeps it locked inside himself.

Is he choking on it, too?

I take shallow breaths to avoid inhaling too much of his scent—futile. It surrounds me. Everything about him overwhelms me.

I chance a peek at him. His jaw looks hard as granite, his full, kissable lips pressed tight together.

It's fucked up how that restrained violence calls to me. Pressing my thighs together, I look out the window. I'm such a mess, and I have no idea how to even begin to make sense of it. Maybe I'm too young, too immature. Too fucking inexperienced.

I hate feeling like a little girl who's gotten burned from playing with the grown-ups, but it's time to admit that's probably what I am.

We pull into the driveway at my house. I move to unclip my seatbelt.

"Austin and Jennifer are fucking."

Brayden's comment stops me. I keep my eyes lowered. "You've fucked her, too." And I saw it once. On a night when I'd needed him more than anything.

"I haven't touched her in years. He fucked her recently, from what I can tell."

Tears flood my eyes again. Goddammit, I don't even know why I'm this upset. I feel something for Austin, but it's definitely not love. Not even close.

I try to exit the car.

Brayden grabs my wrist. When I turn to make him release me, I'm hit with the pained, tender expression on his face.

"Do you want me to fuck him up?" he asks me in a serious, fierce whisper.

Is he . . . is he offering to beat Austin up for . . . I don't get a chance to finish the thought.

He drops my wrist, slamming his back into his seat. Restless, he throws his head back. Exhales. "God. Fucking asshole. I'll rip him apart for fucking hurting you like this!"

Oh. My. God.

He punches the steering wheel.

I grab his hand before he can deliver another hit. "Brayden. Stop!"

There's a madness in those inflamed eyes. A frightening madness that makes them glitter like green gems. "I know I've hurt you, too. That I have no right. But I'm going to fucking kill him for hurting you like this." A pause. Several harsh breaths. The madness expands, a palpable mix of hurt and need that drags me in. Then . . . "I'm going to kill him for taking a piece of your heart away from me and then breaking it."

Pain. God, so much *pain*. Why am I not desensitized to it yet? I can't harden that piece of my soul that's forever exposed to Brayden, and the emotions he's struggling with poke at it. Pierce it. Make it bleed all over again.

I start trembling, tears leaking down my cheeks, too torn apart to control it.

Brayden exhales like I've sliced him open, too, his jaw clenched against the torment.

It's the very last thing I should do, but I let myself squeeze his hand. His big, warm, tanned hand, with its broad, strong palm and long fingers. "I once would've given anything for this hand to belong just to me," I whisper. For his whole body, but I don't say it. I don't need to.

He tightens his hand around mine, his hold anxious. "It does. Every part of me."

I shake my head because we both know I'll never let that happen again. Right now, I don't hate him, but in the next few moments I will once more, and nothing he does or says will change that.

I loved him too hard, too young, and he warped that for me. Ruined my ability to properly love. I have no clue what a healthy attraction even looks like and that's all thanks to him.

There's no other option for me. I'll have to learn, start from scratch. Scrape away years of negative association and somehow convince my mind to trust again.

How could I ever do that with the same man who broke me in the first place?

A man I can't even publicly have.

But right now, he's hurting because I'm hurting. Willing to avenge a wrong he perceives had been done to me—he, the very man who has hurt me so bad—and I can only blame my weakened, messed-up mind for what I do next.

Wiping the tears off my cheeks, I look into his narrowed, stormy eyes, and tell him the truth. A truth I shouldn't tell him, but one I *need* him to know nonetheless.

"I'm not crying because Austin hurt me. Not like that. I could never feel for him that way." I rush out of the car as soon as the words are out of my mouth, and I don't stop until I'm inside the house, locked in my room.

Holy. God.

What did I just do?

I don't think I'll ever forget the stunned look on Brayden's face.

Fuck. Why did I tell him that?

Now he knows. Now he knows how I feel for Austin.

And it's probably only a matter of time before he comes to the conclusion that I still feel something for him.

I fall back on my door and slide down to the floor, staring off into space, wondering what the hell I'm going to do now.

FIVE

Kira

April 25th, 2015

Saturday is not going how I wanted it to. I'm alone and bored.

Ashley and Marilyn are at a family reunion, while Jenna is grounded at home for missing curfew. Mom and Steve went to some event downtown and are probably going to be gone all day.

I could go shopping, or to the gym, or half a dozen other things, but instead I'm sitting in front of the TV with Netflix up, trying to decide on what series I'm going to dive into.

And keeping my mind off everything that happened last weekend.

School helped distract me all week, but now I'm at home with silence, and I feel it. The itching in my chest, the tightness, the growing . . . despair? No, that's not the right feeling.

It's all jumbled, disorienting. I don't know *how* or *what* I feel. It's all a big freaking mess.

After deciding on breaking down and watching *Vampire Diaries*, I hop up to grab something to munch on from the kitchen. Staring into the pantry leaves me with multiple options: chips, crackers, popcorn, trail mix, and cereal.

Fruit Loops sounds like the perfect moody munchy, and I grab the box and plop back down on the couch.

I hit play with the remote and reach in for some fruity, crunchy goodness when the doorbell chimes. I contemplate ignoring it, but instead hit pause and go to find out who's here.

The moment I have the door open I want to shut it again. I want to slam it hard in his face.

"What do you want, Austin?" I cross my arms over my chest.

He looks nervous, which he should be. "Can we talk?"

I turn from him and walk into the living room.

"What?"

"I want to talk about what happened last weekend," he says. I can hear him step forward. "Kira, please look at me."

With a huff I swivel around and glare up at him. "I don't want to hear about how good of a fuck Jennifer is."

He shakes his head. "I made a mistake, a huge one. I like you, and—"

I push against Austin's chest. "All you motherfuckers are the same!"

"Kira—"

"No. I don't want your lame ass excuse. Every time a guy tells me he wants to be with me, the next second he's fucking that slut. Why?"

He stares at me, fear in his eyes. "I was drunk and . . . Fuck . . ."

"Drunk? That's your excuse for sticking your dick in that clap trap?"

His lips form a thin line and his expression hardens. "Yeah, an excuse, but I know you don't want to hear the reason."

"Try me."

His jaw twitches again and he looks away, then back. "I saw it."

"Saw what?" I ask with a huff.

"The way you looked at him. The way he looked at you."

I shake my head. "What are you talking about?"

"Brayden."

My eyes widen and I stare at him as my once boiling blood turns to ice.

No. Brayden is *not* a subject I want to talk about.

"When you told him to leave . . . That wasn't the way you act with a brother or a even a friend. It felt like I was the one intruding on some intimate scene between lovers."

I take a step back and shake my head. "It's not like that."

"Then tell me what it's like." He steps forward, staying in my personal space, suffocating me with his interrogation.

"It's complicated."

He lets out a strained laugh and lifts my chin, forcing me to look up at him. "Complicated? Screw complicated, then. I want you. I've wanted you for years, but him and your brother were always there, blocking everyone. Then I *finally* get the chance to be close." His jaw ticks and he looks around. "I'm laying myself out here—I like you, a lot. I want you to be my girl. Do you feel anything for me?"

The blood in my veins heats up again to a raging boil. "Really? You're asking me out *after* having sex with her?" I can't even say Jennifer's name. I want to rip her hair out, slam her face into the ground, and kick the shit out of her.

He shakes his head, but I don't know if it's at me or at himself. "I'm sorry."

No. Not that. "Fuck your sorry! I'm fucking tired of that word!"

His head hangs. "Please, Kira, I'll do anything for a chance with you."

"Another thing I'm tired of hearing," I hiss. "I thought about it, you and me. I really did. I wanted to give you a chance, to see if we could be something." He looks up, eyes meeting mine, a mixed look of happiness and horror. "Then you stuck your dick back in that slut. So tell me, what the fuck is so great about her pussy that it always seems to win out over feelings for me? Why am I not enough to win out over an easy, well-worn pussy?"

His expression morphs, eyes narrow on me. "You seem to think I've been with sleeping with Jenn this entire time. The last time we were together was years ago, Kira. *Years ago*."

I blink back at him, my hands shaking. Oh, no.

How could I be so stupid?

He steps forward, making me back up. "And you're really worked up about it. Now I'm left wondering . . . or more like realizing, that all your anger is about Brayden. Is that what happened between you two?"

I gasp and look away. "I don't . . . It doesn't matter anymore."

"Yes, it obviously does. Brayden used to be my friend. Used to be." He stresses the last bit, and it dawns on me how much their relationship has changed. "The second I showed interest in you, I lost my friend." The sorry, feeble Austin is gone, replaced with a strong, angry version. "And I didn't fucking care. Do you want to know why?"

He steps closer, but this time I don't back up. His body almost presses to mine and I'm forced to lean back to look up at him. There's a spark in his blue eyes that were so dull moments ago, and an energy radiating off him. Part of me wants to reach out and calm him, but another part is afraid.

I'm stuck, captivated by him, by the curiosity.

His hand rests on my hip, but I can't seem to slap it away. "Because all I want is you."

The words snap me back to focus on how close he is, and I press my hands against his chest as I glare up at him. "Then, again, why sleep with her?"

"Because all you want is him, and I couldn't take it and got shitfaced. All I can tell you is I'm sorry that I did and that it was with Jenn, who you clearly hate."

I stare up at him, at a complete loss of what to say. I'm tired of this conversation. I feel like I've been having it for years.

"Stop. Just stop."

"No." He grabs hold of my chin and makes me look at him. "No more of this bullshit. I like you, a lot."

He leans down and presses his lips against mine. I gasp against them, slow to respond, but I do. His kiss is soft, tender, and so different from Brayden's. When our tongues meet, there's no spark.

This kiss is still good, just . . . lackluster.

"Your indifference kills me," he whispers against my lips. "Pick me. I can help you get over him. I can love you better than him." He steps back, releasing me. "Think about it, Kira. Please promise you'll think about it."

I nod, staring after him as he walks out of the room. The telltale thump of the front door closing is my signal to fall back onto the couch.

Why does my love life have to be so freaking complicated?

Brayden

May 11th, 2015

"What hasn't sold yet?" I ask as I tape off another box of clothes, wishing I had a bed to crash onto and could take a break.

We've sold off most of the furniture, not that there was a lot, but there seems to still be a lot of crap we've accumulated over the last three years. I didn't think packing was going to be a near three-day event.

Ryan is across the hall, doing the same, cursing at something as he searches for his laptop. "Umm, there's two guys coming for the couch at one. Jill from next door is coming to get the table after work at three." He's silent as he scans over the spreadsheet he made. "Did you get the money for my bed?"

I freeze and look over, thankfully seeing a wad of bills sitting on my nightstand—one of the few furniture pieces going with us. "Yeah. A hundred bucks."

He cranes his head into the doorway. "Lunch?"

I nod. "Fuck, yes."

We both climb out of our respective messes of bags and boxes, and head down the stairs. The main floor is mostly packed up: a couple boxes of kitchen items and half a dozen boxes for electronics, games, and DVDs.

"Microwave?" I ask as we head out the door.

"Jordan's picking it up."

I shake my head and laugh. "I can't believe he and Ella are moving in together."

"He's so freaking grateful I think he's going to name a kid after you."

We don't even have to talk about where to go. Jersey Mike's is always our go-to sub shop, and only a few blocks walk from our apartment.

"So, we're done, then? Nothing left to sell?"

He nods. "Finish packing, that's it. Oh, and clean."

"What time is Dana coming?" It's just after eleven, and I want to get out of town by two. That leaves a lot to do in the next few hours.

I'm itching to get home to Kira, to see her again. It's been almost three painfully long weeks.

He pulls his phone from his pocket and turns the screen on. "Shit, I missed a text. Looks like she'll be here any minute." His fingers hit a few keys, then he raises it up to his ear. We keep walking, already to the parking lot, then his tone changes and a smile lights up his face. "Hey, baby. Yeah, I'm sorry, I just saw it." He pushes the door open to the shop. "We're at Jersey Mike's, want me to get you something?"

He nods and hmms before saying he'll see her soon and hangs up.

With only one car, there's no way we'd be able to move all our crap in my car, so since Ryan's moving in with Dana, she's going to help out. Most of his boxes are going straight to their apartment anyway. I haven't had a chance to look for one, so all of my stuff is heading back to my dad's.

"Have you told her?" I ask after ordering, turning to him. Changing schools, moving to Columbus, is all to be closer to Kira, to win her back, but I'm not ready for her to know yet. She doesn't respond to eighty percent of my texts, but I keep sending them, all in hopes of breaking her down.

Ryan shakes his head. "She's excited that I'm going to be there, but she hasn't asked about you. Not that I'd tell her anyway."

"Thanks, man."

"I just hope leaving it as a surprise doesn't bite you in the ass."

"She'll know soon enough. I'm not going to hide it until August."

Ryan orders for him and Dana and we find a spot to sit.

"I just hope Austin hasn't moved in on her too much."

"Nah, Craig said he's been studying, too."

"Then I just have to beat him home." I'm actually getting worried. The vibe was off with Kira when I left her. She was upset, and all I know is that it has to do with him, even with her last-second confession.

Ryan smiles, not even responding to what I've said, and gets up from his chair. His arms open up and Dana's wrap around his waist. It's sweet, almost sickly, when he kisses the top of her head, but I know that's more jealousy than anything.

I want that with Kira.

Even the way she looks at him, her blue eyes sparkling, is full of love. All I get from Kira is disdain, but I know it's all my fault, so I take it . . . for now.

"Hey, Brayden," she says as she sits down next to Ryan.

The fucker's beaming. I've never seen him like this before.

He loves her, and she loves him.

And I'm green all over again.

Fuck. I've become a lovesick pussy.

My future with Kira is on such a tenuous thread that I've been an agitated, nervous wreck for weeks. Ever since her birthday, I'm not sure of the one thing I've always been sure of—does she still love me?

From the moment I met her, she's been mine, but even more so, I'm hers. No matter how things play out, I'll always belong to her.

I shake my head.

Fuck, that's no way to think.

She *is* mine. She loves me—she always has. My Kitty is just angry and hurt by me.

"Here, I brought this for you," Dana says, thrusting a case at me. Neither of them seem to be aware of the siesta I just took. Hell, I don't even remember picking up my food.

"What's this?" I stare down at the CD in my hand.

"Whale song."

I quirk my brow at her. "What the fuck do I need whale song for?"

"Listen to it."

"Explain it to me, man."

She rolls her eyes. "You keep pawing at Kira every time you see her."

I pull back. "That's . . . probably true. How do you know, though?"

"Grapevine. Anyway, you need to calm down and stop

mauling her every time you see her." She points back to the CD. "A counselor told me about this when I was freaking out during finals. Now, I listen to it everyday to relax."

"I'm not fucking listening to whale song."

"Fine. Then jack off."

I chuckle and shake my head. "Doesn't work."

She purses her lips. "Do it twice. Just do something so you're not jumping on her the moment you see her."

"Hey, I'm not that bad."

Her brow twitches up. "Really?"

Fuck.

"I'm serious about this, Brayden. You're being obnoxious with your affections, and it's pissing her off. If you back up, she'll see that she can't deny this thing you have, and it will eat at her."

"What, act like I don't care? I've done that, and it's only pushed her away."

"No, you have to show her you care, but show her you respect her and her personal space as well. Trust me, Kira's got it bad for you, but she needs to remember what it's like to like and want you again."

I stare at her for a minute and take another bite of my sandwich. "I fucking hate it when your girlfriend is right," I grumble

Ryan just shrugs, a smile pulling at his lips.

They were years in the making. From the moment she moved to town, I knew he was hooked. Dana isn't like some of the girls in our circle of friends. She's cool, and doesn't just roll over.

It takes another three hours to pack the cars and clean up, getting me out a little later than I wanted. It's weird to head home without Ryan, but I'll see him in a few days.

The entire drive home, my body is buzzing. I haven't seen Kira in weeks. Finals took up all my time, along with all the crap to change schools.

I stop at a rest stop just before the Ohio border on I-74 and take a break, munching on my leftover sandwich.

Are you home? I text Kira. It's long after three, so she should be, but I need to know. I need to see her.

Another bite, and my phone buzzes. *No. Why?*

I'm amazed she responds.

What are you doing?

I'm working out.

I can almost hear her give an exasperated sigh. *Any plans after that?*

Not that it's any of your business, but no.

Perfect. I merge back onto the highway and head straight to the house. She should be home by the time I get there.

If she's even going home. I play with the idea of asking, but in the end decide not to. She'll know I'm on my way if I do, and I want to catch her by surprise.

Hopefully the parents aren't home. They shouldn't be at this time, but you never know.

SIX
BRAYDEN

Almost an hour later, I finally pull into the driveway.

Empty.

Perfect.

I can't tell if Kira is home, but at least no one else is.

I get out of my car and stare up at my father's house. Where Kira lives. And I'll be living here for the next few weeks. Back under the same roof as her, until I find an apartment in Columbus. Even then, I'll be across the hall from her half the week due to my summer job.

It's going to be hard, yet I'm also excited about it. Yeah, I'm supposed to behave, take it easy on her.

I'll try my best. Doesn't mean I'm not happy as fuck that I'm going to have her so close to me again.

I walk up to the house and grab the doorknob.

Odd. It's unlocked.

Oh, well.

I open the door and step inside.

Kira's voice stops me.

"Why are you here again? There's nothing left to say between us."

At first, I think she's talking to me.

That is, until I hear *his* fucking voice responding to her.

"There's a lot left to say between us, Kira."

Rage immobilizes me.

And curiosity. Sick, sick curiosity.

I know Kira told me she wasn't hurt about Austin sleeping with Jenn, but I can't help but wonder.

"You told me what you have to say," Kira tells him. "And I told you I don't want to hear it."

They're in the living room, I can tell now. It's wrong for me to stand here and eavesdrop.

Not that I make any move to make my presence known.

"You don't want to hear it because you're angry, and I hurt you, and I'm so fucking sorry—"

Kira interrupts him. "You said it all the last time you were here trying to explain."

That piece of shit came to grovel to her?

Of course he fucking did.

"You promised me, Kira. You promised you would think about you and me, about being my girl."

Fucker said *what*?

"I did think about it, Austin."

I can almost feel the ground start shaking beneath my feet with the force of my rage.

This . . . I did this to her. Made Amanda my girl. Shoved her in Kira's face, knowing it would slice her apart.

I deserve this.

I deserve this.

I. Fucking. Deserve. This.

A thousand times I repeat it to myself.

My fury continues to clash with my pain, and regardless of the fact that I understand the situation logically, I can't stop from asking myself:

Kira agreed to think about being his girl?

He slept with Jenn, and yet she'll forgive him that easily?

Austin only hurt her once.

I hate myself because I've done it way too many times.

"And what, Kira? . . . talk to me," Austin *begs*.

"Every time I thought about it, all I imagined was you with Jennifer."

Austin blows out a breath, silent for a few seconds. "Sometimes, Kira, all I imagine is you with Brayden."

He knows about us. Really knows.

Son of a bitch knows, and he doesn't give a fuck. He's still determined to have her.

"I never fucked Brayden. I gave myself to *you*, Austin."

The hurt in her voice slices through me.

There's only so much pain I can take. Yes, I know I'm a hypocrite, that I should just stand here and take every hit like a fucking man, but I fucking can't.

I head to the living room.

"Tell me the truth," Austin says. "Were you thinking about him when we slept together?"

There's nothing but silence from Kira.

Come on, Kitty. Answer him, and answer him right. Save his fucking ass from my fists fucking up his face.

"I'm sorry, Austin, but I don't want to keep rehashing this with you. I'm going to tell you what I've told Brayden many times: if you truly cared about me, you never would have done it."

I come to a halt at the entrance to the living room, reeling.

She's *comparing* us to each other?

The look on Austin's face tells me he feels as disgusted by that as I do.

Kira crosses her arms and stares him down. "At the end of the day, there's a reason why you were both such close friends once."

Don't say that, Kira. Don't even go there . . .

"In my eyes, you're both exactly the same."

"We're not the fucking same and you know it," I growl.

Kira jumps.

Austin's head turns in my direction, his expression furious.

I ignore him, staring Kira in the eye.

She gives me a look of utter disgust, obviously realizing that I've heard a good portion of their conversation. "Oh, really? Explain to me the difference."

Really? She wants to go there? Fine. "You've never felt for him what you feel for me. You never fucking will."

She turns white as a ghost.

It's like instant medicine for my anger. The perfect response to calm me.

The proof I need to know that my words have hit the truth.

Kira *does* still love me.

It's almost enough to make me smile.

Then I see the big asshole heading my way. I meet him in the middle of the room.

"You keep forgetting you can't have her," Austin spits.

Kira calls out both our names—the only thing that stops me from breaking this motherfucker's face.

"You keep forgetting I already do." I promised Dana and myself that I'd back off. Take it easy, not push too hard, and what I said is just that: me verbally pushing too hard.

But it's the truth. The hardcore, brutal truth my soul keeps screaming out, and one I know Kira feels deep down.

She runs up to us, trying to push us away from each other, to work her way between us. She can't. We're too big for her to move, and we're too busy wanting to kill each other for her to make us want to.

"Both of you! Stop!" Kira cries out.

"Just walk away already," I warn him, for her sake more than anything.

"I'm never going to walk away from Kira unless she makes me."

My vision turns bright red.

"If you guys fight, I will never forgive either of you. I mean it!"

At her words, Austin and I instantly take a step back away from each other.

I want to kill him for it.

I can see in his eyes that he wants to kill me, too.

His eyes flicker toward Kira, and he runs his hand through his hair before heading to the entrance of the living room. There, he stops, turning his head to glare at me over his shoulder. "Don't forget you're her stepbrother. You can never give her what she deserves."

It's a perfectly aimed blow.

I want to see him fucking bleed at my feet. "You ever ask her to be your girlfriend again, and I will kill you."

"Brayden!" Kira slaps me in the chest.

I don't turn away from Austin's stare. I'm dead serious, and I hope he sees that.

He laughs, a bitter, mirthless sound. "I'd like to see you try. After all, you're not the only man willing to kill for her." Before I can say anything, he walks away, and I hear the front door slam shut shortly after.

Kira hits me again, harder this time. "You're such a fucking asshole!"

"Why? Because I told him the truth?"

"It wasn't the truth!" She storms away from me.

I follow her. "Kira, wait."

"Just leave me alone."

We end up on the second floor, outside the door to her room. I catch up with her and grab her arm.

"*What*?"

"Look at me." I don't drop her arm until shes does, that seemingly permanent anger in her gaze. "Did you really agree to think about being his girl?"

Silence.

The same silence she gave Austin when he asked her if she was thinking about me the night they slept together.

"Kira." I can't hide the slightly broken tone of my voice. Shit, it's nothing compared to how I feel about this shit situation.

"Don't look at me like that," she says.

"Like what?"

Her little jaw twitches. "Like I'm tearing you apart."

"You are." My voice drops so low I wonder if she even heard me.

The shocked expression on her face tells me that she did. Her nostrils flare slightly and her disbelief becomes rage.

"You fucking asshole." She points at my room. "You stood in there, packing your bags to go to your girl."

I flinch. Knew this was coming.

She's not done. "You stood there, looked me in the eye, and you took that fucking call."

I remember. God help me, I do.

"You told her, while staring at me, how much you missed her—"

"I lied," I mumble.

"Did you?" She jams her finger into my chest. "Did you?"

"Yes!" All I want is to hug her right now. Hug her tight. Somehow erase all the bullshit so I can get my sweet Kitty back.

Fucking shit, it's like I barely see her smile nowadays.

"And when you went to her? How many times did you fuck her? How many times were you with her after that?"

Too fucking many. "I had to think of you. Every damn time, I had to close my eyes and imagine it was you just to get through it."

She slaps me. "Fuck you, Brayden."

I grab her before she can storm into her room. "Hate me for it, but I loved you. Every minute that I was with her, every minute that I wasn't, I still loved you."

"You don't know how to love, then."

"You're right. You're so fucking right, baby." I want to run my fingers over her skin, comfort her, but all I can do is offer her the truth. "I had no idea how to love you. I know that."

She's silent as she contemplates what I've just told her. What seems like sympathy flashes in her eyes. "Your parents fucked with your head growing up, I get that. But you had no right to fuck with me."

"You're right."

"I fucking cared about you so much. Forget what I felt for you as a girl, I was your *friend*, you asshole."

I would love to fall to my knees and beg her forgiveness. Would, too, if I thought it would help in the slightest. "I know. I *know*. That's why, no matter how much you feel you need to hurt me, I'll still be here. I'm not going anywhere."

She murmurs my name sadly, eyes glittering with unshed tears.

Needing something—anything—I reach for her and pull her into my arms.

She lets me, but she doesn't hug me back.

"I mean it. Do everything you want to me, hurt me any way you want. Hell, I want you to. Maybe then it'll make the guilt a little easier for me."

"You're a masochist," she mumbles into my chest.

I smile and kiss the top of her head. "Yeah. Especially when it comes to you." No response. Sighing, I hug her tighter. "You can do whatever you want to me, and I'd still forgive you."

"Because you hurt me."

"And because I adore you." In my mind, she's my girl, no matter what happens. I can't undo the thought, was never able to. And in my mind, she's still my best friend, even if I'm no longer considered hers.

"You'd forgive me anything? What if I decide I want to be with Austin?"

"You're so good at hurting me with that." She tenses. "He was once my friend, Kira."

A fact she was very aware of when she decided to give herself to him. The one boundary I never crossed. The one boundary I'm damn sure I never would have. I would have never gone after any of her friends.

Kira pushes at my chest.

I move back slowly. "It's okay if you chose him that one time. I get it. I forgave you for it the moment I found out." Her, yes. Him? Never. I can't.

Her beautiful, sad eyes stare up into mine. "And if I decide to give him a chance?"

"I'll forgive you for that, too." No clue how I'll stop myself from trying to kill him, though. "I'll wait for you. I just . . ."

"You just what?"

Fuck. Does she understand how hard this is for me right now? "I need to know I'll have you someday." My brain can't even begin to imagine an entire life without her. Never could. I just fooled myself into thinking it was possible once.

I watch her, trying to read what's going through her mind.

And I get nothing but her pain.

Kira starts heading into her room. Against my will, I make no move to reach out for her.

At her door, she stops. "Let me know if you need help unloading your car." She walks into her room and closes the door.

SEVEN

Kira

May 25th, 2015

The bell rings, signaling the great escape. The stampede funneling through the classroom door is greater than usual. Then again, only nine school days remain, and an hour and a half of world history review has everyone crawling the walls.

"Boo!" Ashley pops up behind me as I pull my phone from my back pocket.

"Hey! How was Spanish?"

"Muy boring," she says with a sigh, then turns to me, her blue eyes sparkling with mischief. "Did Lyn tell you what she's doing?"

I shake my head. "No, she wasn't in class."

Her eyebrows shoot up. "Really? Where, oh where, is my little sister? And whose face is she sucking?" She pulls out her phone, typing away.

I wake my own up, turning the screen on and seeing why my ass was vibrating all morning long.

Six text messages.

Over the last few months I got used to tons of messages per day, and today was no different. My daily dose of annoyance from Brayden.

Though he isn't the only sender, and I check out Jenna's first.

Sam is sooooo hot. I would seriously jump him.

Followed by,

What party are we going to this weekend? Maybe he'll go.

And then . . .

What are you doing? Answer me!

I shake my head. Study hall must have been extremely boring.

The next is from Austin, and I find myself hesitating to open it. I haven't forgiven him, and the whole explosion the day Brayden moved home still makes me sick.

Hi. How's your day? Did you hear about AJ Henricks party next month? It's costume. I want to take you. Let me know.

I sigh and back out of the message, deciding to worry about it later, because there are two more messages waiting for me and they might make me go crazy and tell Austin yes.

Hey, baby. Did a little manscaping today. What do you think?

I stop walking, stop breathing, even stop thinking. My jaw is slack, and I could be drooling. Because attached to Brayden's message is a picture that has my blood pumping, thighs clenching, and clit twitching.

I'm a pile of goo in the middle of the hallway, forced to lean on the bay of lockers next to me for support.

It starts with his sexy smirk that drives me crazy, even though I don't want it to, and is nothing but hard, smooth, taut chest and abs. He's wearing a red hoodie. It's covering up one of his huge pecs, but that doesn't matter, it's a tease, making me want to see it all. What's showing trails all the way to the bottom of his abs, down to his very low-slung grey sweatpants. So low, the base of his dick is almost showing. The hoodie is open at the bottom, highlighting his V.

The V!

A sound I can't identify leaves me at the sight of a highlight and definite shadow in his sweatpants.

His cock.

Oh, holy fuck, his cock.

Missing you, if you couldn't tell. ;)

The head is hanging low and long, perfectly outlined.

He's hard. For me.

My mouth is dry, hands shaking, pussy pulsing. I'm a fucking mess.

"Yo, Kira, are you okay?" Ashley's hand waves in front of my face, and I blink at her. "Girl, what is it?"

She moves to look at my phone and I snap it close to my chest, making her eyes pop open in surprise.

"Kira, show me."

"No."

Her gaze narrows, then she leans forward and snatches the phone from my hand, turning away before I can grab it back.

"Ashley!" I reach for it, but it's too late.

Her eyes are glued to the screen, just as I'm sure mine were.

"Oh, my God." She glances up at me, then back down at the screen. "I think I just came."

My body goes rigid, and I grab the phone back as an unwanted rage boils in me.

Ashley's whole face is in shock. "I think I may have to switch to team Brayden."

"Shhh!" I hush her, grabbing her arm as I drag her into the bathroom.

I need a minute to calm down, to collect myself. The bell goes off, and I don't care that I'm late to calculus.

I had to tell my girls some of what was going on after what happened over my birthday, but I didn't tell them everything, all the crap that's gone on over the years, so I told them he asked me out. That alone caused them to form sides. Jenna and Marilyn are team Brayden, while Ashley makes up team Austin.

"Seriously, girl, you need to have that hot-as-fuck male specimen, if just for scientific research."

"Research?"

"Yeah. See how many times that beast can make you come, and report to us so we can live vicariously in your bliss."

Fuck. Bliss.

I hate to admit that she's probably right. It's bad enough my body betrays me every time I'm near him, even just hearing his voice.

I don't want him . . . but I do. Scratch this itch that takes over and forget who I am, forget about the world.

Fuck him out of my system and be done with him.

"That would be bad."

"No, it would be good. *Very* good." Her eyes soften and she takes my hand. "Look, I know there's a lot of baggage between you two, even without you saying it. It's obvious. And while I'm still totally team Austin, what's wrong with a hate fuck with Brayden?"

I shake my head. "You're terrible."

"No, I'm right." She steps back toward the door. "Come on, let's get to class. We can talk about it later. I'm sure Marilyn and Jenna want to weigh in."

I let out a groan and step forward. The last thing I want is all of their opinions, let alone allowing them all to view the picture. I'll never get my phone back, and I also don't want anyone else seeing something that was for me alone.

"Wait." I hold my phone up high, hitting the camera function and selfie my response with a middle finger just for him. It's sitting in my cleavage, thanks to the angle. Oh, well.

With my response out, we head to class. It's only five minutes in when I slip into my seat and lean over to my neighbor, Thomas. "What did I miss?"

He smiles and hands me a stapled stack of papers. "Review. I grabbed you a copy."

"Thank you!"

As I turn back, my phone buzzes and a message pops up on the screen.

I'm more than happy to fuck those tits, baby.

I sigh and change my phone over to silent before slipping it back in my pocket. Brayden being home is not a good thing. Three hundred miles away was bad enough, but now? My skin itches, my heart races, and the attraction is overpowering.

When I get home he'll be across the hall, a few feet from me, and no Ryan to shield me because my rat of a brother abandoned me for a girl.

Not that I fault Ryan for it, but I do like to tease him about it. Years of back and forth with Dana and they're finally together. I know him, and that despite what he's put off, he loves her.

76

I stare down at the Calculus review. Only a few more days and school's out, and I can't wait to be done. Then again, that leaves me home alone with Brayden.

Lord, give me strength to stave off this lust.

Kira
May 27th, 2015

The words in front of me blur. Not because I'm tired, but because my attention once again wanders.

I shake my head, trying to refocus. It's exhausting to fight this raging curiosity badgering my mind.

Is he partying right now?

Come on—of course he is. It's his twenty-first birthday. Ryan and Dana invited me to go with them. I declined, of course.

They said they were taking him out for dinner and then drinks.

As per Ryan and Brayden's usual status in quo, I'm assuming that drinks is code for "partying their asses off."

Whatever. I'm used to it. It's not like I was tempted to go or anything.

I uncap my highlighter and set back into it.

Blurs. Nonsense. Some more blurs.

I'm not getting shit done.

Aggravated, I drop the highlighter onto my French workbook. My final is on Friday. I started out French late, but my plan is to continue in college and be fluent in two years tops.

Jenna and the twins are also studying their asses off, but none of them are in French, so they aren't available to offer me any kind of distraction.

Not that studying a foreign language is actually doing anything. I thought it'd be enough to help me forget. Clearly, I was wrong.

I chew on my thumbnail and stare at my dark computer screen.

Just one look. A single peek and my curiosity will go away, right?

I drag my laptop closer and turn it on. Approximately thirty seconds later, I find myself on Facebook, pulling up a profile I haven't checked in forever.

Brayden Hunt.

Amid what has to be close to a thousand birthday posts, I see a picture that Ryan posted and tagged. It's just him, Dana, and Brayden in the picture. They seem to be at some bar.

The picture is totally different from what I expected to see. They seem to just be chilling instead of hardcore partying. The caption reads: *"Had a blast with my boy on his twenty-first."*

Had?

The picture was posted almost two hours ago.

So, the party is over? Ryan and Dana probably went off to do their own thing then.

Brayden . . . I refuse to think about it. In the back of my head, I know what he's most likely doing right now.

It hurts to think that.

Fuck! It actually still hurts.

Footsteps sound out, coming up the stairs.

Wait. Mom and Steve are supposed to be gone until tomorrow. They've been going out on more getaways lately. A desperate attempt to save their failing marriage.

Curious, I get up and open the door to my room.

Brayden stops just outside his bedroom door, fingers on the buttons of his black dress shirt.

He'd been midway through unbuttoning it.

My eyes slide down the length of him, pausing on the bared skin of his chest. I should look away. At the very least, be more discreet.

I can't. His smooth skin calls to me. If it was up to me, I'd lick every part of his chest, then move lower.

"Kira." His voice is strained. Probably because I'm eye-fucking him shamelessly.

I swallow and look up into his eyes. "What are you doing home?"

A smirk tugs at the corner of his mouth. "What? I can't come home early on my birthday?"

That smirk of his is too fucking sexy. Paired with that black, half-buttoned shirt and those black dress pants, he's one fine looking man.

Holy shit. It's official—the little boy I met so many years ago is now legally a *man*.

I look away, throat tight, and jerk my shoulder in a shrug. "I figured you'd want to party all night since it's your twenty-first."

"Nah."

My head jerks back in his direction. "Nah?"

He shrugs and throws me this adorable little smile.

I cross my arms and repeat my question. "Why are you here?"

"The one thing I truly wanted for my birthday wasn't there." He looks straight into my eyes as he says it.

I inhale sharply, trying to hide it, trying to ignore everything I feel. I can't ask him what he really wants because I'm afraid I already know the answer to that.

He lifts his hand and runs his fingers through his hair. It's a slow movement. Almost deliberate.

My eyes lock on the inside of his wrist.

For the last few weeks, he's been walking around wearing that leather cuff. The one that drove me insane, made me want to rip it off so I could sink my teeth into the inside of his wrist.

There's something on the inside of his wrist all right, and it's not my teeth marks.

It's ink. A tattoo.

A dark, gray adorable cat. But it's not the cat itself that shocks the breath out of me.

I only see it for a few seconds, and I'm standing at least five feet away from him, but I still make out the cat's eyes.

The unique color of those eyes.

A color both I and my brother share.

One last smile from Brayden. "Goodnight, Kitty." Turning, he walks into his room and slowly closes the door.

He doesn't lock it.

The urge to follow him into his room leaves me shaking. I don't know how I manage to get back into my room, but when I do, I make sure I lock the door, hoping it'll be enough to deter me.

To keep me inside.

To stop me from going to him as my body so desperately wants.

EIGHT

Kira

June 6th, 2015

Black squares fly through the air. Burgundy tassels twirl around.

I wish I had a camera on me to snap a picture of our caps against the brilliant blue sky. It's beautiful, the moment electric.

Everyone is screaming, including me, jumping up and down. Excitement streams through the crowd, and down the way Jenna pushes her way toward me. Her arms wrap around me and we bounce together, giggling.

"We did it!" Her smile is blinding, and I know my own matches.

"Yes!"

I turn back to the sea of family members, searching out my own clan. I spot Mom first, camera in hand, beaming with pride. Steve is beside her, talking to someone, and Ryan is on her other side with Dana wrapped around his arm.

Next to them I know is Brayden before I even get there, because I can almost feel his stare boring into me. I'm surprised to find a relaxed smile on his face. It makes my stomach flip and confuses me more.

I didn't want him to come, but getting Brayden Hunt to *not* do something is a skill I have yet to master.

"Come on, let's go find Marilyn and Ashley." Jenna grabs my hand and pulls us through the crowd.

Hugs find us on our way as classmates say goodbye, and I realize it may be the last time I see some of them. After a few minutes we finally break out into the walkway and right into Ashley and Marilyn.

More squealing and hugs and jumping before we make our way to our parents.

"I can't wait for tonight!" Jenna says.

"You're just hoping to hook up with Sam," I say with a wag of my eyebrows.

"I hear he's endowed." Ashley grins, causing Jenna to fan herself.

"Kira!" Mom calls out.

I stop and take a step away. "Gotta go. I'll see you in a couple of hours."

"Want us to pick you up?" Marilyn asks. "Or is Brayden taking you?"

Ugh. Bringing him up makes me almost wish I'd kept quiet that there was anything between us.

"No. Austin is, right?" Ashley winks at me.

Jenna sighs. "Lucky girl."

"Lucky?"

Marilyn rolls her eyes. "Kira, you have two of the hottest guys our school has seen chasing you."

"Sshhh!" I hush them. The devil's ears are perking up. I can tell by the way his stupid face is lighting up.

They giggle and make their way out while I squeeze through.

When I reach my family, Mom is almost in tears, Ryan trying to console her, while Steve shakes his head.

"I'm okay." She beams at me, her bottom lip quivering as she reaches for me and pulls me into her arms. "I'm so proud of you."

Ryan ruffles my hair. "Good job, kid."

I slap at him, but I can't connect thanks to Mom's iron grip. "Jerk!"

Mom finally lets go, and I try and fix the rats nest he's created. Ryan laughs and I swat at his stomach, hitting hard. He grabs my wrist and pulls me until I collide with his chest for a hard hug. My feet leave the ground as he picks me up.

"Congrats, baby sis. Love you."

I should beat on him to let me go, but I've missed this, missed him, my brother. "Love you, too."

There's a familiar chuckle beside me as he sets me back down that makes me tingle.

Fucker.

I turn to Brayden, unable to stop myself. His green eyes are bright, almost sparkling.

"Congratulations."

I tuck a strand of hair behind my ear. "Thanks."

I'm almost clear of touching him, but when he steps forward, arms open, I grimace inside. Not wanting to cause a scene, I allow his arms to circle me. It's brief, his restraint obvious in the tension of his muscles, but it's more than enough to cause my heart to speed up.

"What are your plans tonight?" Mom asks as we turn toward the parking lot.

"There's a party."

I promised Mom we'd have a family dinner. Though to me family is her, Ryan, and I'll add in Dana. Steve's not my dad, and even though I've lived with him for three years, we've never gotten very close.

Then there's Brayden, the complicated thorn in my side.

Thankfully dinner goes off without complication. A.k.a. Brayden behaved himself.

When we pull into the driveway, I jump out and run upstairs to change. I kick the door behind me and grab the hem of my dress to pull it above my head and toss it in the hamper.

"Is Austin going to be there?" Brayden asks from the door, scaring the crap out of me.

"Jesus!" I whip my head around as I nearly jump out of my skin.

As his tongue swipes across his lips, I realize I'm only wearing a strapless bra and a thong. Oh well. I don't even bother to cover myself.

"Shut the door, asshole!"

His eyes darken, and he steps in and starts to close the door.

I narrow my gaze on him and stomp forward. "That's not what I meant." I push on his chest until he's back in the hallway and slam the door in his face.

Fucker.

"Is Austin going?" I can hear his anger through the barrier between us.

"Why do you care?" I shuffle through my dresser for a bra, wanting to get out of this strapless.

"You know why."

I roll my eyes, then move to my closet. "He lives down the street, so I'm sure he'll be there."

"Did you invite him?"

I already picked out an outfit for tonight, but his presence has me all over the place.

"Not directly." My fingers work the clasp of the strapless and it falls to the floor. I peek out the door. "Everyone will be there. Ryan said he's going."

"I know." His voice sounds strained, but I think I just gave him some side-boob view, maybe even some nip.

Am I trying to tease him? Always.

Suffer, asshole.

"Are you going?" Damn curiosity.

"Yes."

I pull the dress I picked out over my head. "Why?"

"Because you are."

His answer irks me and gives me the damn happy vibes.

"This is the year-end graduation party. The biggest party of the year. Don't expect me to pay you any attention at all."

"Wow. When did I become the clinger?"

"When you started stalking me." I throw a flip-flop at the door.

He chuckles. "It's not stalking if I love you."

I know he's quoting some meme floating around the Internet, but fuck . . . those words. They stop me in my tracks, which is bent over as I slip on my shoes.

I stomp back over to the door and peek through. "Don't start that crap up again. You had your fun. It's my turn now."

His mouth pops open, anger flaring in his eyes, then it's suddenly gone. "You're right."

The words "I am?" almost slip from my lips. It's such a departure from the norm that my whole system is in shock, leaving me to stare at him, wordless.

"I'm a jealous asshole. I know. I can't stand the thought of anyone touching you, most of all Austin."

I close the door and walk over to my dresser to pick up some bracelets and my wristlet, then throw open the door. His eyes go wide, running up and down my body, setting my skin on fire. "Well freaking get used to it, because you have no say in any part of my life." I push him aside.

Before I can scoot by, Brayden grabs my wrist. The calm demeanor he's mastered all day is gone, replaced by a fury that almost makes him look like a maniac.

"I'll walk with you." The party is only a few blocks away.

I wrench my arm free. "Walk by yourself."

I make sure to push him hard on my way out, giving me time to race ahead and down the stairs.

My heart hammers against my ribs as I stomp off down the street. The party isn't too far, and I plan to drink, so heels be damned, I'm walking. It also helps give me a Brayden breather and time to calm down.

The block is already parked up with cars when I arrive, and I can't wait to find my girls. I pull out my phone to check a text I got on my way from Jenna, hoping she's already here.

Sam IS well endowed. See you . . . sometime. lol!

A smile spreads on my face, and I shake my head. Looks like Jenna is getting exactly what she wanted for graduation.

I wave to some people I know who are hanging out on the lawn as I walk in. The music is loud, thumping all over the whole-house speaker system. There's no view of Ashley or

Marilyn, so I head toward the kitchen where the drink of the day is undoubtedly being served.

After dealing with Brayden before I left, I need a drink. Something strong to erase the tingling I can still feel from where he touched me.

It's still pretty early, but the place has a ton of people, forcing me to weave through and giving the drink hand gesture to a few friends trying to pull me over. Before I can turn back around I slam into someone, my hands out, stopping on a belt.

"Hi, Kira."

I crane my head back to look up at my tallest friend, reigning in at six foot eight. "Hey, Thomas."

If basketball doesn't work out for him, he's got brains to fall back on. That, and classic farm-boy good looks.

"How are you?"

"Not bad. Haven't seen you in a while."

We were lab partners back in chemistry, and he's helped me out more than once when calculus tried to kill me.

He chuckles. "Since Tuesday?"

I shrug. "Hey, in high school terms, that is forever."

"Glad to be missed."

"Yeah, well, soon you'll be some bigshot at IU and you'll forget all about me."

"I'm not so sure about that," he says. "Are you excited about college?"

"Definitely. You?"

"It's gonna be hard, the practice schedule is intense, but I get to play for Indiana University."

"That's awesome." I smile up at him, genuinely happy and excited for him.

"Too bad you won't be there."

"OSU calls," I say with a shrug. "And I'm stoked that Ryan transferred and will be there."

Thomas's eyes dart around. "Is he here?"

I shake my head. "Not yet. That I've seen, at least."

He blows out a breath. "Cool."

"Why cool?"

His eyes go wide. "Oh . . . N-no reason."

I quirk my brow at him. "Tell me."

"It's just . . . I'm talking to you, and the guy is scary protective of you."

Ah, I get it now. The Austin incident.

Jerk is always getting in my way.

"Are the rumors that bad?"

He lets out a nervous chuckle. "He always kept guys away from you, him and Brayden Hunt, but that was next level when he attacked Austin."

I purse my lips. "Yeah, it was."

"Ever since then, it's been kinda hard to work up the courage to ask you out."

I blink up at him. "What?"

He smiles and ducks his head. "You're not with Austin, I hear. Can . . . can I take you out sometime?"

I stare back at him in shock. I like Thomas, and I can totally see him being a great boyfriend, but I've never thought of him that way.

Probably Brayden's fault. I'm sure I can probably blame him for just about everything for the past few years.

"No," I whisper, hating that I'm turning a great guy down. "I'm sorry. I'm a mess right now."

His expression falls and he swallows hard. "Too late, then."

"Or too early." I smile up at him. "If things were different, I would say yes."

He chuckles. "Thanks for the pity yes."

"Hey, it's not like that. I like you, but . . ."

"It's complicated?"

"Extremely."

"Well, if things become uncomplicated, give me a call," he says as he backs away with a wave.

Turning down a guy with so many good points? I must be insane.

I take a left to the kitchen, suddenly bummed. What would it be like to date a nice guy like that? To not have two fuckers being a pain in my ass?

Maybe I should become a nun.

The counters are covered with red Solo cups and what looks like an entire liquor store worth of booze. Then there's the keg in the middle of the room.

Perusing the display of bottles, I spot a familiar label and twist the top off.

Mmm, raspberry-flavored vodka.

"What did he want?"

I jump, the bottle slipping from my lips, vodka spilling down my chin. "Shit!"

Austin steps in front of me, offering up his shirt.

"You scared me," I say, wiping my chin off.

He gives me that sexy smile of his. The one that should turn me into a puddle of goo, but as usual, it's only mild excitement.

"You're cute when you're scared." He looks down at my bottle. "What are you drinking?"

I blink at him, then look down. "Vodka."

"Starting with the heavy stuff, huh?"

I shrug in response and take a few gulps. It burns the whole way down, making my body involuntarily shudder from the strength.

"You know, if you're doing that so you can seduce me, you don't have to. I'm ready, willing, and available for you."

I start to laugh, almost at ease with his flirtation attempt, then I remember what happened and stop.

"Me and every other female."

He cringes. "Ouch."

Did that sting? Good.

"You know if I could go back, I never would have—"

"Fucked that slut?" I'm laying it all out, tired of all the bullshit.

"That's not it."

"What is it, then? Because I'm still pissed, Austin."

"I never would have let you push me away. Then I never would have . . ."

His admission softens me. I know it's Brayden and his past with her that makes me hate her so much. "I just can't stand that of all people, why her? Jennifer's fucked half the school. Who knows what diseases she's carrying."

"Excuse me? What the fuck are you saying about me?" Jennifer asks as she steps forward.

It's then I realize we've gained a few prying eyes and ears, including slutty herself.

I take another swig of the open bottle in my hand. "I was talking about how you've ruined the pool of available guys in the area."

Her blue eyes are wide, jaw tight. "Who are you to judge me? What makes you so special, Kira?"

"I don't fuck every guy in a ten-mile radius."

"No, you're a cock tease who has them running to me when you won't put out."

My eyes go wide and I step forward, practically snarling. "You are so disgusting! Is that how you're going to go through life? On your back?"

"Not just on my back, but on my knees, too. Not that little Miss Priss would know anything about that."

"You don't know anything about me."

"And you know shit about me. So, stop running your prude mouth. Stuff a dick in there, and maybe you'll see the fun in it."

"Fuck you!"

She lifts the hem of her skirt and slaps her pussy. "Go for it, bitch! This pussy knows how to satisfy a man. Maybe that's why guys run from you to me."

I snap, lunging forward, my fingers clenched tight around the bottle, ready to smash it into her skull.

The bottle misses as Austin pushes Jennifer back, and I'm yanked away. An arm wraps around my waist, lifting me up into the air.

"Let me go!"

I turn back to find Brayden's green eyes as he drags me away.

Brayden

"What is your malfunction? I said, let me go!"

Her nails dig into my arm as I pull her through two rooms and out the back door. She doesn't weigh much, but her flailing legs kicking around as she tries to break free make it tough to hold on.

There are a few people out on the deck who scurry away as we exit the house.

I set her back on the ground, and she sways, regaining her balance on her sexy-ass heels. They match her sexy-ass dress, and I want to fucking drag her away.

"Calm down."

She scowls at me. "What the fuck? Couldn't stand to see your fuck doll get hit?"

"It looked more like you wanted to kill her, especially with that bottle." I point down to the bottle, which is in her death grip.

She shifts her weight from foot to foot, jaw locked tight.

"What is it about her?"

"That was about you. I can buy you sexy lingerie, but I don't have enough for bail."

"That's laughable."

"Why?"

"You're my devil, not my knight in shining armor."

My jaw ticks, and I try not to cringe at the sting of her words. "Kira, I love you. I'm always going to protect you, even when it's from yourself."

She stares at me for a moment, then takes a swig from the bottle. "I don't want that."

"Tough. Now, hand over the bottle." I hold out my hand expectantly.

Her eyes narrow, and she steps back. "Fuck you."

"I'm not telling you not to drink, just pace yourself. Give me the bottle and sip on a beer."

She lets out a sigh and holds it out. "In exchange, you leave me the hell alone tonight."

I snatch it from her, glancing down at the label. "For a while." Vodka. She was sucking down vodka like it was water.

"All night." She jabs a finger into my chest. "This is my night. Don't ruin it."

"I'll have my eye on you. No more starting fights."

She crosses her arms over her chest and stalks past. I don't miss the whispered "asshole" as she goes.

My gaze stays fixed on her, watching her as she gets a beer, and her friends, Ashley and Marilyn, come up behind her. Hopefully they can help contain any more explosions.

I twist off the top and take a long pull from the bottle. It burns all the way down as I slump into one of the deck chairs.

Kira has never liked Jenn, but I didn't know it was so deep. If I'd arrived a few seconds later . . . She was just lashing out, but the bottle is thick glass, and heavy with liquid.

I stare at the bottle before taking another drink.

Austin dug up old wounds I'd created in Kira when he did Jenn. That night I royally fucked up. But there's a chance she'll forgive him for a one-time slipup.

I stand back up, setting the vodka on the table, and take my own advice as I head in for a beer.

For two hours I catch up with old friends, but never far from Kira.

Jenn tries to get my attention a few times, but I brush her off. She's just after sex, but there's only one pussy for me.

A movement of auburn catches my eye and I look over to Kira, who's at baby giraffe status on those fucking sexy heels of hers. Her girls insisted on a couple of celebration shots, and now she's tipsy.

Panic sets in as she tells them she'll be right back. I'm out of my seat and following her without a thought. There are too many predators here tonight and no one will be taking advantage of my girl.

A couple of guys notice and start to follow, but immediately change course when they see me.

Yeah, I've still got it. Fear me, assholes.

She steps into the bathroom, and I lean against the wall to wait. When the door opens back up, her sea legs leave her unbalanced and she bounces off either side of the doorway.

I can't help but chuckle. She looks so damn cute.

The sound alerts her to my presence, and her brow knits as she narrows her gaze.

"What?"

I shake my head and hold out a bottle of water. "Here. Drink this."

"I don't want it."

"Just do it." Fucking stubborn as ever.

"What is it?"

"Water."

Her expression softens and she grabs it, unscrewing the top and taking a few long gulps.

"Thanks."

"No problem. Just let me know when you want to go home. I'll walk with you."

"I don't need you to." She thrusts the bottle back at me and stomps off as best she can.

I watch her, my jaw ticking, my hands wanting to grab her. The anger is so great I almost miss Austin spotting her, then making his way through the crowd.

Almost.

There's no way in hell I'm letting him near her.

A few long steps, and I've made up the distance. I reach out and grab her forearm, tilting it so I can reach the wristlet she's wearing. Her keys are clipped to the strap, and before her drunk mind can process what I'm doing, I have her keys.

Dad and Sonia are probably in bed. The last thing she'll want to do is let them find out she's drunk.

"Hey!" she yells, jumping into the air and swiping.

Being nearly a foot taller than her definitely has its advantages, and I will use every one I can get to keep her from him.

I step back, holding her keychain high in the air. "Sorry, something you want?"

"Brayden! Stop being an asshole!"

I turn and start heading to the entrance, praying to God she's smart enough to follow.

NINE
BRAYDEN

"Give me my keys, Brayden!"

She's right behind me, chasing after me.

Just as I want.

I wish she could understand the kind of favor she just did for Austin. She saved his ass.

"Give them to me!"

Oh, she's pissed. But there's no sympathizing. I'm equally as heated. "You're lucky you're not over my shoulder right now."

"Why are you always being such a dick?"

Kira has no fucking clue how nice I'm being considering that Austin was eye-fucking her in that dress all night.

In front of me. No fucks given.

I bet everyone in that party knew he was there for her, and he made no moves to try to hide it.

Kira calls out my name again.

We're only a few blocks away from home. I'm going to make sure she gets inside, then I'll lock her in her room if I must.

I'm supposed to be playing nice. Austin's audacity and the sheer lust clouding my system make it impossible for me to do so.

"Brayden, I'm not fucking kidding!"

"Neither am I." We cross onto our block, passing by her old house.

"Oh my God, just give me my freaking keys!"

She tackles me from behind. The impact of her body takes me by surprise, and I stumble forward.

Four steps, and I slam into the brick fence surrounding her old house. The same brick fence we played behind countless times.

Her arms tighten around my neck. "Last warning. Give me the damn keys."

I burst out laughing and straighten. Grabbing her arms, I try to ease her off. "Woman, we're already here."

She presses closer, wiggling, all the while trying in vain to choke me.

Fire explodes through my veins. I'm already beyond fucking turned on, been like this forever now. The last thing I need is that lickable, tight little body rubbing up on me in any way.

"Give them back to me so I can go back to the party!"

She's drunk, and adorable, and absolutely delusional. I've been good, kept as much of a respectful distance as my hunger for her has allowed. Have tried my best to not push too hard after that day at the restaurant.

That doesn't mean I'm going to let her return to that party. She's done for the night.

I pry her arms off me and turn to back away from her.

Kira's panting, eyes lit up with the challenge, her hair a sexy mess. Instead of anger, I see what seems to be amusement glowing in her eyes.

Fuck, I want to eat her. Don't know if I can control myself much longer.

She points her little finger menacingly at me. "Brayden . . ."

I throw my hands up and back away some more. "Go ahead. Shred me alive. But you know I'm not letting you go back over there." Her annoyed huff makes me smile.

Her lips twitch in response. She's fighting to hold back her own smile, and it only makes me smile wider. "You do know I'm *very* willing to shred you alive, right?" She starts coming toward me, almost like a predator stalking prey.

Fuck, yeah. That has to be one of the sexiest things I've ever seen.

It takes all of my willpower to continue backing away. To remind myself that she's drunk and I have no right to take advantage of that. "You do know I'll probably end up liking it, don't you?" I mumble, even more turned on by the idea of her clawing at me. Biting into me.

I'll even let her draw blood. Whatever she wants.

A drunken giggle escapes her as her lips stretch involuntarily into a smile.

Those lips. God help me, I want them. Want to love on them. Fuck them. Come on them.

The air between us is suddenly hot and playful, and I don't understand where the change came from. It's so sudden that I'm left reeling, clueless how to deal with it.

Is she ready to give in to what she feels for me?

Does she want me to do every single thing I'm imagining myself doing to her?

We've made our way onto the driveway wrapped around the side of the house. Kira stops and tilts her head, staring behind me. "It's still there. Forgot about that."

I turn to see what she's looking at—the large, dark outline of the tree house Ryan and I built almost ten years ago. The new owners of the house never took it down, and I think they even upgraded it for their kids at one point.

Kira rushes up to me and grabs my hand. "Come on."

I let her lead me at first, too caught up in the feel of her small hand in mine. "Kira, wait. The neighbors."

She doesn't slow down one bit, her heels clicking on the pavement. "Driveway is empty. They aren't here."

"That doesn't mean anything."

Spinning around, she places her finger on my lips. "Shhh."

I can't help it. Groaning, I suck her finger into my mouth and Kira lets me, her lips parting, breaths speeding up. I watch her pupils expand, my dick pounding inside my jeans.

She swallows heavily and slides her finger out of my mouth. "Come."

Shit. The way she says that, I almost do.

Christ, if she's planning to take me up into that tree house to seduce me, drunk or not, I don't think I'll be able to resist her.

Kira stops next to where the driveway ends and bends down to slide off her heels. Just that simple act hits me like a punch to the dick. "Kira, this isn't a good idea."

She throws me a playful look over her shoulder. "Oh, shut up. You know you want to."

Damn me, does she even realize how sultry and delicious she looks right now? Barefoot, in that tight-as-fuck dress, that teasing expression making my dick twitch hungrily for her. "I want to do a lot of things I can't do right now." Most of them don't even involve getting her up into that tree house.

Ignoring my murmured comment, she walks onto the grass, hips swaying with every step.

I'm helpless not to follow, my eyes glued to that perfect bubble butt of hers. She stops at the ladder leading up to the tree house. This ladder is brand new, definitely not the same one that snapped with her on it years ago.

It's been ten years since that day, yet my chest fucking tightens, like I'm experiencing it all over again. That feeling of almost losing her chokes me. A feeling I've felt too many times in my life.

Kira places her heels next to the tree and grabs onto the ladder.

I step closer. She's drunk—not falling all over herself drunk, but I'm still worried.

Not that I should be. She climbs that ladder as expertly as she always did. Halfway up, she stops to check if I'm following her.

I'm not.

Her position allows me to see up her skirt clearly, and she's either wearing the smallest thong on earth—

Or she isn't wearing anything under that dress.

My body tightens with more lust.

My blood heats with raw anger.

"You coming up?" she asks me, as if nothing's fucking wrong.

"Kira . . . tell me you're wearing something under that." Fists clenched, I struggle for some semblance of calm.

The insidious question nagging at the back of my mind bursts forward—did Kira dress up like that for Austin?

This motherfucking pain, man. It's the reason I'm willing to take whatever she throws at me. I didn't realize it at the time, but this is what I did to her, what I made her feel for too damn long.

I'll take all of it. Including this hit. I deserve it.

Exhaling, I grab on to the ladder.

She rushes up into the tree house, not answering my question.

Sure, go ahead, girl. Leave that knife shoved inside my chest. Fifty-fifty right?

I follow her up into the tree house, not believing that I let her convince me to do this. We're going to be arrested if we're caught.

When I get inside, Kira's sitting down against the far wall. All I can see is her outline, her long hair falling over her shoulders.

We're not up here to have sex.

I'm having a hard time convincing myself of that. Having an even harder time believing that she isn't entertaining the idea as much as I am. That she isn't thinking of us tearing into each other up here, in the dark, in the same place we spent so many hours playing as children.

Fuck, that thought turns me on. I'm probably a sick bastard for that, but I can't help it.

I move closer to her. Can't have her. She's had too much to drink. The litany runs through my mind. A warning.

If I do anything with her now, she'll have an excuse to pretend it was all a mistake tomorrow.

No. The next time I touch Kira, I want her fully aware that she's letting me. That she fucking wants it as much as I do.

It's still hell. Every inch that I move closer, all I imagine is fisting all that hair and bringing her to my mouth.

I sit down slightly across from her. Her head turns in my direction. "Turn on your phone's light," she whispers in a fucking siren's voice.

"It's not a good idea for us to be up here." I wish she understood how much I mean that.

"It's not a good idea for me to be up here with *you*, you mean."

That comment shouldn't sting as much as it does. "I rather you be up here with me than anyone else," I growl.

"Then turn on the light."

Shit. Mother of fuck. Her voice.

Like the pathetic slave I am, I bring my phone out and do as she says. As soon as the light is on and I can stare into her eyes, I ask her that question. The evil one that won't leave me the hell alone. "Did you dress up like this for Austin?" Damn it, I *need* to know, even if that answer ends up ruining me.

She just stares at me with her big hazel eyes. Eyes that are usually so expressive. Now I can't read them. She's getting good at hiding what's on her mind. Especially from me.

I grind my teeth at that realization.

"It's not cool what you did back there, Brayden. Taking my keys."

My shoulder jerks in a shrug. "I'll apologize for a million things, but not that. I wanted you out of there."

"What if I storm into your life and get in the way of you having fun?"

I laugh at that. She still doesn't get it. At this point, I'm starting to wonder just how far I'll have to go to convince her. "I'm yours. You have permission to do whatever the hell you want to me."

She seems to mull that over. "You wanted me out of there . . . why? Because Austin was there?"

The teeth grinding resumes. "Yes."

"You shouldn't care so much."

"Are you fucking kidding me?" It takes all my self-control to keep from yelling out. "He loves you. You . . . you feel something for him. I don't know what, but it's there. I told you I'd forgive you for choosing him, but don't expect me to just sit back and do nothing to try to stop it. Until you make that choice, I'm going to fight like hell for you." This topic grates. A feeling I can't stand, scratching its way through me.

On top of it all, Kira continues to sit there, calm as can be. "I love how you still think you have any say in that decision."

I run both my hands through my hair. "He went back and slept with Jennifer."

"I'll remind you again—so did you."

"When I was *seventeen*, and not after sleeping with you. You . . . fuck!" Saying it is almost as hard as remembering it. But not saying it isn't going to erase the fact that it happened, either. "You gave yourself to him. He was your first, and he still ran back to her."

Her eyes drop, but not before I see what flashes in them.

"Tell me," I say, voice hoarse. "Tell me to fucking destroy him for what he did to you, and I'll go back and do so right now." It's not the first time I've begged her for this. Probably won't be the last.

Expression calm once more, she leans back on the wall, eyes focused ahead. "You really do care that he hurt me." She sounds surprised.

"Of course I fucking do."

She laughs under her breath. "It's not like he and I were together, so I have no real reason to be upset, right?"

I wish that was true. So damn bad. "You might have not been together, but there was something between you guys. He had no right to do that to you."

"Was there something going on between me and Austin?"

"You were sleeping together." I can't keep the bitterness out of my tone; don't even bother to try.

"I only slept with Austin that one time."

What . . . my mouth falls open, and I can't formulate a response. I can barely formulate thoughts.

Once? He only had her *once*?

Once is more than enough, but hearing that he hasn't slept with Kira since that one time . . . fuck. I feel like I've been hit. Elation bubbles up in me, until I see the look on her face.

It doesn't matter how many times they were together, if she keeps insisting she isn't hurt. Obviously she is, and even though I don't know why, the desire to hurt him in return won't leave me alone. "It's fucked up what he did to you, Kira. Let me make him pay."

"Why is it okay for you to hurt me, but it's wrong that he did so?"

God damn, this girl has a way of cutting me to the quick with her words. "None of the things I did to you were okay. I've told you hundreds of times. I fucked up. I fucked up so bad, Kira."

"So you want me to forgive you, but not him?"

I get why she's asking me these things. I even appreciate the fact that, instead of pushing me away completely, she's actually trying to understand me.

Still, opening up isn't my strong suit. Not even with her. Being put on the spot so suddenly makes me want to shut down, avoid further discussion.

But I know I won't. When it comes to what I want with Kira, I finally have my shit straight. I'm going to do what's right. "You can forgive him if you want. Yet we both know that the one thing I don't want is for you to be with him."

She tilts her head, hair sliding over her shoulder. My phone goes dark. I hurry to turn it back on, needing to see more of her.

Just looking at her is better than any sex I've ever had with anyone else.

"It has to be your pride," Kira says thoughtfully. "That's why you don't want me with him."

Fuck, yeah. My pride is involved. I won't deny it. I'm a guy, and some other fucker is actively trying to take what's mine. "It's not just that. I love you."

"You say that so easily now. But you never stopped to think how much you were hurting me all those years. I'm supposed to forgive you for that? What if his reasons are similar to yours?"

The comparisons to Austin are fucking killing me. No matter how deserved they are, she has to stop that shit before I lose my mind. "You're right, baby. I didn't stop to think about anything."

Kira tenses up at my admission, and I see the anger rise in her. The resentment.

I hurry to add, "I was too caught up in my own pain, and I had to escape. That's what losing you did to me. It fucked me up so bad, and I was already fucked up to begin with." Admitting I'd been a pussy back then isn't easy, but it's true. "I was frantic to numb myself, and I couldn't. In the end, that was the hardest lesson."

"What was?"

"That no one on this planet is you, and you're all I fucking want. I don't care how, what I have to do to earn you." Leaning toward her, I lock eyes with her. "And trust me, Kitty. I've learned my lesson well."

Even in the dim light of my phone, I see her cheeks pinken. Her expression is lucid, focused intensely on me, trying to gauge my honesty, and I start to wonder if she's even drunk anymore.

Kira gets on all fours and starts crawling toward me.

I tense.

Breath leaves me.

Desire collides with that ever-present, insatiable hunger. The force of it burns through my veins and slams into my cock.

My mouth fucking waters with every centimeter that she gets closer.

She's drunk. Definitely still tipsy at the least. There's no way one of my most violent fantasies is coming true this easily.

I slam my head back against the wall. "Kira, why—*don't*."

Her hand lands on the floor next to my hip. Her other hand lands on the other side.

My hips jerk up toward her, seeking. "*Kitty*." Don't do this to me. Not right now. I can't fucking fight it . . .

"You're only saying all these things because you want to fuck me."

I groan at the tone of her voice—husky, low, *hungry* for me.

"And for some reason, Brayden—" She presses her lips to my ear. "—Right now, I really want to let you fuck me."

Oh God. "No, baby. Please."

She drags her lips along my jaw, down to my chin.

Push her away. Fucking hell, do it.

"All . . . this . . . time . . ." Kira ducks her head, kissing the spot under my chin. A sweet, almost affectionate kiss; it sends shocks through me, making my hair stand on end. "Trying to get me to fuck you—" Parting her lips, she drags her bottom one up my chin, toward my mouth. "And now you're turning me down?"

I snap my head back before my lips connect with hers. "If you were fucking sober, I'd have you flat on that floor right now, thighs spread for me."

Giggling, she rubs her cheek against mine, purring in the back of her throat.

My cock jerks at that sexy sound.

"Do it," Kira whispers. "Pin me under you. Spread me wide."

Holy . . . fuck . . .

Such dirty words from my girl . . . I freeze, then reach out and grab onto her waist to pull her back.

Shit. Bad move.

Her waist is tiny, fits right into my hands. I could use it to control her rhythm, how fast or slow she slides up and down my cock . . .

No.

She bites into my neck, right where she marked me before, and her hand lands on my dick.

"Kira, baby. Oh fuck, yes."

Biting down harder, she jerks me through my jeans.

"Fuck, I'm gonna come, Kitty. Stop."

She moans around my flesh, sucking hard, *wanting* to mark me.

My dick pulsates for her.

Her hand squeezes down around me.

Groaning, I lean forward and kiss her neck. Just one kiss. One taste and I'll stop.

My tongue flicks out.

One taste isn't enough. Fuck, it'll never be enough.

I thrust up into her hand, sucking her into my mouth.

She whimpers and bites me even harder.

Fuck yeah, I want it. I want the promise of violent sex between us. Want her claw marks running down my back, her bite marks all over me.

"Fuck me, Brayden. Fuck me hard."

Yes. God, yes. I slide my hands down her slim back, toward her ass.

Sanity shoots through my mind. A momentary burst of common sense.

Not like this. Not. Fucking. Like. This.

I slam back into the wall behind me, at the same time jerking Kira away from me.

On her knees before me, she blinks up at me, expression hazy with lust.

I scramble to my feet, adrenaline pumping through my veins. My cock is so hard he's practically pointing at her. "No." My voice breaks; I clear my throat before speaking again. "It's not happening like this, Kira."

"I don't get it. You keep trying to fuck me."

"I don't just want to fuck you!" Bending down, I run my fingers down her cheek. Smooth. Delicious. If she were sober right now, I'd eat every inch of her. "I want *you*. Not just your pussy. And letting you fuck me while you're drunk doesn't help me wi-th that."

Her calmness evaporates. Jaw clenched, she moves away from me. "I'll never be your girl, Brayden."

It hurts every time she says that. Not that I pay too much attention to it. She wants to believe her words, I see that. Regardless, it's not true. "If you truly believe that, come find me tomorrow. Sober. Come and ask me to fuck you while you're fully aware of what you're asking for."

I watch her get to her feet. "And if I do?"

Impatience rides me, almost overruling my resolve. I don't allow myself to contemplate my answer for too long. "If you do . . . then I'll give you what you want."

God help her, because I will. I'll give her every single thing she's asking for.

"Even if I were to come find you tomorrow, sex is all you'd get from me."

I laugh. Not because I find this funny, but I can hear the doubt in her tone. "You keep telling yourself that."

She doesn't respond. Her stubbornness is almost visible. Without another word, she heads to the entrance of the tree house.

All right. If that's how she wants to play it, I'll continue to go along with it. For now. Eventually, I'll break her down.

When it comes to this—to us—she isn't more stubborn than I am.

TEN

BRAYDEN

June 10th, 2015

"What is he doing home?"

I grind my teeth as I pull up into the driveway next to my father's car. It's past one in the afternoon on a Wednesday. If it wasn't for Kira's car sitting out front, I'd turn my ass back around before walking inside. I'm ninety percent sure he's cheating on Sonia. All the signs are there—late nights working, missing dinner, fighting, and a waning of affection between them.

I'm not even out of my car when the asshole opens the garage door and walks out. He stops mid-step to stare at me before continuing on.

"How did it go?" He shuffles his suit jacket from one arm to the other and pulls his keys out, keeping his gaze from mine.

"Good. I found an apartment near campus in the same complex Ryan and Dana are in."

He gives a curt nod. "How much is that going to set me back a month?"

114

I clench my teeth. "About the same." I hate these conversations. The awkward, stilted flow of forced words from a broken relationship. It's almost like we're strangers, and I don't know if it will ever change. I don't even know if I want it to. I hate him.

After throwing his jacket in the car, he sighs and looks up at me. "I wish you'd decided years ago to go to OSU instead of changing in your last year of undergrad. Would have saved me thousands in out-of-state tuition."

It takes everything in me not to go off on him, to explode out all the feelings I've been holding back for years.

I shrug, the tension thickening between us. "Yeah, well, it's where I'm going to get my Master's, so I figured why not go now?"

"That, and your *sister* is going there." I hate his tone. The way he accentuates that one word.

"She's not my sister." It's an automatic response, and one I've practically growled at my father. Too late to take it back now.

A triumphant sneer forms on his lips. "The law says so, and everyone knows she's your stepsister."

His attitude screams out that he knows I want Kira. Not that it matters. I don't care what people are going to think anymore.

"Fuck that."

His eyes flash as he slams the car door and stomps over to me. We're eye to eye, but that doesn't mean he stops trying to appear larger than me.

"Listen and listen good, Brayden. I am your fucking father, and you will respect me and what I'm about to say."

I let out a harsh laugh and shake my head, my eyes hard.

"After all the shit you've done? You lost that a long time ago."

He grabs hold of my shirt and pushes me back against the side of my car. Face inches from mine, the explosive, testosterone-fueled rage I know all too well—one of his character traits I inherited—emanates from him. My fists are balled up, ready to lay the fucker out.

"Stop acting like a little spoiled-ass punk kid. Grow the hell up. You're twenty-one now, and that means only two more years of tuition from me before you have to pay for it yourself."

He pushes off me and heads back to his car.

"Fine by me."

"One last thing." He opens the door again and points a finger at me. "If you want to stay in this house, make sure you keep your fucking dick away from your sister." He slips into the car, slamming the door, then revs the engine as he backs out.

My nostrils flare with each harsh breath, nails digging into my palms. The pain is the only thing that kept me from hitting him, from getting out all of my anger and frustration. Blood thumps through my veins as I stand there, waiting to calm down before I tear through the house and do the exact opposite of his words.

An anger fuck will not win me any points with Kira, especially for our first time.

Instead I stare down at the concrete beneath my feet, anger boiling off me as I attempt to blow the driveway up with my mind.

When it doesn't work, and I give in to the fact that I do *not* have superpowers, I head inside. Once in the shade of the garage, I notice Sonia's SUV parked there. Another oddity for a Wednesday afternoon.

The thought that maybe they were having a little afternoon delight flies right out of my head when I walk into the kitchen from the garage.

Sonia stands at the kitchen island, shoulders shaking. She gasps at the sound of the door shutting and turns to me, her fingers quickly wiping the tears from her cheeks.

"Brayden, you're back." She gives me her best attempt at a smile. "Any luck?"

I nod, my hands twitching at my sides to offer her some comfort, but not knowing how. The hurt on her face makes me feel bad for my stepmom for the first time. Sonia didn't know what she was getting into when she started sleeping with my father. I've been pissed at her for years, but the sad expression she's been wearing the last few weeks is melting my anger because it reminds me so much of what my mom went through.

That fault lies with my father, not her. I see that now. Vulnerable and lonely, she was easy prey. And I know the only damn reason he married her was to have the perks of a wife again.

"Yeah, I'll be just a few buildings down from Ryan and Dana."

Her fake smile reaches her eyes as it turns into a real one. "That's great. I'm happy you'll be close." Her gaze flickers to the clock on the wall. "I need to be getting back to work."

"Home for lunch?"

She picks her purse up from the counter, along with the keys laying next to it. "I somehow forgot my phone this morning, so your father and I met for lunch."

I step aside, opening up the path to the door.

"Dinner will be a little late tonight."

I give her an honest smile. "Don't worry about it. I know how to feed myself." *I did it for years before he married you.*

She reaches out and squeezes my arm. "Thank you."

After she leaves, I stay in the middle of the kitchen, listening to the sounds of the house, thinking. Lost in thought, lost in memories, lost in dreams. There's a duality going on, deja vu like energy buzzing through me.

The click of a door, followed by the sound of water rushing through the pipes in one of the walls, reminds me I'm not alone.

She's here. Upstairs.

I move without thought to the entry and look up the stairs, listening.

Music blares, but isn't enough to cover the beating of water raining down in the hall bathroom or the unmistakable clatter of rings sliding across the shower curtain rod.

Three seconds later, my dick is hard and leading the way up the stairs. The door is open a crack, the music radiating from her room.

Kira's naked.

Kira's naked a few steps away.

A ripple ignites my body as it moves through. I reach down and adjust my hardening cock as I step into my room.

There's no stopping where my mind has gone and where it's taking me. I pull my shirt up as I toe my shoes off, then pull my shorts and boxer-briefs down, taking my socks with them.

Completely naked with my cock bouncing, I walk over to the bathroom door.

Wet heat, saturated with a sweet, succulent scent of my girl and whatever shit she uses, pours out of the gap she's left. I place my hand on the door and slowly push it open enough for me to slip in, then push it back.

She's singing along with the music, a Maroon 5 song. The combination of sounds is so loud, she doesn't even hear me.

I grab onto my cock, stroking it a few times to calm the fucking raging need for the friction of her pussy.

Was I pissed off? Doing some deep thinking a few minutes ago? I don't even remember, because my dick rules with a fucking iron fist. The directive is simple, one objective.

Come.

And then fucking come again.

All over and inside my girl.

I bite my lip, holding back a moan as I squeeze down on my cock.

The song ends and I hold my breath, listening to the water hit her body, hoping she doesn't hear me. After all, there are some markings on my body I'm not ready for her to see. The most recent is still healing, and I have nothing to hide them.

The next song is hard and sexy, and I can't stop my hips rocking my cock in and out of my fist. Being this close to her naked body is too much for my poor dick. It needs, begs for, skin on skin.

I pull the side of the curtain opposite of the showerhead and peek in. She's facing away from me, her head under the spray rinsing out her hair.

I take the opportunity and climb in behind her.

She hears me this time and jumps as her head whips around. Her eyes go wide, then she's facing away again. "Get out! You can't be in here. Mom and Steve are downstairs."

I freeze for a split second before smiling, not that she can see. She didn't call me names or hit me or tell me to fuck off. No, Kira's worried about our parents.

"They went back to work." I step forward, the tip of my cock pushing into her soft ass cheek before sliding up and landing in the dip of her fucking perfect backside, the tip pressing against her back. The rest of me stops an inch or two before touching her as I reach over her shoulder and place one hand on the wall while the other moves down her side to her hip.

"I said get out." She tries to sound tough, to give a biting edge to her tone, but it doesn't work.

This little bit, caging her in, is enough to turn her on, to take over her body just like she takes over mine.

I'm breaking her down. Little by little.

"Not leaving. The scent of warm, wet kitty is one fucking strong aphrodisiac, and I want to play."

She shoves her elbow back into my ribs, making me flinch but not hurting. "Idiot."

I let out a chuckle as I brush her hair away from her neck. She's more worried about being caught fooling around than me touching her, teasing her, making her come.

"When my cock is finally inside you, that's when you'll get it. After that, no one else will be able to satisfy you. It'll be me and my cock you'll crave. Once inside, you'll never want me to leave."

Her fingers flex against the tile and she lets out a whimper, her hips rotating.

I groan, staring down at the drop of precome, spreading it across her back. "A little more of that, and I'll empty my balls all over you."

Her breath comes out in pants as I rock into her, one hand on her hip, drowning in the friction of her skin on my dick. I snake my hand around her waist and down, slipping them between her pussy lips, finding her clit and grinding down on it.

She lets out a gasp and a strained moan.

"No. No, no, no." She shakes her head and grabs hold of the shower curtain, yanking it open.

I don't even have time to grab her before she picks up her towels and runs out of the bathroom.

The warm spray of water falls on me as the door to her room slams shut.

She left before I could tease her any more, before I could make her come, make us both come. Now, I'm left in a fucking state with my cock ready to burst.

The music stops, but no new song begins.

I'll give her a new sound for her playlist.

The tip of my dick is wet. Wet enough that I don't need to reach for the soap. I palm the head, smearing all that precome around. Once my hand is nice and wet, I slide it across the top of my hard-on, around, squeezing tight.

It's almost enough to make me come.

I let go of my cock and flatten my hands against the tiles. Leaning forward, I try breathing slowly in an effort to calm myself. I don't want to come. Not yet.

The agony of wanting Kira, of not having her, is fucking delicious. Logically, I know I shouldn't get off on this pain, but I do. I want more. I'm already delirious for her, but I want to be pushed so far past the edge that the sickness in me becomes permanent.

Maybe it already has.

Her ass felt so good beneath the sensitive skin of my tip.

My hips rock at the memory, thrusting my cock into empty air.

"Fuck." Reaching down with one hand, I cup my tight balls, tugging on them. Running my fingers in light circles around the soft, ridged skin, I close my eyes and imagine it's Kira's wet tongue.

My dick throbs, and I feel more precome leak out.

She's close to giving in to me. I sense it every day a little more. If I were to get out of this shower right now and chase her to her room, she'd let me take what I want.

She'd let me lay her on her bed and slowly spread her legs open.

I lick my lips, imagining myself licking up and down her inner thigh.

Would she be ticklish there? I'd spend extra time at the juncture of her thigh, teasing her with the tip of my tongue before sucking one juicy, bare lip into my mouth. My lower lip would rub across her clit and it would pulsate for me, tempting my tongue.

Fuccck, it feels like it's been forever since I last had that cute cunt in my mouth.

I could have it right now. Her desire had been palpable. She rushed out of this shower because she couldn't trust herself with me.

But if I go after her, take it now, it'll be a decision made solely by her body.

I need the girl to choose me with all of her.

I want her body.

Her emotions.

I want every fucking part of her mind and soul.

My hand tightens around my balls in frustration; the slight pain only serves to make me hornier.

I want *her* tugging on my balls like this. With her hand. Her teeth.

Clenching my jaw, I fight the urge to jerk myself a little longer. I'm going to make myself fucking scream when I come. So loud that my girl will hear me in her room.

Eyes closed, I let the fantasy in my head play out. Kira pushes me back before I can suck on her clit, making me lean back on my legs. Rising up on her knees, she runs her hands all over my body. Every muscle ripples at her touch.

I let my head fall back, moaning loud as fuck. Water slides down the front of my body, over my hypersensitive cock.

I imagine Kira's hands taking the same path as the water, sliding over my abs, down, down. A hiss leaves me when one of her hands wraps around my dick. Somehow, I manage to withhold from grabbing it in real life.

Her other hand wraps around my aching balls.

I allow myself to squeeze down on them, exactly like I imagine she would.

She leans down, her little tongue licking my shoulders, a path across my collarbone, and each of my pecs. Her hand slides up and down my length the whole time, teasing me. Each light stroke makes me pound harder.

Shit, I can't take it anymore. I wrap my hand around my dick. Come almost bursts out of me. I lock down every muscle, struggling to hold it back.

My breaths are loud in my ears. I wonder if they can be heard over the rushing water.

I open my eyes and look down, amazed by how swollen my dick is. One stroke. Just one more and I know I'll explode.

Damn it. What I wouldn't give to be able to take her. All of her. I let go of my balls and slam my fist into the tiles in front of me. "God, Kira. You make me so hard. Need to pump into your pussy. Make you take every drop." In her mouth. Deep in her cunt.

All over that sweet body.

My come would cover her chest, sliding down her perfect tits, one pearly drop clinging to her pink, hard nipple.

"Oh God. Fuck!" I squeeze down around my cock until all I feel is a fucked up mix of pleasure and pain. "Kitty, you make me feel so good . . . can't fucking take it . . ." My dick swells even more inside my tight, immobile fist. I grind down on my teeth, watching the first drop of come leak out and cling to my red tip—

My head jerks back, my mouth opening on a roar.

Come shoots out of me, hard enough to cause me even more pain, and I fucking love it, growling out Kira's name with each wave. I don't move, coming without a single stroke.

One last shudder goes through me, and I go utterly weak. I fall forward to lean against the tiles. My heart stutters after every beat and I can't breathe.

I hear a door opening and slamming shut out in the hall, then footsteps running down the stairs.

Without a doubt, that was my Kitty, and she's running downstairs before she ends up coming after me.

A smile curls my lips.

Note to self: jerk off in the shower while Kira's home as often as possible.

ELEVEN

Kira

For the past ten minutes I've been staring out the window of Brayden's car wondering how the hell I got here. How did he convince me to go shopping with him?

Maybe it was the way he said please or the puppy dog eyes. Maybe it was the cracks he created in the treehouse the other night.

Maybe I was consumed with the feel of his skin on mine, and my body spoke for every other part of me.

I was stunned speechless. He came out of his room, changed and drying his hair with a towel.

Hypnotized.

Staring at him looking so delicious while still being turned on had me unable to say no when he asked.

I would have given him anything he wanted. Spread-my-legs-for-him kind of anything.

Next thing I know, I'm stuffed in his car on one of my first free days since graduating. This is *not* my idea of a good time.

It's torture.

Ever since he came home for the summer, he's been pushing me. Teasing me and testing me.

Tempting me.

I'm at my wit's end with this annoying want for him. He's driving me crazy, on purpose, but I can't give in, as much as I want him, too.

That's over and done with.

I made it so.

But he keeps bouncing back, chipping away at my resolve, telling me he loves me.

And I see the change, I do, but it doesn't matter. It's been so long I don't know how easy it will be to change the dynamic of our relationship or how I think about him. Especially since he's resolved to make me fall in love with him.

We pull into the parking lot, where he finds a spot near the entrance and we walk in.

As we step onto the escalator to the showroom, he turns and smiles at me. "How's it feel to be done with high school?"

I shrug. "Good, I guess."

"Are you excited for OSU?"

My gaze narrows on him. "Why so interested?"

The smile drops from his lips and eyes, revealing that beaten, hollow look I've seen a few times since he came back. He turns from me to get off the escalator and walks off, forcing me to jog to make up his lead.

I mash my teeth together as we pass by the first few displays to stop myself from reaching out and asking if he's okay. To comfort him.

That's not how we are anymore. I don't care for him the same way. I can't. Sure, my body still reacts to his, but that's it.

An awkward silence surrounds us as we walk, then suddenly, he falls from my peripheral. My head snaps over in time to watch him land onto a couch. He frowns, then stands and moves to the one behind it. By the fourth couch, I'm next to him, arms crossed and brow raised.

"What are you doing?"

"What's it look like?" he asks, then reaches for my arm, pulling me down next to him. "What do you think of this one?"

I bounce on it to form some opinion for him, my head moving back and forth. "It's okay. A little hard."

"Yeah, I agree. Next."

We move to the adjacent row, and I barely sit down before I'm back on my feet.

"Hell no, unless you want to sit on a rock."

There are probably over thirty couches and by the time I'm halfway through, I've lost him. After standing, I look around and spot him a row away and up. As I get closer, I have to shove my nails into my palm.

His long body is stretched out, arms crossed over his chest, and eyes closed.

"Hey." I bump his elbow with my knee. "What are you doing?"

One eye pops open. "Nap test."

I quirk a brow. "Nap test?"

"Yeah, come on down."

He grabs hold of my wrist and tugs, making me fall on top of him. I let out a surprised squeak as his other hand flips my legs onto him as well like they weigh nothing.

"What are you doing?"

"You've got to try it out. Let me know what you think."

"Idiot, I think I'm not going to get a good idea about the couch if I'm on you."

Get off.

Get the fuck off.

Get off his motherfucking perfect chest and the bulge growing in his pants.

My body is unwilling to listen to the signal my brain is sending. It's getting as wet as a bitch in heat and ready to make a scene.

Especially after his stunt in the shower. He made so much noise all I could think about was him tugging on that beast of a cock he's got with enough strength to jack off a rhino.

Bastard.

I manage to push against his chest and slap his stomach. "Sit right, jerk."

The corner of his mouth draws into a half smile.

And I remember.

Back before he knew I liked him, before he kissed me.

The names. The teasing.

Once he's upright I fall down on the cushion, using it to cover the emotions from his stupid face that are forcing themselves on me.

When I look up, Brayden's eyes are heavy lidded. He's rubbing his fingers across his lips, an action that brings back memories I've tried to forget. Those lips eating me out on my birthday . . . and that night in the restaurant bathroom . . . on his bed.

He steps away, moving to one of the stations set up with maps and pencils.

"This one," he says as he writes down the information from the tag.

Once he's done, he holds out his hand and pulls me up.

"Are you buying it?"

He nods and starts walking away, his hand seeming to reluctantly release mine.

We make our way through accent tables and chairs where he writes down another number from some plain square end tables in red. I don't know what he's doing, so I just walk with him, looking at everything and making a mental checklist of possibilities for my dorm room.

The kitchen setups have changed since the last time I was in, and I fall behind. By the time I catch up, he's almost to the dining room displays. I stay behind him, trying to keep my distance, to keep the itch down, when he begins to meander through the tables, pushing on them as he passes.

My brow knits as I walk over to him.

"What are you doing?"

He blinks at me, then puts his hand on my hip, moving me until I'm in front of him. Before I can ask again, he lifts me onto the table and steps between my thighs.

"B-Brayden?"

His lips twitch into a smirk, and I swear my pussy starts gushing. The way we're positioned is so sexual, the urge to link my legs around his waist and pull him closer is impossible to resist.

He looks around before leaning forward, resting a hand beside me, the other on my hip as he rocks into me. His breath is harsh and I grab onto his shirt, but I don't know whether it's to push him away or pull him closer.

"Have to make sure it's a stable surface."

"For what?" I stare into his eyes. They're dark and alluring—hypnotic.

His lips ghost mine, threatening to touch. Threatening to melt me.

"To fuck you on."

The heat of his body, his scent, and his words are a perfect symphony of torture. My thighs squeeze his hips, drawing him closer. I need to feel the hard cock he's keeping from me.

I want him to do what he says. It's the perfect height, and I want him to fuck me on it.

He clears his throat and steps back, licking his lips as my hands loosen their grip.

A small whimper leaves me, the tension in my muscles falling away, making me weak.

What the hell is going on?

I'm turned still on from his teasing me in the shower, that's what. He's using it to his advantage.

I hop down, refusing to look at him as he writes down the table's, information.

"Don't you have a table? Why are you buying all this stuff?"

He glances at me, then away. There's something he's hiding from me. I know his tells.

"For my new apartment," he says, clearing his throat again.

"You're not keeping the old one?" With Ryan gone, I just assumed Brayden would get a new roommate.

Walking back to the pathway, he turns back to me. "No. We sold everything."

"Everything?"

He nods. "The furniture. It was too much to move."

I catch up to him and grab onto his arm, stopping him. "Why didn't you put it in storage, then? That's cheaper than buying all new." What is he hiding from me?

He looks at me, then away, and back again. "I'm not going back to Purdue."

I stare at him, then shake my head. "What?"

"I guess now's as good of a time as any." He pumps his fist in the air. "Go Buckeyes."

My mouth drops open, the blood that he'd forced into my face falling back into my body. "You transferred?" My voice is barely a whisper.

Oh, God.

No.

No.

He can't.

He nods, his fingers brushing a lock of hair behind my ear. "I can't be without you anymore."

My face scrunches up, and I swat his hand away. "You did fine for the last three years."

I swallow back the scream that wants to explode. There's no way I can handle him being on the same campus as me. Not when he can make me want him inside me with just a look. He's wrecked me, and I was finally going to have a chance to change things.

He shakes his head. "No, I was a mess." His voice is just above a whisper, the look in his eyes tears at me. "I've always been a mess without you."

I blink back tears. "I don't believe you."

His lips form a hard line, and he nods. "I'm working on that." He attempts to smile, but gives up. "Come on."

I follow behind him, my emotions all over the place. After all this time, after every way he's broken me, how can he make me feel like this?

My bottom lip is trapped between my teeth as we go. Walking behind him, I can see the way his muscles flex. He bypasses all the bedroom furniture setups, walking right up to the dressers, wasting no time in writing down the information.

Then it's the beds. He sits on each one, lays on a few, and I find myself mimicking him again, just like at the couches.

After about five bounces, I find a good one and lay down. It's soft, but still firm, and makes me want to find a blanket and curl up. I need a nap after the emotional and physical roller coaster that is Brayden.

I'm not alone for long. Brayden climbs up next to me, both on our side, staring at each other.

"Do you have a costume for this weekend?" he asks.

"Yeah."

"What are you going to wear?"

I can barely think, still stunned. "Not telling."

"I'll just have to wait and see then."

"You're going?"

Of course he's going—it's at Jenn's house.

"Only because you're going to be there." He sits up from the bed and writes down the number.

After stuffing his list in his back pocket, he holds out his hand to help me up. I stare at it for a moment, then up at him.

"Why are you doing all of this?"

That sad smile forms on his face again. "You know why." He reaches out and strokes his fingers against my cheek, sending a shiver through me. "I love you, and I'm doing everything I can to make you see it. To see how much I can't live without you."

Right now, I hate the reaction I have to his words. I want to jump him, kiss him, be with him, but I also hate him.

I'm lost, unsure what to do with the war raging inside me.

TWELVE

Kira

June 13th, 2015

"I love you, and I'm doing everything I can to make you see it. To see how much I can't live without you."

He can't live without me. Yeah-fucking-right. After years of doing such a great job at it, he expects me to believe that now.

And he did do a great job. We all know that.

Brayden says he was miserable while we were separated.

I honestly wish I could believe that.

But I don't. I never will. So whatever he has to say doesn't matter.

Speaking of the devil himself, my text notification tone rings out.

Let me see your costume.

I stare at said costume laid out on my bed and swallow.

It's provocative. Beyond sexy. I know that. I knew that when I picked it. No, I hadn't known Brayden would be at the party the day I bought the costume, but now I know he will.

He's going to see me in it.

Damn it. I'm so fucking horny. I've been like this forever.

Thinking about his reaction the moment he sees me in my costume shouldn't turn me on more.

It does.

Fuck, I *need* him.

I can't have him.

This shit has to end already.

I don't want to show you my costume. As a matter of fact, I don't want you at the party at all.

It crosses my mind that I should put my phone down before he responds and I'm tempted to continue interacting with him.

Too late.

I'll let you see a peek of mine if you show me a peek of yours, baby.

I'm smart enough to drop the phone on the bed. I know what's coming through next—a picture.

Not smart enough to stop myself from wondering what his costume could possibly be. Knowing him, he'll look devastating in it.

My mouth waters.

My pussy pounds.

God, what the fuck? I'm even more out of control than usual. It's a good thing he's in Columbus right now.

I fucked myself earlier in the shower. The same shower he jerked off in days ago. Up against the wet tiles, I rode my fingers until I had no choice but to scream out.

I despise the fact that it was his name I yelled out.

Thank God the house was empty.

My phone vibrates on my bed. I try to ignore it, stripping out of my clothes so I can start changing.

But getting naked only makes it worse. Nowadays, I can't take off a single stitch of clothing without immediately imagining his hands on me.

Son of a bitch.

I grab my phone off my bed, frustrated that I'm such a slave to my impulses.

No stopping this. I tell myself I won't do more than look. I won't respond, it'll be just this.

It's a picture of his lower abs. That motherfucking V. He's wearing light jeans, unbuttoned, and his hand is holding them open to better show off his abs.

The leather cuff is on his wrist, but it doesn't matter. I know what's beneath it now.

Want. Christ, how am I supposed to get fucking past this level of desire?

He enrages me to no end.

My legs weak, I walk over to my bed. I can't even think of putting on my costume. I want to send him a picture, tease him back, but I can't do that either.

The beat of my heart is so powerful through my body that it worries me. *Want. Want. Want.*

I sit on my bed, shaking.

My inner walls throb, my clit aching, in desperate need of attention.

I want his tongue all over my clit again, his lips sucking on it hard.

What's wrong with me today? Why is it worse than before?

But I know why. This madness has been building for weeks.

No, lies. This has been building for years.

How am I going to resist him tonight of all nights when the insanity is stronger than ever?

Trembling, miserable, I pick up my phone. I can barely even type. ***Don't come to the party tonight. Please.***

There's no waiting for his response. This pain has turned me into an animal. There's only one thought. I need to come again, and my fingers won't be enough this time.

I reach under my bed and pull out the case I bought to keep my vibrator in. I purchased it weeks ago, needing something thicker than my fingers to fuck myself with.

Because I can't stop wanting Brayden's thick cock pounding inside me.

My phone vibrates on my bed; I continue to ignore it, leaning back, spreading my trembling thighs.

My pussy lips are swollen and wet enough that I feel them slowly part with the movement.

Another notification from my phone.

I play with my hard nipple, pinching it, and slide the head of my silicone dildo across my clit.

My head falls back and my hips arch, my body hungry for that length inside me.

I slide it up and down, letting my juices cover it.

My phone starts ringing.

A small moan leaves me, and my pussy ripples. I know who it is without looking. I can almost feel him on the other line.

Always feeling him. Always sensing him.

God, I want him.

I know where this is heading as I reach for my phone—don't care. Fucking him is impossible. Having phone sex with him will only make things worse in the long run.

My thumb swipes across the screen and I accept the call. At the same time, I turn the vibrator on, pressing it back to my clit.

"Kira—" Brayden's sharp intake of breath tells me he picked up on the sound of my vibrator.

Just the sound of that breath makes goose bumps break out all over me.

"Tell me to come over," he demands in a hoarse voice.

I moan. "No. This is all you're getting." The sound of my own voice surprises me.

"Oh really?" An utterly masculine chuckle leaves him. I can hear the cockiness in it, and I want to be mad at him for it.

Instead, all I want to do is ride his fucking beautiful face. Come all over his gorgeous lips.

Cover him in my scent so that if any other girl tries to go near his mouth, she'll know he's taken.

"This is all I'm getting? Huh, Kira?" He purposely moans my name, drawing the sound out. "Is that why you're fucking yourself with that little bullet vibrator while imagining it's me?"

His voice. Lord help me, I'm hooked.

"It's not a bullet." I slide the tip inside me, slowly, letting myself feel how it parts me open.

Brayden falls silent, breathing harshly in my ear.

I slip the vibrator in deeper.

"Kira, are you . . . are you fucking yourself with a dildo right now?"

I bite my lip, but it's not enough to hold back my whimper. "*Yes.*"

The sound he makes is indescribable. I don't know if it's a grunt or a growl, or maybe an angry combination of both. All I know is that he's not pleased.

"Why?" I ask. "Jealous?"

"How big is it?" he grits out.

Still biting my lip, I let out a little giggle and rock against the head my dildo, teasing myself. "Almost as big as you."

That sound again. Rough. Horny. Aggravated.

"What?" I moan out the word purposely, pushing the vibrator halfway in. "You don't like knowing I'm fucking myself?"

He hums; another frustration-filled sound. "My dick is the only dick that belongs inside you."

That statement shouldn't turn me on as much as it does, but it's too fucking delicious to resist. His dick. *My* dick. The only one with the right to pound into me. The only cock to spurt in me.

I love that thought. I really, really do.

Not that I'll admit that to him. "That's your opinion. I . . . " My breath catches as the dildo slips fully in me and my hand presses into my clit.

"You what, Kira?" His breath races, faster, louder.

Closing my eyes, I let myself get lost in the visual of him thrusting into his fist while he hears me fucking myself. "I beg to differ," I whisper, lost in sensation.

"You do, do you?" The soft, implied deadliness in his voice. That barely leashed fury.

Why do I love it when he's jealous? *Why?* "Uh-huh." My legs shake harder.

"I'm going to ask you again, baby: is that why you're thinking about my dick inside you right now?"

I want to hurt him.

Want to fuck him.

God, I want him to keep talking but at the same time, I just want him to shut the fuck up.

I hate when he reaches inside me, grasping at bitter truths I don't want to acknowledge.

Brayden groans, and the sound is so blatantly sexual that I know he's doing it on purpose again. Fucking with me. Proving once more the power he has over my body. "Slide it back in, Kira. No, only halfway, baby. Soft, shallow thrusts."

It's like he's in the room, watching every move I make.

"Now slide it back out. Go slow. All the way to the tip."

I do as he says, feeling my walls clench around the dildo. My body doesn't want to let it go. It's not Brayden, but with his voice in my ear, I can almost pretend it is.

"Don't thrust it in, yet. Hold it there. Right at the tip."

"No." My head thrashes side to side. I want to disobey him. Slam the cock in my hand into me. "I need more."

"Not . . . yet. Pulsate on the tip. I'm squeezing mine right now, imagining it's your tight pussy."

The way this man talks undoes me. A fresh wave of resentment floods me as I think about all the women who have had that cock in them, his sexy voice talking dirty in their ear.

I could have it if I wanted to take it.

But I hate him too much to give him that.

My chest convulses and a pained cry leaves me.

"Baby," Brayden whispers in a sad tone.

"Let me fuck myself." Why am I not doing it? Why am I still obeying him?

"Not yet, Kitty. Just a little more."

"It hurts," I whine, *aching*.

"I know, baby. But I'm going to make it all better. I promise."

"You can't!" It boggles my mind that he can't understand it. This heartbreak has become warped. Misshapen. It not longer even resembles heartbreak, but something more akin to trauma.

It's unfixable.

I'm unfixable.

There's no going back.

And yet my body is hungrier than ever, my soul grasping at the tattered connection between us.

"Kira, listen to me."

"*Please*," I beg, and there are tears in my eyes. I need him to make me come, to moan in my ear while the orgasm tears through me.

Then, I have to hang up the phone on him and sever this connection once more.

"Then do it. Slam it into you. Use all your strength like I would if I was there fucking you with my cock."

I do as he says, thrusting the dildo deep.

My back arches, body locked up. I'm coming so hard I can't control the loud moans leaving me.

"Say my name, Kira. Say it!"

I do, repeatedly, my hips churning to meet each thrust.

"Oh God, baby. The way you say my name. You ready for me? Ready for my come?"

He'll never know how fucking much.

Brayden yells out. "Fuck, baby! Fuck, I love you."

Pain.

Pleasure.

My soul grasps at the flimsy remnants of that connection again, trying to rebuild it somehow.

"I love you, Kira. I fucking love you. So much. *God*, I need your pussy."

I'm still coming as I hang up the phone on him, cutting off his rambling.

I'm still coming as that first tear slides out of my eye.

I yank the dildo out of me and jerk upright, throwing it away from me. Covering my face with my hands, I struggle to pull myself together.

Impossible. I'm torn apart.

Broken.

Exposed.

No. No. No. I'm not this girl anymore. I no longer fall apart for Brayden Hunt.

I'm stronger than this. I can't go back to being that shattered little girl he left behind.

Sniffing, I wipe at my wet eyes and get up to continue getting ready. I can't stop him from going to that party, but I won't stop myself from going either.

I'll just have to ignore him.

I will.

He snuck past some defenses the last few weeks. I wasn't careful enough.

That's over now.

I'm going to build those defenses back up.

And no matter what it costs me, I'm going to convince that man to move on and leave me alone. I'm going to make him believe he has no power over me.

Somehow.

I expected to get many reactions to my costume choice.

I expected wrong.

Reactions isn't quite the right term for what's happening.

The guys here are practically trying to grope me. As soon as I walk into the large foyer, all heads turn in my direction.

I'm wearing a black bra-top that pushes my breasts out ridiculously. Paired with it is a tiny black and pink tutu, and matching fur leg warmers. The large black and pink cat ears on my head also match the fingerless gloves on my hands.

Yeah, I'm showing a lot of skin, but so are a lot of the girls here. I don't understand why the guys are overreacting like this.

Dodging a guy I don't even know, I make my way to the other side of the foyer. I see Austin to my left, hanging with Craig.

Talk about showing a lot of skin. His gladiator costume leaves most of his body on display.

It's a gorgeous, bronzed body, cut to perfection. A body I once had between my legs.

I felt almost nothing then; I feel the same now.

He catches sight of me and turns sharply in my direction. An eerie stillness falls over him as he takes in my costume with a hunter's eye.

Austin's going to come to me. I sense it.

A hand reaches under my tutu and squeezes one ass cheek.

"Hey! What the fuck?" I fly around, ready to break a motherfucker's nose.

It's Emma, one of the girls in my school. She's dressed as a punk rocker, her dark hair streaked with purple. "Damn, girl, you look fucking yummy tonight." She's blatantly bisexual, and she gives no fucks about grabbing whatever she wants.

This isn't the first time I've been groped by her.

"Emma, I've told you before. I'm a cock girl only."

She sighs wistfully. "Yeah, and every time I hear it, it makes me wish I had a dick to give you, babes."

I shake my head and smile. "You like dick, too. Remember?"

"I'd give it up for you."

Oh, she's smooth. I'll give her that.

"Speaking of dick . . ." Her head turns in the direction I'd seen Austin in. "Looks like you've got an eager one heading straight to you."

Before I can turn toward Austin, I sense an odd silence fall over the foyer. As if everyone's attention is focused on a single thing.

Confused, I look at everyone and see all the women staring toward the entrance. All the guys stare at the girls, then turn their heads to see what they're looking at.

Brayden.

He just walked in and is standing at the large double doors, right beneath the giant crystal chandelier that dominates the ceiling of the foyer.

It hurts. In every cell in my body, seeing him hurts.

145

He's looking around with one eye due to the patch that accompanies his costume, but I know, I just *know* he's looking for me.

I'm drowning. This is beyond what I can handle. The world around me is disappearing, zeroing in on him and only him.

And I can't fight this. I . . .

I have to get away. At least for a few minutes. Gather some semblance of rationality.

I've never been this ready for a man in my life. If I don't leave, *now*, I'm going to grab him, right here, in front of every single person in this place, and I'm going to fucking devour him.

So, I turn around and head straight for the stairs, taking them as fast as I can, hoping there is some place in this huge house where I can hide from him.

Brayden

My phone's dead in my left hand.

My eyes are locked on my right hand. The same hand I'm currently holding up. The same hand covered in my come.

This girl made me fucking come all over my hand and then hung up the phone on me.

And she came, loud as fuck in my ear, while fucking herself with a dildo.

That's the last cock other than mine that's going to go in there. Next time that pussy gets stretched open, it'll be by *me*. My fingers. My dick.

Temple throbbing, I rush to wash my hands and throw on my makeshift costume. Once I'm dressed, I slam into my car and peel out of my parking spot. The drive from Columbus usually takes just over an hour. I make it in less than that, but even that takes too fucking long.

Before exiting my car, I send a text to Kira. *I'm here. Where are you?* I don't even know why I try reaching her phone. Even if she sees it, she won't respond.

No. Because she doesn't want me here.

Tough fucking luck. I'm here.

So is Austin.

Therefore, I sure as hell belong here.

I honestly don't know why I'm so mad right now, but there's this volcanic throbbing in the pit of me. Brutal energy coalesced into an impending detonation.

I need to calm the fuck down. Sure, years of wanting the girl have merged with the torture of the last few months. My mind's totally screwed.

Stepping just inside the open doors, I try to spot her among the dozens of people here. In the back of my mind, I register how most of them stop to stare at me.

My eye bounces off the crowd's faces.

I spot Austin first, dressed in some ridiculous gladiator costume. What a fucking douchebag. He's walking with an intent that's unmistakable. So is the look on his face. I follow his stare.

Fucking knew it.

Son of a bitch, what the hell is she wearing?

Here we go again.

I cut a path through everyone in my way, following Kira to the large staircase.

Don't know who she's running away from, but *I'm* going to be the one to catch her.

She's halfway up the stairs by the time I reach the bottom.

That tutu doesn't cover shit. Her tiny as hell underwear are bare for the whole world to see.

So is her ass when staring from down here.

Goddamn this girl.

That's mine. All of it. Enough is enough.

I follow her, as I'm always doing lately. There's a certainty that grows with every step take, one I can't even begin to describe.

Kira turns left down the hall, and I speed up to catch her. She's halfway down another hallway when I get within a few feet and reach out for her.

The certainty solidifies.

It's over. I'm done giving her the choice. Even if she ends up fucking despising me even more than she already does, this bullshit ends now.

She's going to admit she's mine. Tonight. My mind's made up.

I take that last step, reach out, and turn her around. That beautiful little demon glares at me. Her eyes caress me, anger mixing with lust, and I know I've got her.

We're exactly where we're supposed to be—on the same page. Ready to fucking devour each other.

Locked by the same desire-fueled rage.

"What the fuck do you want?" she growls.

"What the fuck were you thinking when you decided to wear that?" I growl back.

THIRTEEN

Kira

"What the fuck were you thinking when you decided to wear that?"

It's one of those moments when someone's audacity just leaves you utterly speechless. That's me right now. Jaw completely unhinged. Anger skyrocketing to a whole new level.

Who the hell does he think he is asking me that? Did he see himself before leaving his damn apartment?

His pirate costume was obviously put together last minute, probably with clothes he already had in his closet, but that only makes it look more rugged. The light beige shirt he's wearing has a wide-open collar and he rolled the sleeves up to his elbows, leaving his forearms exposed. The black leather vest he threw on top of it has gold buttons and adds the perfect touch, and matches the leather combat boots on his feet.

Mussed-up hair, light jeans, the thick leather bracelets encircling his large wrists . . . the eyepatch covering one of his gorgeous eyes. The exposed eye is narrowed and glaring at me.

He looks just as dangerous as he is.

No, his costume doesn't show nearly as much skin as mine does, but it's just as bad. I *heard* him walk into the house—and by that I mean I heard the collective sighs that left the mouths of every female within eyesight of him.

He knew damn well what he was doing when he put on that costume.

"You have a lot of nerve asking me that."

"You're wearing a *bra*!" he snaps, his expression hard. Vicious. His jaw twitches, and he takes a step toward me.

It requires every ounce of strength in me to step back. "It's not a bra, it's part of the costume—"

"I saw your ass in that fucking tutu while you were walking up the stairs!"

"And?" I knew how short the black tutu was when I decided to buy it, but it matched perfectly with the black and pink cat ears on my head.

Brayden's hand shoots out, latching on to said tutu. He yanks me into him, pretty much growling in my face.

My heart beat drops between my legs, pounding, sending blood rushing to my clit.

"If I saw it, everyone else did," he says, enunciating each word slowly, his breath sliding between my lips. His scent is too strong now that he has me so close.

Oh God. "I . . . and?" Speech has left me and that's all I can give him, because I can barely think clearly. It's a fog—a hot, needy fog. I'm suffocating. I . . . fuck, I want him, and he hasn't let me go.

His fist tightens around my black tutu. He pops his jaw and

150

leans down into me, lips *right there*. So close. "How many fucking times am I going to tell you that you're *mine*, Kira?" His eye flickers up to my cat ears and back. "*My Kitty*. No one gets to see what's mine but me."

My heart gives a wild kick.

No. *No.*

I can't be excited about this. I refuse to admit just how turned on it makes me when he gets possessive like this. I am *not* his. Never will be. He has no right.

"You're going home right now and changing."

Motherfucker. "Get off me," I hiss, anger mixing, churning, reminding me that I can't have him no matter how much I fucking want him.

He doesn't answer for a beat, that single, emerald eye glinting in the dim light of the hallway. Then he shakes his head one time. "No."

I grab his stupid, sexy shirt and push him back, right into the wall. "I told you—"

Holy fucking shit.

I stop mid-sentence, eyes locked on what I've accidentally exposed, my brain misfiring. Brayden's heart races under my hand, but the rest of him remains still. So still. I yank the shirt further aside, fully exposing the left side of his chest—

And the stylized *K* tattooed right onto his left pectoral.

What. The. Fuck?

"Brayden, there you are!"

Brayden tenses and lets go of my tutu as if burned.

All the while, my eyes are locked on that stupid, beautiful *K*.

"I've been looking everywhere for you," Jennifer says, coming closer.

I bet she has. She, like every whore in this house, wants him.

She, like almost all of them, has had him.

That *K* on his chest seems glaringly bright, making it almost impossible to pull my attention away.

But I do, somehow looking away and letting go of his shirt. For the same reason that Brayden rushes to cover his chest—because he's my fucking stepbrother, and no one can really know what's going on between us.

Especially a jealous skank like Jennifer, who will run to tell everyone in town.

"What do you want, Jenn?" he asks her.

Her eyes light up as if he's straight up told her he wants to drag her into the nearest bedroom and have sex with her. Giggling, she twirls her hair and bites the corner of her lip, eyes eating him up just as mine had earlier. "There was something I wanted to show you."

Translation: she's ready to bare her crotch and let him have at it.

I should be immune to this by now. It shouldn't matter.

It does, and I want to fucking tear her eyes out.

I can't.

So I clench my fists and stand here, seething, hating myself because I still care.

"I'm busy talking to Kira."

Jennifer blinks as if surprised and finally realizing I'm here.

Bullshit. She knew. But like everyone else, she suspects something and therefore has no qualms about blatantly laying a claim on Brayden. She knows she can and I can't, and she's rubbing it in my face.

"Oh . . . well, as soon as you're done talking to your *sister*, can you please come find me so I can show you?" The almost innocent way she stares at him, eyes wide, makes me sick to my stomach. But not as sick as what Brayden says next.

"Sure."

What?

Jennifer giggles and gives him this flirty little smile. Her eyes cut in my direction, and I don't miss the way they flash with malice. Nor the way she seems to be silently gloating.

Like I give a fuck. Oh, no. She can gloat all she wants. That's not what I'm focused on right now.

My initial is fucking *tattooed* onto his skin, and he just agreed to go find her after he "finishes" with me?

Jennifer turns at the end of the hall, heading down the stairs.

"Kira—"

I snap.

Later on, I'll probably look back on this moment and hate myself for the way I lose all control, but nothing matters right now except the obvious.

This man has spent months of his life trying to convince me I'm his. He's marked his body with symbols of me. Which tells me he knows the truth.

I'm not his.

He's *mine*.

And he just fucking agreed to meet up with his favorite sex toy in front of me.

My hands wrap around his shirt.

Shock flares in his eye.

I pull him right into me, fist his hair with one hand, and slam my lips against his. If people are looking, I don't care.

All that matters is the way his hands grab my waist, groaning as the shock wear-s off and he starts bending me back with force, grinding his huge, swollen cock into me.

I whimper into his mouth and start pushing him backward, the knowledge of what I'm about to do burning through my veins. Brayden stumbles, a hand leaving me and grabbing onto a door frame to catch himself.

It's open, empty, and I shove him in, slamming the door behind me.

I'm panting, dripping, as I stare at his lusted out face. He opens his mouth to say something—I push him back again, right onto the bed and the dark pink comforter covering it.

Actually, it's too pink. And some of the pillows behind Brayden's head have *hearts* on them.

His head tilts back on the pillows, his eye locking with the large frame on the wall, right above the headboard.

It's a picture of Jennifer.

This is her room.

Growling under my breath, I climb onto the bed next to him.

Brayden's head snaps back to me, his eye huge. I wrench his shirt up to his chest, exposing that gorgeous valley of abs and the waistband of his low-riding jeans. I see the lines of what looks like a really intricate tattoo curving around his side, but I'm too far gone to try and see what it is. Furious, my heart beats like a wild drum in my ears, I pop open the button on his jeans.

He gasps, his hips rising off the bed as his hands ball up into fists.

Using the same force, I tug his zipper open. His cock's right there, hard, exposed.

He's commando, and all I have to do is reach in to grab it.

"Oh God. Oh God," Brayden chants low, watching me in disbelief.

I wrap my hand around his length and pull him out, mouthwatering when a single drop of precome clings to his tip for a second before slowly falling.

His hips pop off the bed, thrusting that hard cock into my hand.

"Fuck, *Kira*."

Desperation falls from his mouth in the form of my name, causing a ripple of fire to move through me, making my pussy clench.

My name.

No one else's, because he only needs me.

And I need him.

Inside me.

Brayden.

My Brayden.

I flip my leg over his hips, straddling him and pulling my panties to the side. My pussy is drenched, the flesh swollen in preparation of having that beautiful dick inside me.

"Shit." He reaches up, right as realization dawns in his eye, and yanks the eyepatch off, leaving his hair an even bigger mess than I'd left it.

I hold his cock steady, looking right into his eyes, and bring it right to my opening.

"Kira. Oh my God, Kira, *please*," he begs me, his expression wild, his big body straining under me.

Moaning, I slide his swollen tip between my folds, covering it in me—

I choke on a scream as I drop down and his cock finally

slams home.

Brayden

White fucking bliss forces my hips up as she slides down, slamming all of my dick inside her.

Inside *Kira*.

Bare.

"Oh, shit!" My mouth drops open as I stare down to where we're joined. "I'm inside you, I'm fucking inside you."

There's only one lift of her hips, then back down before her nails dig into my chest. She's holding in a scream, and my cock is right there with her as I desperately keep from coming. Walls tight, pulsing around me, begging me to come with her.

"Brayden," she gasps, rocking on my cock, shuddering as the wet clutch of her cunt almost forces my come out of me.

Fuck. Oh, fuck. My girl's coming all over my cock, her sexy little lips wide open as she moans incoherently. It feels too good, looks too good, and I can't hold it back.

I'm going to come.

Right here.

Right now.

Deep in Kira's tight pussy.

Painting her walls, exactly how I've always wanted to.

I grip down on her hips, guiding her draining body as I pump up. Fisting the front of that pink and black bra she's wearing, I bring her down, catching her when she collapses on my chest. One hand around her jaw, I kiss her, eating at her mouth, fucking it with my tongue, rotating my hips into her over and over.

She tightens around me, still coming, whimpering as our tongues twirl.

It's all too much and I start coming, the first brutal wave slamming up my cock and into her, choking me with pleasure. "Fuck, baby. I love you. Fucking love you," I hear myself desperately moaning.

Kira shuts me up, fisting my hair and kissing me senseless.

I start coming even harder, my entire world going black, my heart hammering like it's about to explode inside me.

I'm a panting mess, and my muscles give out, relaxing back down onto the bed.

 Her hips continue rocking, pussy fluttering on my still hard dick as she tries to sit up. It's then I see the lust draining from her and reality settling back in.

Not fucking happening.

I'm stronger, faster, and have her flipped onto her back before she even realizes, looming over her, pinning her down with my cock locked inside her. I wrap my arm around her and shift her up the bed so I can climb on.

Her expression clouds over again, arms reaching around me, pulling my lips down to hers. Instead of kissing her, I dip down and lick up the side of her neck, resting on my favorite spot, biting her. She lets out a squeak, and my dick twitches inside her, making her do it again.

"Where the fuck do you think you're going?" I growl into her ear, nipping at it with my teeth. "I'm not fucking done with you yet."

I sweep my hands down her thighs to her knees and push them open, spreading her wide. The new angle lets me slide in even deeper, and I groan as Kira lets out a high-pitched gasp, her back arching. I wrap one hand around her neck, holding her down on the bed, and look right into her eyes, stopping for a single, heart-pounding second.

"You're mine." I tighten my hold on her neck. I slide the length of my dick out of her, slowly, seeing it glisten with both her come and mine.

Kira tightens around me, as if refusing to let my cock go.

And that right there is all the answer I need.

"Fucking mine," I repeat, slamming back in, holding one of her thighs open as I piston into her with every bit of strength in me.

It doesn't matter that I just had the most draining explosion of my life. I have a mission to pump her so full of my come she won't be able to live without me.

Each thrust of my dick into her causes little whimpers and cries and the most fucking erotic come face I've ever seen. Lips parted, eyes heavy and glazed over.

Her pussy keeps milking me, pulling me in.

"Kira." I let my forehead drop onto hers, staring into her eyes, not breaking the connection as my hips slam into hers. "You feel so fucking good. Didn't know—Jesus, girl. You're killing me."

She wraps her arms around me. Her legs. Her pleading eyes never leave mine, wide, emotionally open, finally showing me everything I've been dying to see. She needs me just as close. Needs me to keep going. To give it to her harder.

So I do.

Her pussy is so wet, filled with our come. Each thrust pushes it out the harder and deeper I go. My hips move, driven by the aching need for more friction.

It's unbearable, mind wiping, animal driving instinct that keeps me going.

Fill her.

Again and again until she's overflowing with my come.

More than she already is.

Soaking wet tightness pulls more from me. I can feel my balls pull up.

She tries to close her eyes. To block some part of herself from this unbearable connection. Her head turns to the side. I grab her chin and bring her back to me, nipping her bottom lip hard enough to cause her eyes to snap open.

"Those eyes, baby." I push deep into her and stop moving, letting her feel each throb my cock gives. "They turn me on so much. Can't live without them anymore."

Her walls ripple around me. "Stop," she begs me in a whisper, eyes watering.

"No. Never again." I'm going to come. God, I'm so fucking close.

Her back arches, eyes rolling back and fluttering. The silent scream from her parted lips gains volume, leaking out shuttering whimpers and keening cries. Coming again, all over me. My fantasy is finally coming to life, and the real thing is so much more erotic that I start coming with her, unable to hold back.

I stop for a single breath-stealing second, feeling the come rising up my length, the explosion building at the base of my spine. Then I lose control, grabbing her hips to slam into her, my back arching to push me in deeper. "Fuck. *Fuck*! Ah, baby. I'm fucking—holy shit. Kira. Kira. God, I love you. *Fucking love you*!"

My hips pump until there's nothing left in me. Weakness

sets in. I lose the strength to hold myself up and fall onto Kira, my mind going utterly blank.

FOURTEEN

Kira

Brayden's sprawled on me, completely boneless. The weight of him is more than I can handle; I don't care. Moving him is the last thing on my mind. Layers of clothes separate the majority of his body from mine, but I don't think I've ever felt closer to anyone.

I tense with panic.

He groans, shifting, and his cock slides out of me. "Wherever you're at in your head right now, come back. Don't start pulling away." His voice is nothing more than a hoarse whisper in my ear, destroyed by all the roaring he did while coming inside me.

I stare up at the ceiling, my mind starting to detach. I'm too attracted to this guy. Too into everything about him. Being here, present in this moment, isn't an option. I can't allow myself to feel what he's trying to make me feel.

Brayden kisses my cheek softly.

I flinch and tense more. Hot fluid leaks out of me, and I gasp when it doesn't stop, realizing what it is.

Oh God, that turns me on. Knowing he pumped all that come into me is so fucking sexy.

Seeming to read my mind, he runs the head of his softening dick against me, smearing his come into my skin. "You're the first girl I've ever fucked without a condom. It's so fucking good, baby."

"Liar." I struggle beneath him, angry that he would dare lie to me about that.

"No, baby." He pulls back to look at me and runs his fingers down my cheek. "I swear to God, you're the only girl I've ever done that with, and you'll always be the only one."

I'm not looking at him. Refuse to do so, eyes still locked with the ceiling, but I feel him jerk.

"Wait. *Fuck.* Kira. We didn't use protection. Holy shit!"

"I'm on birth control." I went on it two months ago, telling myself I wanted to be safe when I went out there to experiment. Be with other guys.

It's pathetic how I never got around to that.

An eerie stillness falls over Brayden. "You're on . . . birth control."

He says it like it's such a bad thing.

What-the-fuck-ever. I just want him off me. I want to run away, hide, scrub the memory of this night out of my brain.

There's a shift in weight, then he's on his knees above me, his face blocking my view of the ceiling.

I focus on his lips because I refuse to look into his eyes.

"Why are you on birth control?"

Rising up on my elbows, I slide backwards away from him.

His hand lands above my knee, squeezing down.

I should break his hold, but for some reason, I don't. Head bowed, I stare at his large hand, unable to move.

"Why, Kira?"

"Isn't it obvious?"

Silence.

I know he can read into my tone, guess the answer to my question. He doesn't like it, but does that matter? Yes, I went on birth control planning to have a back up once I went out there to sleep with other guys.

So what? He's no one to judge me for it.

His sigh brings my eyes back to him. I'm shocked by the amount of sadness I see in his gaze. Anger I expected. Maybe even disgust. But he's downright anguished now, and I don't know why.

"I see." He nods. A slow, resigned movement. "So I'm not the first guy to come inside you, either. Austin was."

Whatever distance I'd managed to build between us collapses on my end. What I should do is get off this bed, exit this room, and leave him with that belief.

I can't. It hurts me to see that expression on his face. To know the reason behind it.

God help me, I'm such a fool.

"Austin never came inside me. No one but you has."

His eyes meet mine, and I hate the glimmer of hope I see in them.

I hate it because it eases my pain. It makes me *happy*.

Biting my lip, I stare back at him, my head spinning.

"Are you serious?"

There's only a smidgen of doubt in his tone. He wants to believe me so damn bad.

That's the problem between us. How broken we are. He doesn't fully trust me, and I sure as hell don't trust him.

Unless he's inside me. Then nothing seems to matter but

163

us.

"I have to go." It's the last thing I want to do.

And that's exactly why I have to do it.

I scooch back a bit more.

Brayden's head falls down, eyes on the bed. I follow his stare and can't help the gasp that leaves me. That gasp only makes yet another round of wetness gush out of me and onto the pillows I'm sitting on.

There's so much of it on the bed—thick, white—that it's impossible to mistake what it is.

The hand around my knee tightens. Dark eyes meet mine. "Damn, baby. That just makes me want to pump you full of it all over again."

I go weak all over.

My eyes fall to his lap. His dick is still exposed, sticking out of his open jeans. Even semi-soft, it's long enough to lie on his thigh. I watch it bounce twice, then start to harden.

A hungry moan leaves me.

He slides his hand beneath my tutu, cupping my pussy. Staring at me, he braces one fist on the bed and leans into me, lips parting.

I ache to kiss them. Own them. Never let them go.

Fucked.

I'm so freaking *fucked*.

"Come here, baby. I have more to give you."

I start leaning back against the headboard, spreading my legs to give him more access—

"What the fuck do you mean you heard someone screaming in my room?"

Brayden and I freeze.

It's her. Jennifer.

And I want her to find us like this. Want her to see that Brayden just pounded me into *her* bed. Want her to know that I was the one who milked him dry.

Brayden wants it too. I see it in his eyes.

It can't happen. We can't get caught.

He's my stepbrother, and that hoebag will have no problem letting the whole world know we're fucking if she finds out.

Brayden jumps off the bed. Before I can process what's happening, he has me up in his arms. Three large strides and we're in front of the door to her closet.

"No. Not in there. She might catch us," I whisper frantically.

"No choice. Nowhere else to go," he whispers back and opens the door. He steps inside, puts me down, and manages to close the door just as I hear the door to the bedroom open.

"See? The bed's a mess."

I can't make out who's talking. It's dark in this closet, barely lit by the sliver of light leaking in through the bottom of the door.

Brayden pulls me to him, hugging me. We're chest to chest, my bare tits squeezed into his bare chest. I choke back a gasp, tensing.

"What the fuck? What's that on my bed?"

That screech makes me cringe.

Until I realize what Jennifer's talking about. I hold my breath, waiting for it . . .

"Oh my fucking God, is that—Someone came all over my bed!"

A laugh bubbles up my throat, and I have to press my face to the crook of Brayden's neck to smother it. I don't know why I think this is so funny, pretty sure this makes me a very

165

sick person.

"Who the hell was up here?" Jennifer's scream is loud enough to crack glass, I swear to God.

I hear her friend mumbling, trying to calm her down.

Brayden cups the back of my head, holding me to him, and I feel his chest bouncing with his silent laughter.

"I am not going to calm down. I want to know who the hell was up here so I can kick them the fuck out of my house!" Jennifer yells. "Go out there and start asking around. Get the other girls to help you. Or else I'll kick all of you out, too."

Jesus, what a bitch. I don't understand how she has a large group of girls ready to jump at her beck and call.

Brayden shifts, sliding his hand between us and wrapping it around one of my breasts, his thumb swiping underneath, moving between the pulled down cup of my bra and my skin. As I try to pull away, he slowly tugs on my nipple.

Shaking, I bite down on his neck, trying to hold back my moan.

"Come back to my place with me, baby. I'm not ready to let you go."

I shake my head.

He tugs on my nipple again, soft, slow, and rolls his hips into me, making me feel his fully hard dick. His lips graze my ear. "I need you again. All fucking night."

My skin breaks out in goose bumps. I want nothing more than to have him to myself all night. "I can't," I whisper into his ear. I really can't. We had sex, yes, but it's not meant to be a repeat.

It's all my body and soul want: multiple repeats.

Brayden sucks on my earlobe, just as slow as he's playing with my nipple. "Please, baby. My cock's aching for you again."

My pussy is aching for him, too.

Willpower disintegrates.

The hunger rises.

My common sense is seconds from checking out completely.

I don't hear anyone in the room outside, didn't even register the fact that Jennifer and her friend had left. This is my chance. I can force Brayden to let me go, get the fuck out of this house and party.

But there's no escaping this—*him*.

His thumb presses into the bottom of my chin, lifting my head up to him.

I don't resist him.

Our lips meet, perfect fucking friction, and the moment I feel his tongue sliding along mine, I know I'm done for.

This is happening again. And again.

I'm going to use him, fuck him until I can't take anymore. Gorge on him until the thought of touching him becomes unbearable to me. "Fine. Take me home with you."

His chest rises and falls with a deep breath. One more kiss, and he opens the door slowly, making sure to peek out and see if anyone is in the room. The lights are still on, but it's empty. Jennifer must have stormed out of here in her search and forgot to turn them off.

Brayden exits first and turns to stand in front of the door, blocking me from exiting. He reaches down to slide his dick back into his pants and pulls on the zipper. I reach up to adjust my boobs, making sure they're covered by my bra-top, and his eyes flicker down to watch. "I'm going to take a separate way out of the house. My car is parked a block away, but I'll drive around and meet you at the end of the driveway."

But of course. We can't let anyone see us leave together. How could I have forgotten?

More importantly, why does knowing this bother me so much?

"Kira?" He leans toward me, eyes wide and questioning.

"I heard you." My voice comes out a lot harsher than I expect it to.

Brayden eyes me warily. "You're coming, right?"

Swallowing nervously, I nod.

He kisses my forehead, lingering for a few seconds, then turns to head out of the room.

I wait by the closet, watching him stop at the entrance and look both ways before walking out. Less than two seconds later, I'm following the path he took, my heart pounding at the fear of discovery.

Sneaking out of the room isn't the hard part. The hallway on this side of the house is just as empty as it'd been earlier when Brayden caught up to me. I already know I can't head down the main staircase. Too many people. Besides, Brayden turned to head in that direction.

Thankfully, I find another set of stairs heading down toward the back of the house. It's packed here as well, especially the kitchen as I pass, but I don't see anyone I know.

Don't give a fuck if they see me.

I don't care about anything, actually. I just want to get out of this house and into Brayden's car so he can get me to his place and fuck me again.

Analyzing that thought is dangerous, therefore I don't

allow myself to even try.

I keep my head down as I walk outside. Like most parties I've ever been in, there's almost as much people lingering outside as there are inside. Dodging past them, I make my way down the seemingly never-ending driveway.

A part of me still can't believe I'm doing this. I'm sneaking out in plain sight to meet up with Brayden.

Because I fucked him.

Because I'm planning on doing so again. Several times, in fact.

FIFTEEN
Kira

At the end of the driveway, I pause, my heart dipping. There's no one here. No car . . .

A blur drives by me, slowing down to a stop half a dozen feet away from the entrance to the driveway.

Seeing Brayden's car makes me way more excited than it should.

With one last look over my shoulder, I run out of the driveway, turn right, and run to the passenger side of the car. Yet another look to make sure no one's around to see me open the door.

Emerald eyes lock on me as soon as I'm inside the car.

I clench my thighs together, ignoring how every inch of me is shaking. The sound of my seat belt clicking fills the car, almost as loud as his harsh breaths. I expect him to take off driving immediately.

He doesn't.

"Spread your legs."

God, how can his rough voice be enough to make my clit

tremble?

"Now, Kira."

Shifting in my seat, I open my thighs. He reaches between them, pushing my tutu out of the way and sliding my thong to the side. My swollen, wet pussy is exposed to the air.

"Stay like that, baby. I want to be able to see what's mine while I'm driving."

He waits until I give him a shaky nod before taking off at full speed down the road. At every red light, he practically has to slam on the brakes to stop the car in time.

And at every light, his head turns back in my direction, his eyes eating up the sight of my exposed pussy.

By the time we hit the fifth light, I'm a quivering, wet mess, my pussy begging for more of his attention. Uncomfortable, I try to close my legs.

Brayden's hand slaps around my thigh, squeezing down. "Ah, ah. Keep them open, baby." The light changes, and he takes off like a demon again.

"But you're driving. You can barely look anyway," I mumble, beyond fucking horny. He was inside me less than fifteen minutes ago, wrenching soul-shattering orgasms out of me. This kind of hunger doesn't make any sense.

"That's my pussy. If I want it exposed, you'll leave it exposed for me."

I should be aggravated by that kind of possessive comment.

God help me, I'm not.

When I spread my legs open once more, he hums under his breath, sounding pleased.

"How far is your apartment?" I ask once he merges onto the highway, my temple now throbbing like the rest of my body.

"Usually an hour. On the way here, I made it in forty minutes."

It hasn't even been ten minutes yet.

Angsty, I wiggle on the seat, two seconds away from rubbing my aching pussy into the leather beneath me. "That's so far."

His left hand tightens around the wheel. His other hand tightens around my thigh. I don't even try to close my legs since his hold makes it damn obvious he won't let me. "I know. Fuck." He speeds up even more.

We must be past eighty, possibly pushing ninety by now.

I can't even find it in me to be worried for our safety. *Faster. Faster.* Brayden must pick up on my silent urging because he presses down on the gas even harder.

Within seconds, we're practically flying down the highway at an unholy speed. His hand starts inching its way up my thigh. I latch onto his wrist, squeezing tight. "No, Brayden. Keep your eyes on the road."

"My eyes are on the road, Kitty." He merges from the middle lane onto the right one, not slowing down one bit. "Now let me grab what's mine."

Heart in my throat, I let his wrist go. Adrenaline pumps hard through my veins. My eyes are locked unblinking on the road speeding past us. Every beat of my heart seems to echo in my ears. Brayden slides his hand between my legs, the tips of his fingers finding my clit.

I flinch at the fierce shot of pleasure his touch sends through me. "Br-Brayden . . ."

"Move your cunt on my fingers, baby."

Is he crazy? I can't believe he wants to finger fuck me while driving at almost a hundred miles per hour! "You're

172

insane. Stop. We can't right now."

His fingers thrust into me roughly and his palm hits my clit. "Yeah, we fucking can. I want my pussy riding and coming around my fingers, and you're going to give it to me."

My back arches on the seat. I'm too turned on to fight this. Closing my eyes, I give in, forgetting everything but the feel of those two thick fingers stretching me wide. Three thrusts, that's all it takes, and suddenly I'm coming, my mouth open on a silent scream.

Brayden growls under his breath, fucking me faster. I feel the car change lanes again, another acceleration, my juices gathering on his hands and the seat beneath me. The world goes quiet after that, my senses gathering into the calm darkness.

The tires screech beneath the car, jolting me out of my semi-trance. I open my eyes in time to see him taking the exit ramp at almost maximum speed, blowing through every light that comes after. What seems like seconds later, he practically slams the car into a parking spot in front of an apartment complex.

"Is this where you live?" I ask, breathless.

He slams out of the car without answering. I catch a glimpse of his expression as he turns to head around to my side. Unclipping my seat belt, I open the door right as he reaches me. He practically lifts me out of the car and kicks the door closed.

Grabbing my hand, he pulls me straight across the parking lot, his much longer strides making it difficult for me to keep up. We reach the door to one of the two-story buildings. He opens it and guides me inside. "Second floor, baby. Hurry."

I take the steps as fast as I can, hearing his pounding

footsteps following me. At the landing, I turn.

"The door on the left," he says, grabbing my arm and leading me.

I'm dragged into his apartment and barely get a second to take it in before he's pressing me to the wall next to the door. He crowds me, giving me no room for escape. Eyes ablaze with emotion, he stares at me.

What is he looking for? Permission?

But I know very well what he wants from me, and it's not permission. What he wants is something I refuse to give him.

"This is just sex between us," I tell him, breathing hard.

"Keep telling yourself that," is his answer.

Nothing else is said between us.

Nothing else needs to be said.

We both know where we stand—what our end goals in this situation are.

And we're still going to fuck each other's brains out because we have no other choice.

His thumb grazes my lip, a perfect, tantalizing touch. He knows just how to work me, even with such a simple caress. "Tell me you're dying for my cock. At least give me that."

I open my mouth, eyes locked with his as I suck him inside. My pussy ripples, hungry to replace my mouth. "I'm dying for your cock, Brayden. As much as you're dying for my pussy."

He can't hold back his anguished groan, nor the bone-deep yearning I see in his expression.

Killing. Me.

No pity. No remorse.

It's starting to feel like soon, I won't have any choice in how this ends.

To silence the annoying thoughts going through my mind, I pull his head down to me, sucking his bottom lip into my mouth.

He doesn't move, letting me take the reins, but every small groan he gives me pounds straight in my pussy. Licking my top lip lightly, he whispers, "Tell me you love my lips."

I'm too far gone to process what that really means, what my answer might divulge. "I love your lips." Humming, I suck on them again and lift a leg to wrap it around his hips.

His body shivers against mine. "Admit that you live for them, baby." He lets the tip of this tongue flick mine, but doesn't give me anything more.

I rock my hips into him, rubbing my aching slit along his rock-hard cock. "Live for them." I pull on his hair, trying to urge him to open his mouth for me. That tongue. *Fuck*, it drives me crazy.

His big hand slides down my back to tightly grip my bare ass under the tutu. "Yeah? What else do you live for, baby? This?" He punctuates the last word with a thrust, blatantly rubbing that monster between his legs into my cunt.

"*Brayden*." I jump up and lift my other leg, wrapping both around his hips. He wraps his arms around me, holding me up as I roll my hips in circles. I kiss his cheeks, his jaw, the corner of his lips, silently asking him to open his mouth and give me what I need.

Tightening his arms to the point of pain, he thrusts up, his chest heaving beneath mine. "Answer me, Kira. I want to know you need me just as bad as I need you."

Can't give him that. No way. And it doesn't matter, because he feels so fucking good right now that I'm already close to coming again. I let my head fall back, riding each thrust of his hips. His dick presses into my clit, delicious friction.

"Talk to me, baby."

I moan, but refuse to do as he says.

He cups the back of my neck and bites into it as hard as he can.

I scream out, eyes opening at the pain—

An orgasm starts ripping through me. Hot. Wild. Perfect.

Brayden pulls my hips away from his, taking away the pressure I so desperately need.

"No!" I cry, clawing at him like an animal.

"You won't admit it? Fine," he growls, lifting me up over his shoulder.

My pussy throbs, still on the verge. I kick my legs and beat on his back, maddened from the frustration. "Fuck you, asshole! Fuck you!"

He takes four massive steps across the living room and flings me violently onto the couch. "No, fuck *you,* woman." Reaching down, he rips open his jeans. "I adore you, and you won't fucking admit it to yourself."

I hate this motherfucker. I hate him more than he could possibly ever understand.

His vest lands on the floor.

I rise up on my knees.

Reaching over his head, he yanks his shirt up and off, throwing it God knows where.

Moving closer, I slap his chest with both my hands, trying to push him back. "No. You don't get to decide when you fuck me."

He steps forward and reaches around me to clasp the back of my top. One rough yank and I feel it rip open. "Yes. I.

Do."

I try to hit him again but he grabs my hands, forcing them down to his open jeans. "Get these off me." He goes to work pulling my tutu and thong down my hips.

His pants are pushed down his legs. I glare at him the entire time, hating this feeling of powerlessness. "I really can't stand you."

He lifts me up like I weigh nothing, slides the tutu off my legs, and places me back on the couch. "And I really can't live without you."

Ugh!

"Stop lying to me, damn you." I rip my gloves off.

"Stop lying to yourself." He kicks off his shoes and jeans, standing before me in nothing but that sexy leather cuff and all the ink covering his body.

And dear God, there's so much of it now. I try to fully make out the tattoo on his side but I'm too unfocused to do so.

When I reach up to pull the cat ears off my head, he stops me. "No. Leave them on."

Kinky motherfucker.

My nipples stiffen painfully. I reach for his cock and give it a brutal squeeze, using the hold to pull him to me. "Fine. Just shut the fuck up and come fuck me."

He laughs, his smile so beautiful that my heart punches at my ribcage. Pressing me into the back of the couch, he climbs on, braced on his knees just like I am. He grabs onto the back of the sofa and leans down to kiss me.

I accept his kiss, but sink my nails deep into his shoulders, making sure he knows I'm not fully ready to give in.

Smiling against my lips, he slides his body up and down,

his erection trapped between us. The damp head wets my abdomen. *Goddamn*, I still can't get used to the fact that I can make him leak precome that easily.

I clasp his face with both hands and run my tongue over the seam of his lips. His hands slide down my sides, stopping briefly to cup my ass.

Then I'm in the air again, the world spinning as Brayden turns around and sits on the couch. No time to think. He forces me back on my knees until my pussy is aligned with his face.

He moves lower.

I fist his hair. "No. I want your cock. Now."

Shaking my fist loose, he latches onto my thighs and forces me closer. "And I want that clit on my tongue."

A man who doesn't like to be denied.

Damn it, why does everything he does turn me on even more?

His eyes gleam up at me wickedly. "Either grab the back of the couch, or hold onto the back of my head. But *don't* try to stop me."

Considering he's only giving me those two options, of course I lace my fingers in his hair.

He licks his lips. "That's my girl."

I'm not going to last. One touch of his tongue and I'm going to fly over the edge. "You better fuck me as soon as I come."

"*Hmmm.* I'm going to fuck you all over this apartment." His soft lips press against my pussy and his tongue snakes out, licking a slow path from my entrance to my clit.

I exhale a shaky breath, moving my pussy up and down that luscious tongue.

But he takes it away from me too damn soon. He blows lightly on my engorged clit, teasing me.

"Brayden, come on!"

Smiling, he tugs my clit between his lips. He cups my ass in each hand to hold me still as he sucks it into his mouth. This asshole has me right where he wants me, and I can't even fight him! I'm throbbing on his tongue, my mind focused only on the pleasure.

I grab onto the back of the couch with one hand and use the other to press his head to me. He torments me with light flicks of his tongue, never giving me the exact amount of pressure I need to come.

My hips writhe frantically, trying to get him in the right spot.

"Yeah, baby. That's what I want. Ride my face."

He doesn't have to tell me twice. "Suck me harder, Brayden. Please. I need to come."

His eyes snap open, flashing up at me with all the hunger of a dangerous predator. With a frustrated growl, he sets in, tonguing me hard, so hard I almost can't take it.

That pain, the pressure, it's too much—

He softens the strokes of his tongue, kissing me tenderly.

It sends me over the edge. I lock up and whimper incoherently as the wave crashes over me.

Brayden licks up every bit of my orgasm. The horny, frantic sounds he makes leave me bucking wantonly on his mouth.

I just came, and as always I need more, *more*.

When will it ever end?

He rips me off his mouth. My thighs shake. It's impossible to hold myself up. Hands wrapped around my waist, he lifts me again, maneuvering me under him on the couch.

I whisper his name, my heart hammering in my rib cage.

Brayden crawls over me, cupping my face. "I'm not done with you, baby."

Fuck, I remember what happened the last time he said that to me.

Oh God, can I even take any more?

He lowers his mouth down to mine, feeding me my own taste, and I know without a doubt that I can.

I'll take everything he can give me.

And then I plan on taking even more.

I plan on taking everything I can from this man.

SIXTEEN

BRAYDEN

My eyes snap open as my whole body jumps with a jolt. I'm in my bed, on my side, curled around a pillow. Light tickles on my skin, tracing lines around my ribs, around my tattoo. The touch is soft, familiar, soothing, and instead of swatting it away, annoyed someone dare touch me there, I relax back into my pillow. I open my eyes again as it clicks who could be touching me and crane my neck over my shoulder.

Kira.

She's completely naked, sitting on her haunches, staring down at my tattoo as her fingers trail around. Her hair is a wild, tangled mess, evidence of the many times I fisted it, the ends resting just above her nipples.

It feels like a dream and I wait to wake up, staring at her.

I can't help the smile forming on my face as the memories of last night come back. My cock stirs as I remember being inside her.

My Kira.

"Morning." My voice is rough, throat dry.

She looks up, her gaze meeting mine, but my happiness doesn't reflect back.

"When did you get this?" she asks.

I swallow hard and rest my head back on the pillow while still looking at her. "Last August."

Her brow scrunches, and she turns back to it. "Why? I mean, why this?"

I clench my jaw and draw in a breath. "Can we not, right now? Can you just lie back down?"

She shakes her head. "What does it mean?"

I reach out to bring her attention back to me. If I'm going to tell her, she needs more than just her ears to hear it. "At first, I was just drunk and getting a tattoo, but I saw this in the guy's notebook. My drunk mind knew what my sober one couldn't admit, so I didn't even understand why at first."

Her fingers stop. "That's not an answer."

"It's part of the story, so let me finish." I pinch her side and she swats at the closest part of me, which happens to be my ass.

"What does it mean, then?"

"You're into art . . . don't you see it? Ryan told me recently he knew what it meant."

She huffs, annoyed. "Just tell me, jackass."

"It's us."

Her eyes widen and she stares back down at it, crawling around the mermaid's hair.

"You know I'm not into that sickly sweet romance crap, that I'm emotionally stunted, but when I saw the drawing . . . It was the perfect representation of us, at that time." I brush the backs of my fingers against her cheek. "Both have feelings for each other, but it's an impossible relationship. A man in a world he can't live, wanting a woman he can't have."

Her face twists, and I wonder if she's about to cry, wonder if I've finally gotten to her. Instead, she grabs my wrist and pulls my arm away from the pillow, sending me onto my back, spread out. There are no tears, but anger as she straddles my hips and places her palms on my chest.

She slaps at the *K* over my heart. "And this? What the fuck is this?"

This conversation needs to happen, but my cock is hard and twitches at the feel of her pussy on my lower abs, so close to its home inside her. I want to push down on her hips and slide in.

My seething, hissing Kitty is so angry at me, and I realize that last night did not win the war, just the first of many battles to come. The pain I etched in her is too deep to fill in only one night. Even after the mending we've done.

"Your brand on me."

"I didn't put it there."

"Maybe not this physical representation, but you did eleven years ago. What lies beneath, my heart, has been yours since then."

Her teeth are bared at me, eyes on fire and boring so hard into me. "Liar."

I reach up with my left hand to cup her cheek and she flinches away, then slams my arm back down to the bed. All of her weight rests on it as she stares at the little grey-wash kitty with her eye color. Her face twists again, and a single tear begins to slide down her cheek.

Finally, she sees them, understands that all of my tattoos represent her. Nailed into my flesh for all to see her ownership of me.

I reach up with my other hand and swipe away the tear with

my thumb. For the briefest of seconds, she leans into my touch before pulling back and sitting up.

Both of us gasp as her pussy lands right on my cock. I can't help but arch my hips, sliding it along her wet lips.

Fire fills her eyes, different from the rage, darkening them as she moves her body with mine. A shudder moves through her when the head of my cock slips across her clit. Placing her hands on my chest, she picks up her hips and reaches between us, gripping my dick and placing the tip at her entrance.

I'm entranced by the vision, waiting for her to sink down, watch it disappear inside her. When she moves, sitting down on me, taking my cock in her, my eyes roll back, lids fluttering. I don't even get to see it due to the sheer intensity of my Kira's wet warmth wrapping around me.

She draws in a trembling breath, nails digging into my skin. Hips up, then down a little. Up and then down again until she has all of my cock shoved up her cunt.

I stare down, watching as she sits back, resting her hands on my thighs, letting me see my cock stretching her fucking tight pussy. There's never been a more perfect sight, but when I look up and catch her gaze, it's cold, even with the lust.

"I'll fuck you, use you, but I'll never be yours."

She sits forward again and raises her hips before dropping again. Up and down, riding me, taking from me.

I curl my fingers around her waist and squeeze, then trail up her sides until I reach her tits. Her nipples are already hard, and she lets out soft little moans as I lightly run my fingers over them. A loud gasp leaves her, eyes popping open when I pinch them and pull, flicking as I let them go.

I want to reply, but every thought I have gets blasted away

each time I bottom out in her.

Her moans and squeals grow louder when I thrust up, pushing her down with one hand while the other continues to play with her tits.

She's close, and so am I.

Sitting up, I tangle my hand in the hair at the base of her neck, drawing her close.

"Fuck me, use me all you want. It won't change the fact that I fucking love you, and I know you love me." Her face scrunches up in the most erotic come face. I grab onto her ass, pushing and pulling her along my cock as I thrust up. My teeth are bared, scraping against the column of her neck as I fight off the urge to come, waiting for her. "I'm yours, and you. Are. Fucking. Mine!"

Her walls clamp down on me like a motherfucking vice, her screams filling the room. A roar rips out of me, my arms clamped down on her, holding her tight as I empty in her.

Bare.

My boys released, searching for their target—one they won't reach. Not yet, but one day, I kinda like the idea of them finding it, filling her body with the perfect combination of the two of us.

I fall back down to the bed, taking her with me, chests expanding as we gasp for breath.

Kira

I wake with a start. I'd been flying, then falling, crashing down to the earth. Now I'm shaken, confused. Where am I?

Something squeezes me, pulls me in. It takes a split second

to gain my bearings.

A fraction to realize where I am—in Brayden's bed, tangled up in his arms. His breath is soft against my neck.

And I remember I'm naked.

He's naked.

We had sex more times than I can count on one hand.

It was . . . a million times better than my fantasies.

His hands, his body, his cock.

The electronic vibe that pulsed through me.

Being so close to him is misery—heaven and hell.

I need closer to him.

I need away from him.

With a deep breath, I maneuver my way out of his iron grip, trying my best not to wake him.

I need to get out of here unseen.

Slow and steady, I break away, sitting up. Looking behind me, I'm stunned by the sight of him, of Brayden. He's more beautiful and perfect than one of Michelangelo's statues.

A modern day David.

I have to get away from the spell he has on me. It always turns me into a stupid girl ruled by a childish fantasy of a bygone love.

My steps are soft, silent, and on the wobbly side as I make my way out of the room. I'm so weak I can barely stand, my legs no longer made of muscle and bone. Somehow I make it to the bathroom, once again keeping the noise down.

I try and remember how I got here and where exactly *here* is. It's all a blur, lost in a lust-filled haze. I hadn't even been drinking yet, but I was obviously drunk off Brayden.

We're in his apartment, I know that much.

But how the hell am I getting out of here?

I sneak out of the bathroom and into the living area of his

apartment. It's a small one bedroom with a kitchen and living area. Not very big, but just right for one guy.

We started out on the couch, and I curse when my pussy clenches at just that small thought. Somewhere near that cursed couch, the one I helped him pick out, should be my belongings. I hope my phone still has some battery.

The room is a wreck, dashing my hopes I'll find everything. Boxes of furniture everywhere, remnants of packaging, along with a lot of his stuff, including our clothing strewn everywhere. The search for my clothing results in nothing but a few rags.

Panties—lost.

Tutu—hides nothing.

Bra—torn.

Fuck.

I try to push the memories away of *how* they ended up this way, but the pulsing pain won't let me. Every movement reminds me.

His body.

His need.

My own.

I was right. I always knew—Brayden isn't a one time fuck.

Not for me.

The absoluteness of this sends me to the floor. This was why. I miss him inside me, now that I know how good it is. I want more.

No. Not a want. A *need.*

An itch I scratched and shouldn't have, because I knew my body has always known I'd want more.

I can't be here when he wakes.

I spot my phone under a makeshift table and reach for it. Waking it up, I sigh in relief. There isn't much power left, but it's enough to contact someone. My fingers fly on the screen as I text my girls.

911 I need a ride.

I glance down again and groan. Years of pent-up lust is painted all over my skin, and I'm still naked with nothing to wear.

Across the room is Brayden's duffle, the one he always travels with, and I pray it has something I can wear inside.

As I unzip the bag, I sigh with relief—everything is neatly folded. Clean. Sitting on top is a Purdue T-shirt I've seen him wear, and I slip it on before digging down further.

Pants are out of the question—he's a foot taller than me. I luck out with a pair of basketball shorts. They still hit mid-calf on me, but at least there's a drawstring to help keep the waist up.

My phone chimes beside me, and I grab for it to silence the ringer.

Recon mission? I'm in. Where are you?

Jenna, my savior.

I type back, needing out now.

Columbus.

I love my friends. It takes seconds for her to respond. I swear Jenna has the fastest fingers I've ever seen.

Damn. Sit tight. Text me the address and I'll get my speedy ass there ASAP.

Address? Shit. I was too absorbed by Brayden to pay attention to where he was taking me. All I knew was that it was taking too damn long to get his cock back inside me.

I walk quietly around for anything that might tell me where I am when a yellow slip of paper catches my eyes. It's a delivery form. Lady luck seems to be siding with me, and I text the address to Jenna.

Just hit Wilmington. GPS says 50 minutes. I say less.

She's already to Wilmington? At the rate she's going, less is right. My phone beeps, letting me know there's only ten percent left on the battery.

Phone's almost dead. Meet you at the entrance.

I find my wristlet and do everything I can to keep the keys from jingling, then pick up my shoes as I head to the door. There are a few bottles of water sitting on the counter near the door, and I swipe one.

With ninja skills, I open the door, turning the lock before just as gently closing it.

I grimace as I look down at my bare feet, the four-inch heels in my hand, and the stairs. I've never liked walking around barefoot outside, but options are limited.

The second I'm outside and walking away, the itch returns.

His tattoos . . .

He permanently marked his body with bits of me.

Happiness floods in, but is quickly drowned by ice.

He hurt me, so many times. How can I trust him with my heart ever again?

I can't.

I know it.

I've said it a thousand times arguing with myself. It would destroy me.

And the fear returns. Because I'm feeling something more than hatred. Different from the rage of the past six months. More than friendship. A feeling I buried long ago, one he damaged beyond repair.

It scares me.

I don't want to be that naive little girl again.

I refuse.

I need to control this feeling before it spirals out of control, before he has a chance to hurt me again.

My eyes squint against the bright sun as I walk. A flare of light catches my eye, and I spot a familiar Toyota Camry across the parking lot. It still has the Class of 2012 bumpersticker on it, in our school's maroon and white letters. There's a dent in the bumper from when Dana backed it up into our mailbox as she stormed off after a fight with Ryan last summer.

I forgot that Brayden said he was a few buildings down from them.

I think about going over for about two seconds. Ryan's there. I haven't seen much of him this summer. He's barely been home.

Not that I blame him. That place is *not* a good environment. Toxic.

Then again, if he came, he might see how unhappy Mom's become and convince her to do something about it.

And that's why I won't go over. I don't want him to see me in Brayden's clothes, sneaking out of Brayden's apartment, thinking too much about what it means.

It means nothing.

Sex.

And that's all it's going to be.

Yeah, no denying it. I already admitted to myself I want more. And I *really* want more.

But just for the sex.

Fuck. The sex.

Better than every fantasy of it I'd ever had.

I can do it—use him. A few more times to get him out of my system, and then bye for good.

I make it to the entrance of the apartment complex and sit on the brick landscaping wall.

The wait is killing me because all I can think about is Brayden. Why can't I stop? Over and over.

One second with his skin on mine held more pleasure than every second I've ever had with Austin combined.

It's so strong I know I can easily get lost in it, in him.

But I won't.

I set the rules.

I set the time.

I'll use him and when I'm done, I'll walk away.

As I take a sip of water, a car turns in and pulls up next to me. I jump up and open the door, sliding in next to Jenna.

"What are you wearing?" she asks.

I roll my eyes. "Just drive."

She eyes me up and down, grinning so big it almost looks maniacal. "Team Brayden for the win!"

I shake my head. "No winner. Just a really good fuck."

She stares at me for a minute. "I'm not one to begrudge a girl a booty call."

"But?"

The car slows down and as we stop at a red light, she turns to me. "Is it really that bad to be his girlfriend?"

I shake my head. "Brayden doesn't do commitment. He's a human Pokemon collector when it comes to women."

Her brow furrows. "What the hell does that mean?"

"He's gotta have them all."

Jenna's head falls back and she lets out a loud laugh. I laugh a little as well, but then there's that itch at the back of my mind.

He's changed, I've seen it. He says he hasn't had sex in many months, and I actually believe him.

But belief isn't the same as forgiveness. While I believe some of the things he says, it doesn't change the past.

SEVENTEEN

BRAYDEN

June 16th, 2015

Three days.

Three fucking days since I've seen her.

Kissed her.

Fucked her.

Three days of absolute torture. Of keeping my distance, giving her space.

I woke to an empty bed and no messages. She wouldn't answer my calls or texts. She regrets it, but at the same time, I know she wants more.

If sex is how I'm going to get through to her, to reconnect with her, then so be it.

I told her she was mine.

Showed her I was hers.

Now the challenge was to make her believe both.

I've listened to Dana's damn whale song CD since Kira left as I put together all my furniture. Anything to help keep me calm and from going after her.

Not anymore.

I gave her space, breathing room, time to think about it. I've been patient above my normal tolerance. But after having her, I can't stay away.

As cheesy as it sounds, I need her like I need air. She's my everything, and I can't live without her.

I'm also out of projects and clean clothes. Plus, I have to work tomorrow. It's only part time, but being in marketing, it pays pretty well.

The drive home seems longer than normal, but it's just over an hour from my apartment to home. With only a few exits left, I'm getting antsy.

My cock is already hard.

Days of nothing but me and the memories of fucking her—which was all over my apartment—had me so horny for her. If she's in the kitchen, I want to bend her over right then and slide in. Hanging in her room? I've always wanted to fuck her on her bed.

If I didn't already know I'm ruined for any other woman, it's obvious now. Kira owns all of me. I don't want anything from any other female.

There are two cars parked in front of the house when I pull up, but the garage is empty.

"Hello!" I call out as I step into the kitchen from the garage.

Silence.

The backyard is empty, but there is evidence that Kira was out there with her friends from the towels and bags spread out on the chaise loungers. That explains the extra cars.

Fuck. She's not alone. Dad and Sonia are still at work, and my perfect opportunity to corner Kira is gone.

Giggles float in the air as I make my way upstairs. I swear I hear my name as I throw my duffle onto my bed.

"You have to tell us!" Someone squeals as I walk across the hall.

"No!" Kira says.

With her resistance, I'm pretty sure I did hear my name and that I'm the current topic of conversation.

I push open the door, and four heads snap my way and a couple of shrieks are let out.

"Oh, shit!"

I smirk and lean against the doorframe, my arms crossed in front of me. "Ladies."

They're still in bikinis, hair hanging damp down their backs. Kira's cheeks and shoulders are pink. She probably forgot sunscreen again.

"You scared us!" one of the twins says. I think she's Ashley, but I'm not sure.

"Sorry. What are you girls up to?" I stare at Kira and her mouth, which had been hanging open in surprise, snaps shut and her gaze hardens.

"Get out," Kira says. Her friends turn to look at her, then back to me.

"What? I can't hang with you?" I ask, my bottom lip jutting out a little bit in mock hurt.

Her expression is neutral, giving me nothing. "No boys allowed."

"Payback? We were kids, and that was your brother."

"Well, as an adult, I can say I don't want to play with you."

Ooh, my snarky girl is out. "Oh, I doubt that, baby."

Her eyes widen, jaw clenched tight. By the giggles of her friends, my suspicions were right—they know. In fact, one of them probably came and got her the morning she left me.

Kira lets out a huff, and my gaze zooms down in reflex to watch her tits give a little jiggle.

I really hope she doesn't wear that thing in public, because I'm two seconds from throwing her friends out and ripping it off her. If I'm like that, I can imagine the reaction she receives, and it makes me homicidal.

She adjusts the strap, and I groan at the pale line on her pink skin. Does she have similar pale triangles on her chest? I *really* want to find out.

"Are you going back in the pool?"

"Yes," her friend Jenna pipes in. "Want to join us?"

I push off the door and grab the bottom of my shirt, yanking it off. "Let's go."

"Oh my God, is that a *K* on his chest?" one of the twins gasps.

"Look at that tattoo on his side. Don't tell me that mermaid's hair isn't the same color as Kira's," the other twin says.

"Yo, this man is *so* owned," Jenna pipes in.

Kira glares at me. "We're not going now, dipshit. We just got out."

I give them a pout. "We used to have so much fun in the pool."

She rolls her eye's and I know she's reaching her boiling point.

"Fine. Have your girl time."

"What are you doing?" the twin that commented about the *K* on my chest asks me.

"Packing."

"For your apartment?"

I nod. "I think it's missing a woman's touch." I wink at

Kira, who flips me off.

"Oh, really?" Jenna turns to Kira, who is now beyond pissed.

"Out!" She points to the door as she glares at me.

I hold my hands up and back away. "Yes, mistress."

After passing into the hall, I pull the door closed and wait. There's giggling, but it's silenced by Kira.

"Shut up! You three are terrible."

"Seriously, Kira, how can you turn that down?"

"She can't!"

I step away with a smile. No, she can't.

I'm really beginning to like her friends.

As I enter my room, I close the door and lean against it. My dick is so fucking hard and I'm sure they noticed, especially when I took off my shirt. I rub my palm against my jeans, right over my shaft. A shiver runs through me and my hips rock against my hand as I let out a hiss.

I need to get off, but I don't want to do it without her.

Instead, I pick up my laptop bag and climb onto my bed. I started a list of things I need to take back with me this weekend so I can continue getting my apartment set up. Right now, it's just a shell with furniture, but at least I've got that.

As I scan over the list I notice there's one thing missing— Kira's name at the top.

I'm turning into such a pussy for the girl, but I'm perfectly fine with it.

Most everything I moved home last month is stacked up in the basement, and a good majority of it will go with me. There's the rest of the summer to get it all there, not that there's a ton. Every week I have to spend half of the time here for my job, but I have a feeling more than that will be spent here.

This is where Kira is.

I pull out a notebook and begin writing down the boxes that are higher priority. I'd love to simply print it off, but my printer is somewhere in one of the boxes.

There are still giggles going on in Kira's room as I head down to the basement. Once there, it doesn't take long to pull aside what needs to go back with me and sort out what isn't going at all.

On my way back up, I hear Kira's friends shouting and Kira replying. She's at the bottom of the stairs. I didn't even hear her on the steps above me.

I stay hidden in the basement doorway and crane my head around the frame. She's walking into the kitchen, and I nearly bust my blue balls all over my shorts.

Kira in a bikini does so much more to me now than it did six years ago, before she had tits and ass to fill it. Before she morphed into the petite, sexy woman I want to pin to the wall with my cock. I can't help but follow the sway of her hips.

She turns and jumps a little before glaring at me. "Are you following me?"

"I just came upstairs and I'm thirsty."

She eyes me, then notices the paper and pen in my hand. I set them down on the counter and take in her fuckable body in the most blatant manner. My lips pull up in one corner, and I reach down to adjust my dick. Her gaze darts down, staring, transfixed, for a beat too long.

Yeah, I know what you want, baby.

She huffs, then turns around, throwing the fridge door open, blocking me.

But it doesn't hide all of her, and I'm stuck staring at her perfect ass.

So easy. All I have to do is slip a tiny piece of fabric aside and I'm home. The one place I've always belonged.

After pulling out some sodas and closing the fridge door, she continues trying to ignore me.

Not a good idea in my state. I'm left staring, unable to rip my eyes away from every square inch of exposed skin begging to be licked.

Begging to be covered in my come.

So entranced, I'm not even paying attention to what she's doing, only her movements. I move without direction. Pure animal instinct leads me until I'm standing behind her.

She stops moving, stops breathing as I grab onto her hips with both hands, unable to stop from grinding into her sweet ass.

"Brayden." She chokes out my name. "Stop."

It's such a feeble request. No strength at all, especially when she pushes back against me.

"There you go, vibrating again for me. I can feel it. I know how much you need it."

I trail my hand along the edge of her suit and slip under, right at her mound. She draws in a shuddering breath, and my hips jerk against her.

Slick and smooth skin lies between her legs, and I'm salivating for a taste. It's been way too fucking long since I've eaten her out that I have to force myself to stop from dropping onto the floor and sucking on her pussy until she's juicing all over my face.

"Do you miss me here?" I ask as I slip between her pussy lips, pressing in.

"N-no."

I growl at her answer and shove two fingers in. "No lying, baby. You wouldn't be this wet for me."

She shakes her head. "That's from my swimsuit."

Her protests are so cute.

"Nice try. This . . ." I slide her juices over her clit, flicking it, making her squirm. ". . . is not water."

I trail my other hand up her stomach and under the flimsy piece of cloth hiding her nipples. Her breast is so soft in my hand and a contrast to her nipple which is hard and begging. The moan Kira lets out as I pinch her nipple between my fingers is exactly what I need.

That sound tells me she needs this as bad as I do. These three days were just as hard for her as they were for me, despite her words.

I slide my fingers out of her pussy and rub up against her clit. At the same moment, I flick her nipple. She bucks against me, another moan slipping out, and her head falls back onto my shoulder.

"That's it, Kitty. Feel what only I can do to you."

No protests, but I don't let her.

She's trapped by me. One hand fucking her pussy, hips rocking into her, the other hand groping her. My mouth is latched onto her neck.

I need to mark her. A reminder for her to see every time she looks in the mirror.

"B-Brayden." Her hands latch onto me—one in my arm, the other in my hair. She moves against me in a rhythmic, desire-driven pulse.

I'm so close to bending her over and fucking her.

"What do you want?" I ask as I nip a trail up her neck.

Her eyelids are heavy, her juicy lips hanging open. So far gone, so close to coming she can't even respond.

I let go of her tit and slide up to her jaw, grabbing hold and tipping her face toward mine.

As soon as my lips find hers, she searches out my tongue.

It sets off a spark, and I pull her so hard against me that my palm grinds into her clit.

The kiss is wet and electric, and I can't stop devouring her. The second I find her g-spot, she screams into my mouth before tightening her grip and biting down on my lower lip.

It's so strong—our intensity, our want.

All I want is to crawl inside her.

Grinding, purring, my Kitty can't stop moving. Her pussy clamps down on my fingers, and I know what's coming.

My hand stops and I slow my kisses, despite her protests.

It's fucking hard, torturous even, but necessary.

Her whimpers and pleas cut through me, but it's a lesson I need her to remember—she needs me as much as I need her.

"I know you want more, Kira."

"Please!" Her hips grind against my hand, searching for more.

"You were so fucking greedy for it, and you still are."

I slip my fingers back in, and she shivers in my arms.

It takes every bit of strength in me to pull away from her. So difficult when I know how close she is, how bad she needs it. Her hands are braced on the counter as she turns around.

Her expression . . . Holy fuck, I'm almost coming in my jeans from the strength of her lust.

"Please."

The desperation in her tone tears at me, makes me want to

surrender. But I can't.

She has to see, has to remember, has to feel our connection at its strongest. Soak in it until it permeates every last part of her again.

"Not right now."

Her brow scrunches up, eyes watering in what I'm guessing is sheer frustration. "Why?"

"When your friends leave, when you can't stand it anymore. When you need to finish yourself off, find me."

She steps forward and grabs on to my shirt. "I want it now. I can't go up there like this."

"Later," I press, despite my dick begging to put her on the counter and drive into her.

"Now."

"Five minutes ago, you didn't want anything to do with me."

"And now I'm like this, and it's your fault."

I smirk at her. "Then come find me later. Find out just how good the buildup can be. Come to me, and I'll make you come harder than you ever have before."

Her jaw locks, and she slaps her hand against my chest. "Asshole!"

"Oh, I'll be taking that soon, baby, but not tonight."

She stares up at me in shock, giving me the opportunity to step back and out. I turn around when I reach the doorway and give a couple strokes to my cock.

"See you soon."

Her thighs clamp together as she bites down on her bottom lip, making me second-guess my leaving.

I take a few deep breaths on my way to the staircase.

"Oh, hi," a voice says as I start climbing.

I look up to find Jenna coming down. "Hey."

"Have you seen Kira? She went to get some snacks, and it's been a while."

I nod. "Yeah, she's in the kitchen."

Her gaze narrows on me. "Why do you look like the cat that ate the canary? Or in this case, the Kira?"

I smirk at her and lick my fingers. "I don't have any idea what you're talking about."

She laughs, but when it dies down and I'm about to leave, she stops me.

"Brayden, look, I don't know what went down with you two, and all joking and teasing aside, that's my best friend."

"Hurt her and you'll kill me?"

She shakes her head. "You've already done that." I grimace and hang my head. "What you just did right there shows me you're hurt too. Make our girl happy so I don't have to chop your dick off, okay?"

"That's all I want to do, but she's fighting it, which I completely understand."

"Keep fighting."

"Always."

She smiles and punches my arm. "Guess I'll go pick up whatever mess of a girl you left."

"Hey, Jenna."

She turns back to me. "Yeah?"

"Thanks for being such a great friend. I know because of me she didn't really have many friends that were girls."

She giggles. "I forgot about that."

I head back to my room and shut the door, then collapse down on my bed.

My dick is still hard, thumping in my jeans.

I check my watch—it's already almost five. Unless her friends leave right now, I'd be lucky to see her for a long time, let alone tonight.

Fuck.

I rub against my shaft with my palm.

There's no way I can make it through work tomorrow like this. I'll be a raging fucking lunatic.

I really want to come in Kira, but for my own sanity, it's best to rub out a quick one. But next time, it *will* be smeared all over her pussy lips and oozing out of her tight cunt.

EIGHTEEN
Kira

My friends left just before dinner, abandoning me. They're all on my shit list as I think they're conspiring with him.

Then again, I've never told them everything.

Somehow, by some miraculous means, I made it through dinner. Brayden stared at me almost the whole time, our parents clueless as they ignored each other.

The conversation was stifled, and that's putting it nicely. For the life of me, I don't understand why Steven even tries to engage his son in conversation. The dislike on both ends is so obvious that it felt like a heavy presence in the room. I had to physically restrain myself from reacting every time Steven spoke to him in that forced, slightly condescending tone.

Brayden gave as good as he got, but it still wasn't easy.

My mother didn't say one word to Steven, which made everything worse.

I always disliked the man and I won't deny it. Lately, though, I've begun to truly hate Brayden's father.

At one point, Brayden brushed the back of his fingers

lightly across my upper thigh.

Did I mention that I hate him, too?

Now, I'm alone, staring at my laptop, trying to force myself to *stop* looking at the door.

It's not working.

My thighs clench, trying to keep them from moving, to keep me from thinking about the man across the hall. The one who drove me to insanity earlier and left me like this.

I'm so horny. Clawing the walls, so far gone I'm not thinking straight.

My pussy keeps twitching, aching to be filled. Stuffed by that huge cock of his. Spread open as he pounds into me.

I glance over to my nightstand and contemplate pulling my vibe out. The problem is, I know it won't be enough. A hollow orgasm. Unfulfilling and frustrating me further.

But I don't want to go to him either. I don't want to prove to that cocky bastard that he was right.

Even though he is.

I can't stop thinking about him, about his touch. How freaking perfect he feels inside me. How much I want it.

These are his terms, not mine.

I press my fingers against my clit as my thighs rub together. My nipples are so stiff every shift of my hips has them rubbing against my tank top. Then it hits me, smacks me in the face.

It was on a day close to this, maybe even this same day last year, that I got my first taste of him.

My first addictive hit.

The day he almost took my virginity.

I wanted him to do it. He was almost there.

Mom has the worst timing.

I won't even allow myself to get into thoughts about how things would be different if he had.

Instead, I wonder if he's high right now, just like he was then. Did he get off after he teased me this afternoon?

I feel like I'm going out of my mind.

What is this?

I can't do anything but fantasize about him touching me.

No, that's not true.

I can go across the hall and take what I need. Not because he told me to, because I want it. Me fucking him, not the other way around.

I'm off my bed and to the door. It's eleven, so Mom and Steven should be asleep. The hallway is dark by their room, no light from under the door, but there is a small sliver coming from Brayden's room.

I sneak across the hall and stand outside his door. It's silent inside, and I wonder if he's asleep.

Only one way to find out.

Slowly, I twist the knob and push the door open.

He's awake, sitting in just his shorts with his laptop on his lap, headphones on.

As soon as he notices my movement, his head snaps up. The illumination from his laptop highlights his green eyes, which seem to glow, thanks to the thick black frame of his glasses.

Damn, I forgot how sexy he looks in those.

He takes off his headphones. By his expression he's surprised I'm here, which makes me nervous.

He's been chasing me for the last year, ever since I came to him, just like this.

Maybe it's déjà vu, but it feels so much like then.

He closes his computer and sets it on his nightstand. His tongue wets his lips as he watches me.

Then, he reaches out for my hand. "Sit."

Fuck.

I can't help it. I straddle his hips, right over his cock which seems to suddenly harden beneath me.

I rock against him, staring straight into his eyes. "Finish what you started here a year ago."

His mouth pops open, eyes darkening.

I reach out and slide his glasses off, setting them down on his laptop. "You won't be needing these."

I may have come to him, asked him to fuck me, but I'm still in control, and I make sure he knows it as I trace the line at the edge of his shorts. I grab onto the band and pull, inching them down. He shudders beneath me, his hands running up my thighs.

When my fingers brush against his shaft, he bucks, pressing right against my clit.

It's hot and as I pull it out, I see how hard and ready he is to give me what I need.

Only three days, but it feels like a lifetime since I've had him in my hands.

His fingers reach my shorts and dip in, slipping across my slit.

He smirks at me. "How did my little pussy get so wet?"

I grip his cock with one hand and yank his shorts off with the other.

"You know damn well how. Maybe I'll get back at you and leave you on the verge," I say, taunting him.

His hand grips down on my hip while he shoves two fingers into my pussy, making me gasp. "You really think

I'm going to let you get away? I'm bigger and stronger than you."

Cocky jerk.

I tighten my grip, and he cringes. "I know your weak spots." I loosen up and continue to work his shorts down.

When his whole cock is out, balls as well, I stop.

I'm transfixed, unable to look away. It twitches, and I lick my lips. The damn thing is hypnotic.

How did he ever get this thing all the way inside me?

There's a clear drop of fluid coming out of the tip, and I can't stop myself. I lean down and lick it.

I have little experience with giving head, but that doesn't stop me from swirling my tongue around the tip.

He jerks beneath me, cursing as he throws his hands up, then down and into my hair.

He's so big I can't get much in, so I use my tongue, which only makes him move more.

"Fuck, Kira! So fucking good."

I look up at him, and my pussy twitches. His eyes are wild. Pupils blown, mouth open. Muscles so tight like he's ready to spring on me. It makes me moan around him, sending vibrations through his shaft.

I swallow around him, and it forces him to make the sexiest grunts and groans.

He pulls me off him with little effort and flips me under him. "Shit. Kitty, you're going to get a mouth full of milk if you keep that up."

I draw in a breath as my head lands on a pillow. "And?"

A growl-like sound vibrates in his chest before he slams his lips to mine, our teeth crashing together with the force.

Lips. Tongue. Hot and wet.

Grinding.

Fuck.

He slips my panties and shorts to the side and slides his length against my pussy. He's panting as he pulls back and looks down. We both stare, watching the tip of his cock pop up between my puffy lower lips.

Each zing on my clit makes my hips move against him. The zinging sensation moves through my body with each thrust.

I grab hold of his shirt, fisting it, pulling his mouth back down. An action that only makes it worse. Or better.

Everything is mixing together. Intensity ramping up.

His teeth nip down my jaw, tongue licking down my neck before biting down on his favorite spot.

He moves, making room to pull my tank top off.

No longer pressing against my clit, I let out a little whimper. His mouth continues down my chest until he's flicking my nipple with his tongue.

I'm a confused mess caused by the wavering strength of pleasure. He's pulsing it, drawing it out longer.

With a final pulling bite and suck of one of my very hard and aroused nipples, he moves down.

All I've ever heard about is how guys hate to go down on girls.

Not Brayden.

He seems to make it his life's mission to eat me out as often as he can.

Those dark, almost dangerous eyes look at me, then he yanks my shorts and panties off, tearing them down my legs.

"Jesus!" I nearly jump off the bed when he dives down, latching onto my pussy and digging in.

I squirm from the force of the sensitivity as he sucks on my clit, tongue licking at my opening. I fist his hair, unable to control myself.

"Brayden!"

He sucks on my whole pussy and runs his tongue up my slit.

"Shhh, baby. Don't want the parents to hear you coming, do you?"

A strange moaning whimper makes its way out of me.

I can't stop moving against him. So right. Tense. His hands keep me right where he wants me.

Unable to move.

Forced to take everything he gives.

I'm a panting, writhing wreck. So freaking close to coming, but it also feels miles away.

An almost numbing sensation.

My back arches, body shaking. His fingers move faster in and out than his cock ever could.

No more thoughts. Only feels.

His hands.

His tongue.

Him.

All of him.

My vision goes blurry, the ache between my legs escalating.

Suddenly he's gone, and I'm about to go crazy or break.

"Make sure you come all over the sheets."

Before I can even think to say something, his lips are on mine and his cock is stretching me open.

And I'm screaming into his mouth as I stare into his dark eyes.

My whole body convulses.

Uncontrollable.

Unbelievable shocks that light up everything.

Quaking bundle of pleasure-intensified nerves.

It doesn't stop.

I'm whimpering, thrashing in his arms, begging him with my eyes to slow down.

Before I can even register, his dick is out and he's slamming it back in. Smacking into my still shuddering cunt.

"Come on, baby. One more time."

"Haven't . . . stopped." Tears stream down my cheeks, and I pray he comes before I go insane.

His thrusts somehow pick up in pace, and he cages me in his arms.

"I know. Your pussy won't stop squeezing me."

"Just . . . come."

He hooks his arm under my knee, making my eyes roll back as he hits even deeper.

"Where?" He slows down to long, deep strokes, his hand locked onto the base of my skull, keeping my gaze to him.

"I . . . I . . ."

"Where, Kira?"

His words come out in a desperate growl, while my own are a high-pitched keening.

"In my pussy."

Teeth lock down on my neck, stifling him as he cries out, holding me closer, tighter than he ever has before. I'm clenching him so tight I can feel each throbbing eruption deep inside me. His whole body jerks from the force, and my pussy feels like it's sucking him in.

He collapses down on me, his weight making it hard to breathe.

"Brayden." I tap on his shoulder and he pulls his knees up, taking some of the weight off while keeping his cock buried.

His chest is still pressed against mine, but I can breathe again.

It takes a few minutes for us both to calm down. When he is calm again, he sits up, back onto his haunches.

He looks down at me with a goofy smile and heavy eyes.

I narrow my gaze at him. "You think you won, don't you?"

He wets his lips and nods. "Oh, yeah."

"You di—" I suck in a breath as his thumb rubs against my clit. My walls clamp down on him. "Not fair."

"I know your weak spots," he says with a smirk.

His hips give a little thrust, and he stares down to where we're still joined. The look on his face . . . Jesus, I want him to fuck me all over again.

"Come on, pull out."

He shakes his head. "I don't want to leave."

"What?"

He looks up at me. "You don't want me to leave."

"Come on, jerk face, I need to clean up the mess you made."

"Mess *I* made? Oh, baby, the huge wet spot under your ass is all you." He pulls back, his cock slowly pulling out. The second he's gone, I let out a whimper. It feels like a light has been turned off in me.

His cock bounces, shiny and still hard, making the void in me even greater and the calling to shove him back in even stronger.

"Fuck. That is the best sight ever."

I'm about to ask him, but then I feel the liquid sliding down my ass cheek.

He groans, brow furrowed, tortured almost, and he grabs his cock. I look down, watching as he tries to scoop the come back up to my now gaping opening.

The guy who never fucked anyone without a condom has fucked me bare multiple times in the last few days, and is now playing with it.

"One day, I'll stuff you so full of come . . ." He trails off, lost for a few minutes before looking up at me. Something clicks in his brain, I can see it in the change of his expression, and he pulls away. "Let me find a towel or something."

I lay here as he gets up and sneaks out into the hall. The things he said, or rather, the last thing he said, rings out in my head. He didn't finish the thought, but my pussy twitched, knowing where he was going. The primal level thoughts.

Fuck, was he really thinking like that? Breeding? Making me pregnant?

One day, he said.

But why does him wanting that, even *one day*, turn me on?

NINETEEN

Kira

Avoiding Brayden is easy when he's at work, and I've even managed to avoid him at night, thanks to my girls. Early Friday morning I found him in his room, dressed for work and packing up some clothes to head back to Columbus for the weekend.

I lean on the door frame as he strips his bed, the sheets still stained from the other day.

"Laundry?" I watch as he stuffs the sheet into a bag and not into his laundry basket.

"Nope."

"Then what are you doing?" I ask.

He smirks at me and turns it to show the large spot. "Souvenir."

"That's gross."

He smirks and walks up to me. He leans down, so close that his lips are millimeters away from my own. "Keep telling yourself that, baby. I know you want to make another one."

I mash my teeth together and step back. "Cocky asshole."

The next few days passed without contact from him. Didn't even text or call. Well, he did send another devastating picture of his fuck-hot body.

This morning he returned.

What is with Brayden and these three-day cycles? Three days gone, three home, and three gone again before coming back.

I know he's working and trying to get his apartment set up, but there's just something about it that grates on me.

The problem is admitting why it bothers me.

When he's here I want him, while at the same time I want him to leave.

With him gone, I thought the anxiety would lessen, but instead, with each hour that passed the itch, the anticipation of the next time, increased.

I hate this. I hate that all he has to do is walk in the door and my legs are ready to spread willingly for him.

He got home an hour ago. and I'm trapped all alone with him. Our parents are at work, and while Ryan did come home this past weekend, he left yesterday.

The little shit even revealed to me why I haven't seen his brotherly ass around—he's giving his best friend space to defile his sister.

I'm not sure I love my brother anymore.

One day, big bro . . . Payback is a bitch.

With the knowledge of Brayden returning today, Mom left a list of chores for each of us to do. There wasn't much on them, but enough to keep us from going at it the moment he walked in. Especially since I was teasing him over text yesterday.

I got him back with a pic of me in my bikini.

I've been dusting this table for way too long. The surface is so shiny I can see my reflection.

All that I'm doing is moving my hand back and forth across the wood, because I'm glued to the scene happening outside the window beside the table.

Brayden shirtless as he mows the backyard.

He's got a hat on—a rarity for him—and his headphones as he cuts path after path through the grass.

The only sounds I hear are the racing beats of my heart and the loud buzz of the mower.

It's hot and sunny, and I can't tear my eyes away from the sweat rolling down his naked chest. I want to lick it up, lick him all over.

Fuck.

He wasn't working five minutes outside when his shirt came off. Now I'm hypnotized by him again, watching his shiny muscles strain, pushing the mower around. I'm so entranced I don't even notice when he turns it off.

I jump as he walks toward the house. Frantic energy buzzes through me as I search for something to help me look busy.

As I stare down at the cloth in one of my hands and the Pledge in the other, I want to slam my head against the wall.

I take a calming breath and look back out. He's taken his hat and headphones off, and drops them along with his phone, onto one of the lounge chairs.

I'm drawn in again, watching with rapt attention as he pulls his shoes and socks off. I half expect him to keep stripping, but he leaves his jeans on. They sit so low on his waist, showcasing that perfect V of his that I want to lick and nibble on.

Two large steps and his arms draw above his head as his

body launches forward, arching into the pool. When he surfaces, he shakes his head, flinging water around. He seems to struggle in the water for something before holding up a wad of dark blue and tossing it onto the concrete.

Fuck.

That's his jeans, which means . . .

Look away! Look away! I yell at myself.

It doesn't work. I should have done that twenty minutes ago. Now is too late. I'm aroused past rational thought.

What was I saying about wanting him to leave? No, I want him to come.

Inside me.

All over me.

Give me the soul-shattering pleasure only he can.

I drop the can of Pledge onto the floor and press my fingers between my legs.

He swims a couple of laps, then stands in the shallow end.

The buzzer to the dryer goes off, startling me, reminding me that I just washed all of the pool towels. When I look back, he still hasn't noticed me. He's barely looked toward the house, but maybe he already knows.

I gawk at him as he climbs the steps out of the pool, the water running down his sexy-ass muscles. The boxer briefs he's wearing are clinging to him, accentuating everything.

Especially the one thing I'm dying for.

He picks up the lump that is his jeans and spreads them onto one of the chairs. Then, he grabs his stuff and heads to the sliding glass door.

I no longer have my busy items in hand, but my pussy and nipple instead. "Shit." I frantically search for my dusting tools.

Instead of heading my way, to the left, he heads right, into the kitchen.

I don't even think as I set the stuff down and walk the same way.

When I get there, he's at the sink, gulping down a huge glass of water.

Droplets cling to his skin, and a puddle forms beneath him.

"You're making a mess," I say, gaining his attention.

After a little jump in surprise, he turns to me and smirks. "No mess yet, just water. Nothing a towel can't fix."

I continue toward him and reach out to his waist. He quirks a brow at me, his abs tensing.

"You're getting water everywhere." I grab onto his waistband and pull.

"Whoa."

I fall down to my knees and work the wet cloth down his hips, over his biteable ass, and the slab of man meat that's getting bigger with each tug.

I'm left eye to cock. It's staring at me, getting harder by the second and begging me to take him in my mouth.

Long, thick, veiny . . . How can something so weird looking turn me on so much and make my pussy so wet I'm probably dripping on the floor with him?

Salivating, on my knees in front of him. Lined up with the head, I lean forward, mouth open, and flick the tip of his cock with my tongue, then close my lips around him.

"Shit," he hisses, hips bucking, pushing him further into my mouth.

He's so big and I take as much of him as I can until I'm gagging, which is about halfway. After a few times moving up and down, I pull back and draw in a deep breath.

"Fuck, you're big."

I glance up at him, and he's staring down at me with that lust-filled look I've begun to crave. He reaches out and brushes my hair back. "Damn, baby . . . This is now one of my top five favorite views."

I wrap my fingers around his shaft, pumping him, taking in how good he feels in my hand.

"What are some of the others?"

"No worries, Kitty," he says as his fingers run down my cheek. "The top fifty . . . top hundred are all of you."

Me? All of them? That can't be true, and so it leaves me with one question, "What's number one?"

He bends over, smiling, and presses his lips against mine.

"Eleven years ago when you came bounding out your front door in a tutu and cat ears and claiming me as yours."

Damn it.

Damn him.

No, this is my show.

I reach up around his neck, pulling his lips back to mine. My mouth opens, tongue finding his in a building frenzy as I stand back up.

His body is still warm from being outside and in the sun, while his skin has patches of cool from the air conditioning on the water droplets drying on him.

I step back, turning, tugging him with me. "Come on."

After only a few short steps I stop and push against his chest. He falls back, landing on one of the kitchen chairs, eyes locked on me.

His cock is so hard it's sticking straight up in the air, bouncing against his abs, leaving sticky trails as it taps against his skin. I press my fingers against my pussy before pushing my shorts and panties to the ground.

"Something you want, baby?" He smirks at me.

"Shut up." I step forward, straddling his legs.

A groan crawls out of his chest when I grab his cock, running it against my pussy lips before lining it up.

"I'm your fuckdoll. Use me," he says, arms held out to his sides.

My brow scrunches, but quickly relaxes as I sit, his dick stretching me and making me forget whatever thought I may have had.

It's dangerous—his cock. A weapon of mass female destruction.

I fell prey, just like so many before me. Finally, I see why they can't stay away. If it's like this, I feel sorry for those who only got it once.

I take my time working my way down.

His mouth drops open as he stares to where we're joined. One hand wraps around my neck, pulling my face down to his. Lips parting, tongues sparking the tingling that flies through every nerve ending.

It takes me to a place where I forget. A live version of fantasies of him.

His other hand sneaks around my back, grabbing, pulling me down hard as his hips flex up, impaling me, filling me.

My eyes and mouth pop open, then a shuddering moan rips through me as my eyes roll back.

"You're being a tease," he says as he begins lifting me at the waist, moving me up and down his shaft.

I push against his chest and pry his hands away.

"This is my show. You're just here to get me off. Shut up, and be a good dildo."

My thighs flex, lifting me up, then dropping me back down.

Each thrust rubs against my insides, driving me insane with each small move we make. It drives my body to search out more.

How is it so different with Brayden? With Austin there wasn't really anything.

Fuck. Why does this feel so good?

Brayden's head leans back against the chair, abs tensing as he pushes his hips up each time I fall back down.

For some reason it pisses me off, almost as much as it turns me on, to see the blissed-out expression on his face. I pick up my pace, riding him harder, faster. Make him feel how angry I am that I need this, need him.

His green eyes open and bore straight into me. "If you're trying to hate fuck me, you have to do it harder."

My lip twitches up. "I said, shut up."

His hands grip my waist again, burning my skin and making my pussy clench.

He leans forward, snarling at me. "Harder."

He lifts me up and pulls me back down like I weigh nothing. Thrusting up, fucking me like we're going to die if one of us doesn't come in the next thirty seconds.

I'm a rag doll in his hands, crying out, no control.

"This is what you wanted." He breathes against my lips. "You think you're in charge, but what you need is my cock to dominate you. For me to possess you."

"Fuuuck . . ."

I can't take anymore. My muscles lock up, pussy squeezing down as I convulse on top of him.

He somehow seems to get deeper, almost painful. Long, hard thrusts followed by a frantic pounding. I grab him, holding on for the ride.

He lets out a roar, holding me down as he explodes at the same time as a loud crack rings out in the room.

We crash to the floor in a pile of chair bits and bodies. Chest to chest, both breathing hard, neither able to move. His cock still twitches inside me, making my walls clench.

"Smooth move, Cassanova," I eventually manage to get out.

He starts laughing, almost a cackle. "Shit. Ow! Fuck . . . I think I've got a splinter in my ass."

"Are you sure it's a splinter?"

His fingers tickle my sides as I try to sit, landing me back down on his chest.

"Oh, motherfucker!" he groans.

"Serves you right." I laugh, smiling down at him.

"You're mean. I'm in real physical pain here."

I can't stop, snickers erupting as I push off his chest, even more so when he glares at me.

I gasp as his cock and come leaves me, spilling a mess down on him. What's worse is I can feel more coming out and dripping on him.

He smirks, watching it. "That is so hot."

"It's so gross."

I stand and head to the sink for a washcloth. When I turn back around he's rolling onto his side, the goo sliding down onto the floor.

"Eww, stop!"

But I'm the one who stops. As he turns more, I see it.

Sticking out of his sexy ass, near his hip, is a piece of wood.

"Oh, my God!" I rush over and kneel down next to him.

It's about the size of my finger.

Brayden's fingers wrap around it and before I can stop him, he yanks it out. There's blood now, and I run to the bathroom for the first-aid kit and bottle of rubbing alcohol.

When I get back, I stare down at him, looking at the mess on the floor, and start laughing.

"What's so funny about this?"

I kneel beside him and soak a piece of gauze with the alcohol, then put it against the bleeding hole.

He hisses, slamming his fist against the floor. "Motherfucker!"

"The so-cool Brayden Hunt laid out on the floor. What would your adoring fans think if I snapped a picture?"

His eyes narrow at me, then his lips pull up, making the hairs on the back of my neck stand up.

"Then I'll just have to let everyone know how I ended up like this. First, I'd tell Ryan how his sister is such a pain in my ass."

I hold the bottle of alcohol above the hole in his skin and pour it in. He screams out, smacking the floor again.

"Abuse!"

"Oh, shut up. It's not that bad."

"Says you." Another hiss, his eyes screwing shut. "I need another nurse. Your bedside manner sucks."

"Well, I have a difficult patient." I look closely at the wound. It's not bad and the bleeding is slowing down.

I finish cleaning him up and dress the wound while he continues to look at me. When I'm done, we both stand and look down at the chair damage.

"What are we going to do about the mess?" I ask.

"I'll get it and come up with a story for your mom."

I nod. "Okay." It's suddenly awkward, and we're both still naked. "I'm just gonna . . . go to my room."

I run upstairs, needing to get away from any visual evidence of what I've just done, and grab my phone off my nightstand.

I tackled your best friend.

The words are out to my brother before I can even think. I need to tell someone. I need someone to stop this, to stop me, because I don't think I can do it on my own.

ewww.

Ewww? That's it? A guy just fucked me and all my big brother has to say when I tell him who it was, there's nothing more than mild disgust. I get nothing.

Go kick his ass.

Please. Give me something to think about other than him. Fuck him up for coming near me. Tell him to stay away like you've told all the others.

No

Traitor!

Aren't you going to be mad about it?

You've been mad about all the other guys who've shown interest.

More grossed out. Do you want to hear about me and Dana?

Ewww.

No.

I sigh and fall onto my bed.

Unprovoked. *I* did it, acted first, went after him.

I'm turning into someone else, and it's scary.

But it's also exciting on a level I don't even want to think about.

225

TWENTY
BRAYDEN

July 1, 2015

That itch is back, pulling at my skin, making it feel too tight.

I need her again.

It never stops.

It never will.

A shot glass is slammed down onto the table in front of me. "Drink that shit and stop fantasizing about my sister. I can only take so much."

I grab what's undoubtedly a shot of tequila and grumble, "How the fuck do you know what I'm thinking?"

Ryan pounds back his own shot. "You look like a starving animal."

That's because I am.

"It's disgusting."

I agree, but only because of how little control I have left.

It was bad before I had her. Now?

God help me.

"Leave him alone, babe. He's in love." Dana rubs her hand

into Ryan's shoulder.

"Yeah." I pull out my phone—nothing. No text. No calls. Is she even fucking thinking about me? "Besides, you get the same damn look on your face when you think of your girl."

"My girl isn't your sister."

"You'll learn to live with it."

"No, I won't. Trust me. I've already considered investing in some long-term therapy to erase the images in my head."

"That's your own damn fault for being such a pervert."

"It's called having an overactive imagination, you asshole!"

Dana laughs at the two of us.

I offer her as much of a smile as I can, then look back down at my phone. Kira's been opening up more to me lately, but it's moments like this when I realize that there's still this huge wall between us. An entire day without reaching out to me. I text her, as usual, too.

Another drink is slid in my direction. I grab it without looking up. Opening up Facebook, I go straight to Kira's profile, needing a hit. Any kind of hit.

No posts. No new images.

I don't know whether to be happy about that or not.

My leg starts bouncing as impatience chokes me. Where is she? What is she up to?

Why can't she just open up to me already?

If she doesn't reach out to me soon, I'm going to snap and hunt her down. I know myself.

"Yo, give her some space, man."

I glare at Ryan.

"Let him be, baby. He isn't stalking her down. That's an improvement, I'd say."

Dana gets a glare next.

I'm about to crawl out of my fucking skin. I know this isn't normal. My blood is literally boiling with hunger, frustration.

Being angry with Kira isn't an option. I have no right.

I can't help it.

Damn it, girl, just miss me as much as I'm missing you.

Running a hand through my hair, I stand up. "I'm going to get another drink."

Ryan eyes me warily. "You sure that's a good idea? Maybe you shouldn't get drunk. We all know how you get."

I give him the finger and walk away without responding. Getting drunk tonight isn't a part of my plan, but I do need a bit more to try and numb myself.

Making my way to the bar takes longer than it should. That's because it's crammed with people who came to see tonight's game. I weave my way through the crowd, my hand in my pocket and wrapped around my phone.

I'm waiting for it to vibrate. To give me a fucking hint that what I've seen the last few weeks is true. That the girl does care for me. I'm starting to suspect that she'll never move past using me for sex.

It's sick and painful, but fuck, no, I won't stop. Even if it is true, I have no plans of going anywhere.

I told her I was her fuckdoll. Asked her to use me. I want that, more than I can fathom.

But I'd be lying if I said the need for more than that isn't clawing at my common sense.

I'm practically her dildo. She said so.

So why the fuck isn't she searching me out to use me? I'll fucking take anything at this point, but the radio silence from her end is fucking with me.

Some guy backs up a step, bumping into me. I stop in my tracks, jaw twitching. The guy turns around, chest puffed out, like he's about to do something stupid.

One look at my face and he backs down immediately, mumbling an apology.

Thought so.

He steps out of my way, head bowed.

Before I can continue on my path, I feel someone fist the back of my T-shirt.

The fuck?

I'm yanked backwards, straight out the door leading to the back of the bar. A door I'm pretty sure is for employees only.

"Get the fuck off me." I jerk my shoulder, releasing the person's grip, and spin around to face them.

Hazel eyes.

Auburn hair.

The sexiest face and body this planet has ever been graced with.

My obsession.

The one person I wanted to see more than anything right now.

Kira grabs my shirt again, pulling me to her, away from the door, then pushes me so I'm walking backwards, heading God knows where.

And I let her. I'll always let her. "Fuck. You're here. You have no idea how much I needed to see you right now."

She doesn't say anything. Her facial expression is tense. She's angry.

"Baby, what's—"

Hands on my shoulders, she pushes me down into a sitting position. It's a bench against the wall, in the darkest part of the back of the bar.

I get a brief glimpse of what she's wearing, how short that tight, dark blue dress is.

Kira flips a leg onto the bench.

I lose my train of thought.

She straddles me, her hands shooting down to practically rip at my jeans.

My cock's already hard and pounding for her.

I cup her beautiful face, breaths racing. "What's wrong, Kitty? Talk to me."

"Shut up." She almost tears my zipper as she pulls it down, her hand reaching inside for my dick. This isn't a playful *shut up*, like the one she gave me the day she jumped me in the kitchen. My girl's raging mad. In control, but ready to cause me harm if necessary.

Okay . . .

What the hell did I do to her now?

Her hand wraps around my length and my thoughts shut down entirely, focusing only on the sensation.

"So that's it? That's how you're playing it? You just came here to fuck me?"

She fists my hair with her other hand and tugs my head back. "Yeah. Now shut the fuck up." Her lips meet mine, teeth sinking in.

I thrust into her grip. Fuck, I'm already close, dying to empty my balls all over her. Moaning into her mouth, I grab her ass to bring her down on me.

She slaps my hands away and bites me again.

So that's how this is going to be? Really? She isn't planning on giving me any say on how this goes.

Jesus, that drives me crazy.

Her hand wraps around my dick, guiding me. She places my tip right against her entrance.

Warm, wet skin.

This girl isn't wearing any panties.

I moan like an animal. She did it for me. Because she wanted me that bad. Nothing could get in the way.

Grabbing onto the edge of the bench, I thrust up into her.

Her sexy little mewl echoes around us and she drops her hips, slamming me all the way in.

That pussy's already throbbing for me.

I rotate my hips in small circles, covering my cock in more of her juices. "You're so perfect, baby."

Her arms come around my neck. Harsh breaths hit my lips. She feeds me another kiss, hugging me tight, her body betraying her once again.

"This body missed me." I let go of the bench and grab her waist, holding her down on me. "This pussy missed me." Her walls ripple around me, and she tries to move her hips. "Shit, babe. I bet even those nipples missed me." It's dark back here, so I can barely make out the outline of her tits in that dress.

I tug down her dress until her breasts spill out the top. I can't see her nipples, but as soon as I wrap one hand around her tit, one pebbled nipple presses into the palm of my hand.

Kira cries out, jerking on me. She moves her hips hard, trying to force me to let her go so she can take what she wants.

"Another hate fuck, baby?" I ask, pinching her nipple and rolling it between my fingers.

"It's always a hate fuck between us."

Holding her gaze in the dark, I nuzzle her nipple and flick it with the tip of my tongue. "Not for me."

"It definitely is for me," she breathes, her pussy twitching around me. "Let me fuck you."

Hugging her to me even tighter, I suck on her nipple, my cheeks hollowing out with the force.

"*Brayden.*"

Sliding my hand down her back, I tug her skirt all the way up to her hips, exposing her gorgeous ass. I cup one cheek, spreading her, then reach my fingers into the crease.

She tenses on me, panting, her entire body vibrating with anticipation. "Brayden?"

I switch to her other nipple, tonguing it. Bypassing her ass, I slide my fingers down to where we're connected. Fuck, feeling her lips hugging my cock is amazing. I play with us both, using all that wetness to lube up my fingers.

"What are you doing?"

The slight whimper in her voice makes my dick jerk inside her. She knows what I'm about to do. She's looking forward to it.

Fucking needs it with every fiber of her being.

Moaning around her nipple, I tug it slightly with my teeth and reach back up to press a finger between her ass cheeks.

Kira freezes on me. Her heart explodes into an even harder rhythm inside her chest, pounding beneath her breast. It's a beat that's echoed inside her pussy.

I release her nipple, dragging my bottom lip across it. She's throbbing so hard that I feel it echoing against her puckered opening. I'm so fucking turned on my cock's literally shaking, dying to slide into her tight ass. "Does this feel good, baby?" I rub her in soft circles.

A broken gasp leaves her, and she curls around me,

shuddering.

Can't even answer me.

She's so fucking horny for it, she's losing all control of her body.

God, I'm going to come if she keeps this up.

"I'm going to fuck you here one day. Fill this tight little hole full of my come."

She bites into my ear, moaning uncontrollably, her fingers digging into my back.

"Relax for me, baby," I whisper into her ear. "I just want to finger you."

Rotating her hips as much as she can in my hold, she sucks on my earlobe. A shiver tears down my spine. "Slam that big cock into me. I'll come so hard. Just one thrust, baby."

Baby.

Something uncontrollable pounds through me at the sound of that word leaving her mouth. She's never called me that before. I didn't think she ever would.

Love.

Pleasure.

Pain.

Rage at the fact that I can't publicly make this woman my girl.

Overwhelmed, I mash my teeth together and mentally struggle to hold my jizz back. I suck lightly on her neck, enjoying the way she trembles for me, and push my finger against her opening. "Don't move, baby. Just let me in."

She spreads her legs wider for me. The move somehow slides me in deeper. She's fully spread for me, her ass and pussy begging for my touch.

"Relax, Kira. Let me in. I'll make it so good, Kitty. I

promise."

She makes a delicious sound and melts around me more. Reaching for my arm, she pries it off her and slides my hand around to her pussy. "Play with me there, too."

My cock is thick and heavy inside her. One thrust, and I'll come as well. But I won't let that happen yet. I'm determined to feel both her pussy and her ass coming around me at the same time. I rub my thumb into her luscious little clit.

Her cry echoes out into the night.

Cupping her breast, she brings it back to my mouth, rubbing her tight nipple along my lips. "Lick me."

Fuck me, she's the sexiest thing alive. I suck her into my mouth, groaning in the back of my throat.

My finger pushes past the tight ring of muscles, slowly easing in.

She's so tight that I have to use more force than I want to in order to get my finger inside her. Her body clamps down tight, and a pained whimper leaves her.

I freeze. "Do you want me to stop?"

"Hell, no," she grits out, taking deep breaths. "Just give me a second to adjust."

More proof that she wants me in her ass as bad as I want.

Girl's going to be the death of me.

It takes her a few seconds to relax for me again. Once she does, I pet her clit softly and suck her nipple again, waiting for the pleasure to take over.

"Oh my God, Brayden. My pussy hurts. I need to come."

The cue I need.

I play with her clit a little harder, distracting her.

It takes one more thrust for my finger to slide all the way into her.

235

We both freeze, breathing harshly.

"*Fuck*, Kira. I'm going to come as soon as I get my head in here." No exaggeration. Her ass is a tight, perfect heaven. Even tighter than her pussy.

She jerks my face up, slamming our lips together. Her tongue slides erotically over mine, taking without permission. In an instant, the pliable Kira is gone, replaced by nothing but force. Her hips rock in my grip, sliding my cock and my finger in and out of her.

A scream gets caught in her throat.

My vision burns bright white.

There's no thought of stopping her. Of trying to regain back the control.

Her pussy's so tight like this, and it's only my finger inside her ass. She goes frantic on me, thrusting back and forth, her body pounding hungrily.

I can't fucking breathe. I rip my mouth away from her, gasping for air. It does nothing. The pleasure is too intense. My entire world's spinning and Kira keeps riding me, her head thrown back.

She's moaning too loud, bordering on screams. Someone's going to hear her, and I don't give a flying fuck.

"Kira, your pussy feels amazing like this. Holy shit, you're so tight."

Her head falls back, her body lost to the pleasure.

"You want another finger, baby? Want to be even tighter for me?"

"*Yes, yes, yes!*"

My balls draw up painfully. I thrust my finger in and out of her and stroke her deep with my cock. "How about I fuck you with a dildo in here one day while I fuck your pussy?"

A violent shudder goes through her. Her pussy, her clit, her ass, it all tenses up.

She wants me to take both her holes at the same time, pound her deep. It's so fucking dirty, too fucking sexy. She mewls my name repeatedly, riding me faster.

"Co-coming. Oh . . . *fuck*. It's—Brayden, *fuccck*."

"Kiss me," I growl, thrusting up into her harder, loving her so fucking much right now that I can barely take it. "Kiss me, and I'll pump this pussy full of my come."

She takes my mouth over and over, slanting her lips. Greedy for my tongue. My cock. Everything I have to give.

A split, agonizing second. That's all it takes for my dick to freeze up inside her, come pounding it's way up the shaft.

Her pussy gushes around me. Her scream slides down my throat. The muscles around my finger tighten up. That orgasm explodes through every muscle, securing me to her, keeping me right where she needs me.

I bite down into her bottom lip, snarling, my hips pistoning. I fuck her until there's nothing left in me, my dick giving empty jerks.

And then I fuck her some more, unable to stop, my erection still as hard as ever.

I have no idea when we eventually calm down, but Kira leans into me, her head on my shoulder, her panting breaths in my ear. Arms loose around her, I lean my head on her shoulder too, the world spinning.

"Shit, baby." Chuckling, I kiss her shoulder. "I missed you too."

One second, my arms are full of warm, delicious-smelling girl.

The next, she's off me, reaching for her skirt and pulling it.

I can't clearly see her expression in the dark, but it seems to be calm. Collected.

Shuddered.

Kira adjusts her dress and turns to leave without sparing me another glance.

My dick twitches on my thigh. In a daze, I look down on it. Now that she's not in front of me, there's enough light to bounce off the shiny surface of my cock.

Still wet. Drenched. From her.

She came so hard I'm pretty sure there's a wet spot on my jeans.

And she's leaving.

Wait. What the fuck? She's *leaving*?

I shoot to my feet, blood rushing back to my head. Calling out her name, I hurry to tuck myself in and take off after her.

She's inside the bar already. I open the door and go inside, looking for her.

Lost. The crowd's too thick. I took too long. There's no sight of her.

This girl just gave me the best sex of my life. Considering every time with her has been the best so far, that's fucking saying something.

She came. She fucked. She conquered.

And she left.

Goddamn it, I asked her to use me, but seriously? Come the fuck on.

The nerve of this fucking sexy chick.

Heart racing, I push through the throng, looking for her. She's not leaving me after what just happened between us. She doesn't get to ignore me again, not when both her ass and pussy are dying for more of this dick.

I pass the table where Ryan and Dana are at, but don't spare them a glance. Don't know if they saw me pass by, nor do I care. Something tells me Kira's either at the entrance or already through it, and I need to catch her.

I'm halfway across the bar when I see her. I was right. She's heading for the door.

Speeding up, I open my mouth to call her name over the noise.

Motherfucking Austin.

Fury unleashes as I watch him seemingly appear out of nowhere and follow Kira out the door.

I didn't even know that dick was here.

He won't stop showing around. Won't stop chasing after her. Doesn't matter that I made it clear I'm willing to fuck up my entire life by killing him, he won't. Fucking. Stop.

I make it to the door and rush outside.

Gone.

They're both gone.

I jog out to the parking lot, searching them out.

What has to be at least ten minutes later, I'm smack in the middle of the parking lot, my mind in tatters.

She didn't leave with him. She couldn't have.

I refuse to believe it.

Calling her phone is useless. She doesn't pick up.

Running my hand down my face, I try to calm my breathing and sift through the mental turmoil.

Impossible.

I stare off into the night, knowing that I have to track Kira down, find her. That I have no choice.

But I can't bring myself to move as the possibility that she just fucked me and is now with Austin drills through my thoughts.

I stand here and for the first time ever it occurs to me: How much fucking more of this can I humanly take?

TWENTY ONE

Kira

July 8th, 2015

I'm a mess. A complete and utter freaking mess. The summer is half over, and I'm miles closer to the loony bin than I was when it began. I don't know if I'll know my own name in six weeks when I move to Columbus.

Sex with Brayden has changed me. I've become a succubus. Insatiable for him.

Every single time I see him, my pussy becomes a whore on the prowl for his cock.

Anywhere, anyhow.

Who am I anymore? Not even sure I know the answer.

What I do know is that I can't stop. The fact that I don't want to is what scares me the most.

I've been on a Netflix binge all day, packing in one- and two-star scary movies. Anything to keep my mind off Brayden and the memories of hunting him down last week, or our time in the shower yesterday, or any time with him in the last month.

My choice of preoccupation is why I jump out of my skin

when the front door slams. I grab hold of my chest and turn to find Mom.

"Jesus, Mom!"

Her eyebrow quirks, and she looks from me to the freeze frame of a demon ghost on the screen.

"Scaredy cat."

"It's your fault. Why didn't you come through the garage?"

Yeah, pussy's disappointed. Only me, Ryan, and Brayden use the front door.

She sighs as she sets her purse down and toes off her shoes. "The damn garage door is acting up again." She falls down onto the sofa chair, sinking down into it. "I've asked Steven countless times to fix it. Guess I'll be doing it again."

"Why don't you just call someone to fix it?"

"Because he doesn't want to spend the money on it. He says he can do it."

My lips form a thin line. "Men are infuriating creatures."

She lets out a laugh. "When did my daughter get so wise to the idiocy of men?"

I freeze for a moment, not wanting to mention Brayden, then give a shrug and a laugh to play it off. "Well, I did grow up glued to two idiot boys."

That makes her laugh more and nod in agreement. "Very true." She stands up and stretches. "I'm going to go change, then work on dinner."

I wave at her and pick up the remote to restart my horror fest, but she turns back around.

"Oh, do you still have my earrings? I can't find them."

Oh, yeah, I wore her diamond earrings to prom. "Probably."

"Can you get them?" She gives me an almost sad smile.

"Your dad gave them to me."

I nod, popping up from the couch and make my way up to my room, not wasting any time. The few things we have left from my dad are precious, especially to my mom. I know she still loves him and misses him, despite remarrying.

Steve can't compare.

Mom's earrings are somewhere in my jewelry box. I took them off after prom, but forgot to give them back to her. I flip the wooden lid open and stare down. Sometime soon, I really need to go through this chaos. It's a tangled mess of shiny.

Every piece of jewelry I've ever owned is in here, and somewhere is my dad's ID bracelet. Ryan still wears his watch and keeps his money clip, with the same initials, somewhere safe.

It's been a long time since I've thought about him, my dad. I was so young when he died. The memories I have are faded, and some I'm not sure are even real or if they're made up by a little girl who was desperate to cling to her daddy. His photo sits on my dresser, and another with the whole family is on my desk.

Mom says Ryan's personality is a lot like Dad's.

She wore his wedding band on a chain for years. It was such a staple in her wardrobe, but I don't remember when she stopped.

Under a pile of knotted chains are the two white dots I've been searching for. I pluck them up, and sitting right beside them is my dad's bracelet.

I pull it out and rub my thumb over the letters, slowly covering and exposing his name—Robert Roth. Mom bought it for him for his birthday when they were still dating. He wore it every day.

Pictures and a few tokens—that's all we have left of him. And since moving to Ohio, we rarely get to see his side of the family.

Something else catches my eye in the box. Small pink beads and sequins. A flower-like shape.

A ring.

It was one of those cheap rings from a quarter toy dispenser.

It throws me back almost a decade. Me, Ryan, and Brayden rode our bikes down to the store. The boys were given a few bucks to pick up some snacks.

I was nine, and they were my whole world.

On our way out, I stopped to look at the machines. I didn't have any money, and I remember begging Ryan for some.

That's when Brayden came up behind me. He put a quarter into one of them and turned the knob. Out popped a plastic bubble case. He pulled it out and opened it up, taking the ring out.

I still remember how he smiled at me. The way he reached for my hand and slipped it onto my ring finger.

"Another pretty for the mermaid chest."

I smiled at him. "You mean another pretty for the kraken to steal from me, jerk."

He shrugged. "Krakens like pretty things."

"Oh, yeah?"

"Yeah." He nodded with certainty.

I eyed him. "Am I pretty?"

"I like you, don't I?"

"Yeah."

"Do I like you most of all?"

"You like Ryan most of all."

He chuckled. "Well, he's a guy, and they aren't pretty."

"Okay . . ."

"So, if I like you most of all, you must be prettiest of all."

I could feel my cheeks heating up, and I ducked my head before swatting him in the stomach. "Suckup."

It felt like my heart was going to beat out of my chest. Is it any wonder I fell in love with him?

I set it back down, then pick up the earrings and head out into the hall. A couple of steps in toward their room, I stop dead in my tracks.

"You're going out?"

"Yes. I'm meeting the guys to watch the Reds game," Steven says.

"Do you have to?" There's a sort of defeat in her voice that I don't like hearing.

"Is there a reason not to?"

"The garage door is still acting up. I was hoping you could fix it tonight." Defeat quickly turns to annoyance.

I don't know why I'm not moving, why I'm still standing feet outside their door.

"I told you I'd get to it."

"You've been saying that for weeks! I'm tired of not being able to use the garage."

"I've been busy, Sonia." Steven's voice rises, an edge to it.

"You've been busy for weeks! Every time I ask you to do something, I have to ask you again over and over and over for days for something that would take you five minutes if you would just do it!"

She's repeating words and talking fast—Mom's sign for *very* annoyed.

"Then why don't you do it?"

"Because I'm not your maid, I'm your wife! And I expect that you care enough and respect me enough to help out around here."

He lets out a harsh laugh. "Who pays all the bills around here? I do. Which means the house is yours to take care of."

What. The. Fuck?

My fingers curl up into my palm, nails digging in. I'm two seconds from bursting through their bedroom door and punching my stepdad.

How could he?

"Are you kidding me? *You* were the one who wanted to do that. Said you wanted to take away some of my stress. I had *no problem* taking care of my children and paying my bills before you came along."

"What is really going on, Sonia?" he asks with a huff.

"You aren't taking me out anymore, are you taking someone else out? Are you *fucking* another woman?"

"Don't be ridiculous!"

"Don't be? Something's changed, Steven, and don't forget, you cheated on your last wife with me. I know the signs."

"This conversation is absurd." Steven's voice grows louder, like he's closer to the door. "I'm going out with Tim and John. I'll be back later. Enough of these bullshit accusations, Sonia."

The door pops open, and so do my eyes. He stomps out and glances my way, jumping a bit.

"Shit." He looks back to the door where I can hear my mother trying to stifle her cries, then eyes me up and down. "What?"

I say nothing, do nothing, though I want to. We've never

gotten much past pleasantries, even after living in his house for three years.

He gives a little huff and makes his way down the stairs.

Halfway down, I step to the edge and yell, "I get it now."

He stops and turns back, looking up at me. "Get what?"

I stick my chin out and glare down at him. "Why he hates you so much."

"You know, Kira, I used to think you were a good girl," he pauses, lip twisting up to a sneer, "but you're just another girl competing for his attention, aren't you?"

I let out a gasp, then freeze.

"You said you were going, so leave, Steven!" Mom yells from behind me. I jump, unaware she's there.

He looks between us, then finishes his descent.

"I'm sorry, sweetie," Mom says, wrapping her arms around me.

"Why are you with that asshole?" I ask.

She pulls back, her lips set in a straight line, brow knitted together. It's her "I don't know look."

I slip the earrings into her palm and head back to my room, leaning on the door as it closes.

Once upon a time, Steve was right—I was a girl vying for Brayden. Now?

The beaded ring is still sitting on my dresser, looking at me. Times were easier then, and I almost wish I could go back to that innocence.

I've got my phone in my hand and I'm texting before I even realize it.

How did you live with the fighting?

It's a question I've wondered for years, and an answer I partially know. But it's also a question I don't notice I've actually texted to *Brayden* until he responds.

I had no choice.

No choice.

It's true. For him, it started when he was young, too young to understand.

But I remember when he was fourteen, when we ran away one night. He'd lived with it for years, the fighting, and I watched it beat him down and tear him apart. Shaped him, hardened him.

I remember, but I'd forgotten and I never, ever went through it until today.

Hot tears slide down my cheeks as I wonder what it was like for a little boy to go through that and worse.

I'm so sorry, baby. You shouldn't have to go through that. Ever.

No one should.

You did.

His response leaves me cold inside. *I'll kill him if he keeps putting you through that.*

He's always threatening to kill people because of me. Anyone else would be scared. I find it sweet, actually, despite the fact that I worry what would happen to him if he went through with it.

I guess that just shows how off we both are. We're slightly twisted. I think we both always have been in a way. We're not normal. Not by a long shot.

Fuck, that connection between us.

There's no denying it—it's still here. The broken pieces of us that bonded and brought us together aren't going anywhere.

I miss my best friend. I always, always miss him.

And I can't have him back. Because I won't allow myself to.

Brayden sends me another text. ***Promise me you'll call me if it gets too bad over there.***

My heart breaks.

I won't promise him that. There's no going back for me. I can't return to that place of soul-sick dependence. Not after all the times he brutally left me hanging. I text him back, feeling nauseous. I know he's offering his help and that it's coming from a good place, but I still have to shoot him down.

Don't worry about this. I've got this. Thanks anyway.

TWENTY TWO

Kira

July 19, 2015

I. Am. A. Whore.

The realization does nothing to calm me.

I'd always known I was horny. My entire life, the promise of sex had taunted me. I *lived* every moment waiting to experience passion.

This isn't passion. This is a sickness. A straight-up plague of epic proportions.

How many damn times do I need to have a dick before I actually start getting tired of it?

I can't stop looking. My God, those red swim trunks were made to obliterate my clit.

Correction: you are a whore for one man only.

Ugh, don't remind me.

Why can't I react like this to another man's dick?

Noooo. It's all about this one. It's always about this one.

Holy. Fucking. Shit.

It's twitching for me. Hardening right before my eyes.

Hunger.

Madness.

The existence of this man pisses me off so much.

I bite my lip and press my thighs together, feeling like I haven't had it in centuries. Fucking *centuries*.

"Kitty, are you wearing that to kill me? Your tits look fucking amazing in that bikini."

Blindly, I reach behind me, clutching at the kitchen island. "You're the one that wanted to hang out. In the pool." Why did I freaking agree to this again?

Oh yeah. He came over. My bedroom door was open. He left his open while he changed. I almost died as I watched. He came out of his room, nothing but those red swim trunks gracing his muscular, tattooed body, and asked me if I wanted to hang out in the pool with him.

When I agreed, he told me he'd meet me downstairs and gave me one last, hungry look before walking away from my door.

Viola. Kira changed at the speed of light.

To be fair, I think it's clear that my pussy took complete control. Shit, I don't even remember which bathing suit I picked out, but clearly it was picked out on purpose.

Brayden's standing at the door leading to the backyard, his smoldering eyes locked on my chest. He reaches down and adjusts his now fully hard dick, and I die a little more inside. "Get out here, baby. Before I decide to fuck you up on that island."

I barely check the urge to jump up on it and spread my legs wide. "After you."

With a deep sigh, he turns and heads out into the backyard. It's night out. I don't even know why he wants to go for a swim in the pool, but there's no denying it—as I follow him, all I can think about is him fucking me in that pool.

The sky still holds a few colors from the setting sun, but the darkness is setting in.

The pool glows in the backyard, thanks to the pool light. I expect him to head straight for the diving board; he doesn't. Heading straight for the pool's edge, he looks back at me before stepping off the ledge. He lands inside the waist-deep water, seemingly unfazed by how cool it is.

He drops down into the water, then rises back up, smoothing his wet hair back. The pool's light reflects off his wet body, fucking with me.

No man should be that sexy.

A man like that isn't meant to belong to just one woman.

There will always be too many offers. Too many options.

Even if I could forgive, even if I wanted to keep him, I never could. Not without inviting a buttload of misery into my life.

And there goes my mood.

Scowling, I walk to the edge of the pool slowly, second-guessing my decision to hang out with him the entire time.

He blatantly eye-fucks me with every step I take.

Doing my best to ignore him, I follow his lead and drop into the pool. I'm much shorter than him, so the water goes all the way up to my breasts. My nipples harden immediately.

Brayden licks his lips.

I glare at him. "All right. I'm in here. Now what?" I'm not hoping he lunges at me and presses me against the side of the pool. No, not at all.

He motions with his head to the steps a few feet away from us. There are four small stone benches built into the steps.

I follow him and sit down. He sits next to me, and leans back to brace his arms against the side of the pool. The move stretches out his upper body, enhancing every dip and curve, and I nearly go blind.

How the fuck am I supposed to get over him when he attracts me this much?

We sit in silence for a few minutes. He seems to be contemplating something.

I grow impatient. "Is this your idea of hanging out?"

A smirk tugs the corner of his lips, but he doesn't look at me yet. "You're never going to learn patience, are you, Kitty?"

"Don't make me regret agreeing to hang with you. Besides, you're one to talk about patience."

Laughing, he turns to face me fully. "Baby, I'll be the first one to admit that I'm seriously lacking in that department."

The nickname earns him yet another glare, and my cheeks heat up.

His smile widens, like he knows what I'm thinking.

No, what I'm *remembering*.

I still can't believe I called him baby.

And his reaction. Dear. God. His reaction.

I can't think about this right now. Remembering how we fucked each other behind that bar is the last thing I need to do.

Brayden's smile drops and my stomach along with it. He looks apprehensive. Like what he's about to say next is going to be the very last thing I want to hear. "I want to ask you something."

Yup, heading in a bad direction already. Shifting on the bench, I ask, "What?"

"First off, let me tell you that no matter what your answer to my question is, I'm not going to be mad at you."

Okay?

"I just can't stop myself from asking because . . ."

I raise my eyebrows. "Because?"

His jaw twitches. That ever-present pain floods his eyes as he focuses fully on me. "I'm sick from not knowing."

Life would be so much easier if his pain didn't affect me. If it didn't make me hurt equally as bad. "What do you want to know?"

"Did you leave the bar with Austin the other night?"

I'd had a feeling he'd seen Austin follow me out. He's been a bit distant, which should please me, but doesn't. My first thought is to deny him an answer and let him know it's none of his business.

Surprisingly, I can't do that. The urges to hurt Brayden are hitting me less and less lately. I'm still hurt and angry at him, but it's not the same anymore.

"I didn't leave with him." I can't stand the way his expression melts with relief. It makes me want to curl into his lap and hug him. "Is that the only reason you wanted to hang?" *To interrogate me?*

"No. Besides wanting to spend time with you, I want to see how you're doing."

"Meaning?"

He sighs. "Is the fighting still bad, baby?"

Oh. That. I shrug, staring down into the water. "I think your dad's cheating on my mom."

"I got the same feeling."

My head shoots up. Anger sends my heart into a tailspin. Hearing Steven's *son* confirming my suspicions only makes

255

them seem that much more true. "I think I'll kill him if he is cheating on her."

Brayden nods. "I think I'd help you. It would make what he did to my mom that much more pointless. If he was going to break her, the least he could've done was do it for a woman he truly loved." He realizes what he just said too late, his eyes widening and pupils expanding.

The irony of his statement hurts too much to contemplate on. After all, he once ruined me for a woman he claims to have had no feelings for.

Actually, there were a whole lot of women he supposedly felt nothing for.

I decide to ignore the awkwardness and pain between us. "What makes you say that?"

"The signs are all there, Kira. And, apparently, your mom is picking up on them."

"How do you see them if you aren't even living here anymore? You've hardly seen them together."

He scratches his chin, then nods. "I remember what they were like before the cheating. Or, before Mom found out about the cheating. Sonia wasn't the first and she won't be the last because that's who *he* is. He doesn't *do* love."

"Neither do you."

He shakes his head, his green eyes swirling with pain, much like they did years ago. "I don't do emotional pain. To me, that's all love ever was. If I didn't fall in love, problem solved. But there's a flaw."

"Flaw?"

He reaches out and caresses my cheek. "Love isn't a choice. It's a force, and there's nothing you can do to stop it. You can fight it, but in the end all you do is cause yourself the pain you were trying to avoid in the first place."

"So you had sex with all those women, and your father has also run through his fair share, both while claiming to love one woman . . . How does that make you any different from him?"

He turns from me, dipping his hand in the water and splashing it onto his chest. When he looks back, there's a sort of resolve I haven't seen in awhile.

"I couldn't be with you. First due to your age, and then because they got married. I was a horny teenager and didn't make the best decisions for me or for you. That's the power of hindsight. The correlation means nothing, because I don't want anyone else. I want to love you and you alone. I'm not a cheater."

"Yeah, right," I grumble and place my hand on the edge of the pool, preparing to get out.

Brayden stops me, grabs my chin, and forces me to look into his burning eyes. "I'd rather die than ever cheat on you."

"I'm not in the mood to fucking deal with this right now."

"You never are."

"Damn right. I don't owe you shit. Now let me go."

Clearly, "let me go" translates into "don't let me go" in his book. If I tell him to keep his hands on me, will that somehow register in his dyslexic brain and make him release me?

"I haven't been with any woman, except you, since I decided I was going to do right by you this time. Since the day I told Ryan I would wait for you, come to you at your eighteenth birthday." His eyes beseech me.

I shake my head, and his hand falls away from my face. "So?"

"Do you believe me that I haven't been with anyone else?"

"What?"

Brayden moves closer. When I try to look away, he moves back into my line of sight. "Do. You. Believe. Me?"

The cynical, injured part of me doesn't, but . . . "Yeah, I do."

His shoulders fall, and he sighs as the tensions leaves him. "I will not be with another woman now that I've had you. You're the best I've ever had in every fucking way. No one's ever owned me like you do. I can't even bring myself to think of another woman."

My cheeks heat up again, and I'm grateful it's night out. Even with the pool lights, I doubt he can see me blushing. "That's impossible. You're a *human* man. I'm sure you still have some sort of celebrity crush, at least."

He throws his head back and laughs. "Baby, celebrity crushes? Sure. Why not? But even if one of those chicks somehow appeared in front of me, I doubt I'd be interested in the real life deal. Hot women are everywhere, but in my opinion, I've got the hottest. The sexiest. The best girl in bed and out of it. Why the hell would I look elsewhere?"

Giddiness floods through my veins, overwhelming everything I consist of. It's the perfect thing to say. Something every girl on earth would *die* to hear. It's too good. Straight out of a dream. I know better than to believe that. He's just reeling me in. Hook, line, and sinker.

Nothing I tell myself penetrates through. I'm freaking *happy*. Happier than I've been in a long time. His compliment sucker-punches me in the gut. No man has ever had the power to make me feel this way with just a compliment. And I've received many, I won't lie.

I . . . Oh, God, am I still in love with this man? Like, in *in* love with him? Is that why his words have such an intense effect on me?

The world spins.

"Kira?"

"I've got to go." It's probably the millionth time I try to run away from him. Rounding him, I half-run, half-swim toward the stairs. I'm about to take the first step when his arms come around me from behind, hauling me into his wet body. The feel of him compounds with the emotions I'm struggling with. Hunger hollows out my soul, begging for him.

I struggle against him; he tightens his arms around me and lowers his head next to my ear.

"Let me go, Brayden."

"No."

"Why, damn you? *Why*?"

"I need to know." His breaths are harsh in my ear.

I grind my teeth, squeeze my eyes closed, and struggle to ignore how much I need him. "Know what?"

"What I just saw in your expression . . . I *need* to know it's real."

My first fear-fueled instinct is to deny. *Deny, deny, deny.* But I'm too tired to play this stupid game anymore. "Please, let go. Just let go of everything so we can both move on."

He exhales roughly and bites down into my shoulder. "Never. Do you hear me, Kira? Never."

This is why hanging out with him is a bad idea. Why I'm so stupid. I can't keep letting him convince me to spend time with him. Fucking him isn't helping to get him out of my system, so there's only one thing left to do.

"It's over," I tell him. "Whatever this thing between us

was, it's done. I'm finished fucking you. We had each other, multiple times. There's no need to continue."

His arms slacken.

I grab my chance and bolt out of them, practically flying up the stone steps and onto the deck.

That's where he catches me. I don't get more than a second's notice. My ears register the sound of splashing water as he rushes out the pool, then his hands are around my waist, spinning me around so fast I lose my footing on the wet deck.

Brayden catches me and slowly lowers me to the ground. He kneels on the first step, still inside the pool, and tries spreading my legs to make room for his body.

I beat on his shoulders. "It's over. Just stop already!"

He takes my hits and forces my legs open. Leaning into me, he kisses my cheek softly.

I hit him harder.

For each hit, he gives me another soft, soothing kiss.

"Why are you still here, damn it?" I want to cry. I've given this man so many of my tears during my life, and it's inconceivable that I have yet more to give him.

"Because I love you. I don't care if you don't believe me. This man right here can't breathe without you. Losing you is certain death for me."

"It'll never get any better. It'll always be this. Us fighting. Me reliving the pain. The never-ending fucking misery."

His lips graze mine. "It's not just misery and you know it."

"Ugh!" The worst thing in the world is coming against this level of stubbornness. I won't budge, and neither will he. "Don't you hear me? It's *always* going to be like this. I'll never be the sweet, innocent, stupid, naive, loving girl with you again."

"Okay. I'll take it. For the rest of my life, I'll take whatever you have to dish out. But I'm not going anywhere."

An entire lifetime of this? I can barely imagine it, so I don't know how he can be this accepting of the idea. My heart's breaking at the thought of never finding peace. Of constantly living in this crazy up-and-down rollercoaster.

How can it be so hard to push someone away when all they bring into your life is pain?

The fight leaves me, and I drop my hands away from him. Panting, I sit here, staring at him, trying to figure out a solution for our fucked-up situation.

"Just forgive me," he whispers, grabbing my hands gently.

"I can't," I whisper back.

"What do I have to do? Why can't you forgive me?"

"Because I don't *want* to." This makes me sound like the biggest bitch on earth, I know that, but it's true. "You don't deserve to just have a happily ever after with me. Not after all of that."

Forgiveness is a choice. A hard, brutal, up-hill battle. In order to embark on that kind of journey, a person has to truly want to do it.

Brayden lifts my hands up to his lips and kisses them like he'd kissed my cheek. "Then I'll wait until you feel like I deserve that forgiveness."

There's no more will in me to fight him. Not right now. I don't know if the anger will return tomorrow, but as of right now, I just don't have it in me. I'm drained. I relax, the hostility draining out of me. Letting my fingers curl around his hands, I stare down at our joined hands.

My gut tells me he's not the one, but my heart wants him

so damn bad.

Not just my heart. At the very least, I've come to accept that I'll always need this man's cock.

Giving in, I slide one of my hands out of his and place it on his wet shoulder. Just touching it is enough to make me tremble with hunger. He stays perfectly still, breaths speeding up, waiting for my next move. Looking away from his eyes, I rub his large, defined shoulder in circles.

I hear his deep swallow, and the sound of it turns me on so much.

Eyes on my hand, I watch it move from his shoulder. My fingers graze his clavicle before moving down to his chest. Beneath my hand, his heart is a wild war drum, a powerful beat that speeds up my own. I trace his nipple, loving the way his breath catches.

"You're fucking killing me here," he grits out.

Laughing under my breath, I let my fingers trail down to his glorious, glorious abs. There are no words to describe this six pack. I've kissed, licked, and bitten it many times, and I still can't get over how sexy his midsection is.

I reach the band of his red swim trunks. His cock is even harder than it'd been in the kitchen earlier. Hard and *pulsing* for my touch. Panting, I dip my finger just inside the waistband.

Like a fucking bullet, that man grabs both my hands and maneuvers me so I'm lying on my back. He does it so fast I barely have time to register my new position and then he's crawling over me, his movements slowing down to that of a deadly predator.

That large body moving over mine with all that barely held-back intent.

I swallow the lump in my throat, arching up toward him.

The cups of my bathing suit top are yanked to the side. I gasp at the feeling of air caressing my exposed nipples. Brayden reaches down and unties his trunks, pulling them down just low enough to slide his cock out.

I wrap my thumbs around my bikini bottoms and begin to push them down, but am stopped by his hands wrapping around my wrists.

His eyes are so dark and hypnotic. The vibe he's putting off has me shaking. There's no will to resist as he pulls my hands up above my head, pinning them with one hand as his tongue moves across my parted lips.

Eyes locked on mine, his fingers shove my bathing suit to the side and he slams his cock in. My back arches, every nerve firing off as my eyes flutter and I clench around him.

Fuck, how does this feel so perfectly right when everything else is wrong?

The concrete stings my skin as it bites in with each thrust. His hips slow down to long, slow strokes, his arm moving under my back, cushioning me. I draw my legs up, wrapping them around his waist, trapping him. Little whimpers mingle with his low moans that turn me on even more.

One hand is fisted in his hair, the other digging into his back, and I bite his lower lip, earning a single hard, deep thrust.

"Fuck, Kitty, you feel so fucking good."

With each rotation of his hips I lock on harder, pulling him closer, deeper. My breasts are mashed against his strong chest. The slower pace is agony. Every inch that enters until his hips meet mine drives me crazy because it's not enough and too much at the same time. When he pulls out, my thighs clench to draw him back in.

"Fucking tease," I whine.

His lips quirk up into that fucking smirk of his. "Just feel, baby."

A strangled cry crawls out of my throat as he winds me tight with each slow thrust.

My walls clamp down, and he lets out a long, low moan that makes me shiver. His forehead falls onto me as he pushes deeper.

Closer and closer, on the verge of spiraling out of control. Just a little more.

"Shit!" he hisses and freezes.

When my eyes pop open, there's light suddenly flooding into the backyard, shining through the windows and sliding glass door. I crane my head back in time to watch Steven's silhouette through one of the windows.

"Oh, fuck!" I push on Brayden's chest, forcing us up, and move the cups of my bikini back over my breasts.

My heart is hammering against my ribs as fear rips through me. Brayden is still inside me, not moving, his gaze locked on the wandering shadows in the house. I can see it in his eyes, kinda like Ryan. He's formulating a plan.

His eyes focus back on me and his look of dread morphs into a soft smile, followed by a tender kiss.

TWENTY THREE
BRAYDEN

Fuck.

Fuckity, fuck, fuck, fucking, fuck.

My dick is trapped in the hot, wet suction of Kira's pussy, practically begging me not to leave. And the parents just arrived home while I'm fucking my stepsister on the pool deck.

That makes my cock even harder. The shock of being found out should drain the desire from me, but somehow, it amps it up.

I want to keep sliding my cock in her, racing to get us both off before we're noticed.

Kira is frozen in place, staring at me, silently begging for direction. My brain is quickly formulating a plan, and step one is to pull my dick from the only place I want to be right now.

"Fuck," I curse under my breath.

Step two is to find a way to get us not only out of suspicion, but also upstairs. I move the strip of her bathing suit back over her juicy pussy that's calling to me and give it a little pat, then take in a breath as I slide back into the water.

My cock thankfully shrinks back some from the cool against the skin. It's a puzzle piece to get it back in *and* keep it from being too obvious I'm sporting a boner.

Kira's still not moving, and I push out of the water and kiss her lips. "Stay here, or find a way upstairs," I whisper.

Nodding, she slowly pulls her legs out and sneaks over to get a towel.

Guess upstairs it is.

My heart is hammering in my chest with each step I take, water sliding down my body. I grab a towel from one of the loungers and do a pat dry of my legs, then swing it over my neck to drape in front of me.

Dad hasn't seen my tattoos, and I don't ever want him to if I can help it.

I pull open the sliding glass door and step in. The air conditioning makes me shiver while the voice I hate echoes off the walls. He steps into the kitchen and jumps when he sees me.

"Brayden, you scared me."

"Sorry."

"Night swim?"

I nod. "It's nice and warm out tonight."

He glances around, his gaze scanning me as I run the towel over my hair.

"Is your sister home?"

She's not my sister.

I shake my head. "She went out with some friends."

He nods, still eyeing me. There's doubt in his gaze, and he's right, but I'm not going to let him know that.

266

"You're home early."

He shakes his head. "Somehow got out of the house and all the way to the restaurant without my wallet."

"That sucks." I hate our small talk. It's too forced. I also hate how his continued presence is keeping me from Kira.

"Steven, did you find it?" Sonia asks, coming around the corner from the direction of the half bath. "Oh, hi, Brayden."

I wave at her as she grabs onto my father's arm. "We should get going, we're already really late."

The lines around his eyes crinkle, and his lips form a thin and downturned line. "You think I don't know that?" he asks through clenched teeth.

There's venom in his tone and my first instinct is to put myself between him and her.

Sonia starts, but quickly recovers. "Have a good night, Brayden." She gives me a soft smile, then turns to *him*. "Come along, Steven."

I watch them walk into the garage, staying completely frozen as I listen both for the garage door to close and their car to speed off.

The adrenaline coursing through my body has me so jacked up that the only way I'm going to both calm down and alleviate the blue balls I've got going on is to go find my girl and finish what we started.

I take the stairs two at a time, rushing up to find her. When I get to the top, only the hall light is on.

"Kira?"

Nothing.

I check my room first, but it's empty, then turn the handle to her door.

She's there, sitting in the middle of her bed, wrapped in a

towel, staring at me with wide eyes that are glowing from her phone.

"Are they gone?" she asks, whispering.

"Yeah."

She leans over and turns on her bedside light. "That was close."

I nod. "Exciting, too."

"No, not exciting at all."

"You're telling me that the thrill of getting caught didn't turn you on just a little?"

She squirms where she's sitting. "No, it didn't."

Her cheeks are flush and as I dip down, I can almost feel how turned on she is. "I call bullshit."

"*You're* full of shit."

I chuckle. "Don't go denying it too strongly." I lean over her, pushing her down onto the bed, my lips running across hers. "Now, where were we?" My big toe bumps into something, causing a stinging pain to zing up my foot. "Shit!"

I pull back and use my foot to feel out what I hit. My toes catch onto the edge of what feels like a frame. Rising up on my straightened arms, I curl my toes around the object and drag it out from beneath the bed.

"Brayden? What are you doing?" Kira stares up at me with those beautiful, confused hazel eyes.

I tilt my head and look down at the ground.

The world shifts in an eerily familiar way.

Silence comes next, the type of silence that comes from deep within. I can't move as my eyes take in the picture at my feet.

A picture that's shredded, only bits and pieces of it hanging onto the frame.

It's the picture I bought her for her sixteenth birthday. The one I picked out after wandering around the mall like a lovesick fool, missing her so damn bad that I could barely breathe from it.

She sliced it up. Ruined it. And it wasn't something done in a single moment of destructive rage.

This was deliberate. The slice patterns are too cohesive not to be premeditated.

I don't know how long she's been cutting that picture up for, but she's done it many, many times.

Kira hasn't budged, nor has she tried to see what it is that I'm staring down at.

I have a feeling she knows very well what it is.

We're quiet for a few minutes. I can sense her staring at me while I continue to look at her handiwork.

"What?" Her tone is low but hard as stone, and there's a hint of mockery in it. "Don't tell me that upsets you."

"It does," I admit, looking up into her eyes. "But not because you did it."

"Why, then?" She's trying to keep her expression neutral.

"I did this, okay?" I motion at the floor. "You think I don't know what this is?"

Kira sits up a little straighter, almost like she's trying to get away from me.

I finally move, my hand snapping around her ankle to keep her in place.

She huffs, but doesn't try to break my hold. "In your opinion, what is this?"

"That's what I did to you."

The comment lays heavy in the air between us. I don't have

to explain what it means. It's so damn obvious that that picture might as well be a visual metaphor.

She cut that thing up just like I'd cut her up over the years. Systematically. One beautiful piece at a time.

I don't know what she sees in my expression, but sympathy flashes in her eyes. "Brayden . . ."

I attack.

There's no real thought behind the movement. Just this overwhelming ache in my balls, heart, my mind and my soul. This all-consuming need to imprint how much I love her into every part of her mind. I *need* to get this girl to a point where she feels how much I adore her so she'll never doubt it again.

Covering Kira's body with mine, I jerk her face in my direction and kiss her. I kiss her like the maddened, agonized animal I am.

At first, she tries to resist me, refusing to open up her mouth.

I'm not the only one that's been brutally reminded of all the pain I caused her.

I don't ease up, determination a heavy presence beating through my body. Softly, I suck on her lips, tease them with my tongue, all the while keeping her pinned on the bed by my much larger body. My hips start to rock in circles into her, a primal, instinctual movement that I have no control over.

Kira whimpers into my mouth, her lips falling open.

Groaning, I slide my tongue in, my eyes rolling back in my fucking head at the feel of her tongue. She lets me kiss her, but there's a restraint in her. She's holding back, refusing to give me everything she can.

Refusing to truly let me in.

270

I climb fully up on the bed and have to practically manhandle her legs open to make room for my hips. She doesn't fight me as viciously as I know she can, but she isn't making this easy for me either.

Fine. I'll fight for this just like I'm willing to fight for everything else.

Four swifts moves, and I have her bathing suit on the floor.

I jack off the bed long enough to get my trunks off, then climb back on the bed.

She's glaring at me, ready to strike, spit venom at me, and run away, but the moment I'm over her, there's a flicker in her eyes, giving me an opening. I cup the back of her head, fisting her hair as my other hand wraps around her waist, gluing her body to mine.

There's nowhere for her to go. No escape.

Nothing to do but take all that I have to give.

"Keep fighting me, because I'm not going to stop fighting for you." Her eyes narrow, full of hate, but that other emotion is also there. The one I saw outside.

It's the same emotion I've been seeing more and more of lately.

There's too much going on inside me. Feeling like I'm about to explode, I lean down and bite into the side of her tit roughly, desperate for an outlet.

I need relief. From this onslaught, from the choking frustration of not owning the woman I love the way I want to.

Only one thing can help ease it for now.

Pinning her thighs open, I find her pussy with my cock. She's so fucking wet I don't even need to prep her. One thrust of my hips and her glare is gone, eyes fighting to stay open as she lets out a moan.

It's fucking heaven inside her, and from the utter bliss on her face, I'd say it's the same for her.

I pull out until just the tip is at her entrance, and watch as the lust starts to fade and the anger creeps back in. Then I ram inside her, all the way, making her squeeze around me.

"Fuck," she whimpers.

Again.

Again.

Long. Hard. Deep.

Make her look at me as she feels everything.

I love this fucking girl so much that it obliterates my control over my body. Always. A few thrusts, and I'm fighting to keep my come in my balls. It needs to be inside her, where it belongs.

If I could give her my blood, I would. I'd give her my damn soul if she asked for it.

"This is everything," I growl, biting her tit again.

She cries out, arching, her pussy squeezing tight.

"What is?"

"This. The connection." Her pussy sucks me in, milking me with velvet, soft wetness that drives me wild. "What we feel when we're together. What we can be to each other."

She shakes her head, trying to deny it. "No. Not anymore."

My forehead falls against hers. "You feel it, I know you do."

Her legs wrap around me, heels digging into my ass and spurring me on. My body begins to shake as I hold back the come that's ready to fill her. Grinding my teeth, I slow down even more, but keep the thrusts hard and deep, desperate to shove the truth into her. "You. You. *You.* It's all about fucking you, Kira."

Her hips rise up to meet mine, each time a little whimper escapes her lips. "This is about fucking."

I slam my hips into hers, pinning her against the bed. She's writhing beneath me, the sounds coming from her begging me not to stop. I look into her eyes, but she turns her head. The grip I have on her hair tightens as I move her to meet my gaze.

"I fucked it up, but I'll fix it. I promise you, I'll fix everything. I love you, Kira. You're the only one I ever want."

She turns her head again, pressing her face into my shoulder. When I try to yank her back, she bites down, refusing to move. I hear her soft sob shortly after.

Then I feel her tears wetting my shoulder.

My chest on fire, I drop my head on her shoulder, hugging her as tight as I can while I continue to rock into her. Deep strokes, staying as close to her as I can. So strong, like I'm trying to fuck my essence into her.

I would if I could, just so I could make her see that the only thing I want is her. That the thing I care the most about in the entire past, present, and future of my being is her. That I can't exist without her.

She is my reason for living.

She is my heart, my soul.

My chest is so damn tight from everything, I can hardly stand myself with how much I *need* her.

"Please tell me you love me," I whisper into her ear. "One day. That's all I need."

Kira sobs harder. Her arms and legs lock around me, and we're nothing but a mass of human need and emotion rocking together. She won't answer me, and her cries are breaking me apart.

But she won't let me go. She's holding me just as I'm holding her—like she'll fall apart if I let her go.

"I'll wait forever, Kira. Just keep giving me this. Don't stop. We can't live without this, without each other. Don't take this from me. At least let me feel this."

She's shaking in my arms, but I'm to the point I don't know what from—the physical or the emotional.

"Don't stop," she says against my skin, her words almost breaking.

I'm not sure what she means, but I pull out just a little bit farther to rotate my hips more.

"I won't ever stop. I'll always love you, want you, fuck you until you can't stand coming anymore."

Her body tenses and she begins whispering my name over and over, making my balls draw up tight.

"Fuck, Kira. The way you react when I tell you . . . you can lie to me. It's okay. Your body tells me every truth I need to know."

A soft growl echoes in her throat and she bites down into my shoulder, as if trying to break through the skin. "Just shut up and fuck me, damn you."

Chuckling, I thrust just a little bit faster, giving her a taste. "This isn't fucking, baby. No matter how dirty or raw it gets. I'm making love to you. Because you're my girl."

Her pussy trembles, tightening more.

Another sob.

A frustrated moan.

Her nipples are so hard they rub against my chest with each thrust. Goose bumps break out all over her arms.

Yeah, she's my girl. She's not ready to admit it yet, but her body and soul know what her mind won't admit.

Sobs make her shake in my arms, but there aren't tears with these ones. It's raw, dry emotion, like there's no more tears for her to give but her body isn't done purging itself. She's on edge, so close to falling. To coming. To accepting all that I know and feel to be truth.

"Let go, baby," I whisper. It's taking everything in me to hold back from coming right now. "I've got you. I've always got you."

Her back arches violently, body locking up. Her head punches back into the pillow, exposing that gorgeous neck. Plump lips part on a silent scream.

Holy fuck, I can't get used to this. Can't believe how beautiful she is.

"That's it, baby. Right there. Come all over my cock. Suck it dry."

"*Brayden*," she whispers brokenly, tensing, tensing . . .

Her walls collapse around me almost painfully, pulling me in. The pressure is so intense that I feel the first burst of come being forced from me. An almost involuntary orgasmic pulse. Agonizing and mind-wiping ecstasy that pumps up my shaft, pouring deep into her.

Left without words, without thought as my body jerks on top of her in an intense pleasure I've never known before.

Her nails claw down my back, and I feel them cutting through skin.

Her teeth bite deeper.

I bite into her shoulder without thinking, fucking her, pushing her into the bed with my weight, pumping all the come into her I can.

Her nails dig into my ass, forcing me to keep going, taking

more from me than I can bear to give.

My back arches, one final explosions of sensation shooting from my cock and arcing up my spine.

Spent.

Emotionally.

Physically.

We're nothing but a heap of bodies mashed together. Hard breaths in sync as we come down.

Her pussy still pulses around me in sporadic jumps.

She says nothing.

Neither do I.

This silence between us, where there is nothing but our mixed breaths and the beats of our hearts, surrounds me. It becomes all I know, feel.

I'd give anything to hear the words from her, but right now she doesn't have to say them.

I live to tell her how much I love her, but that isn't necessary in this moment either.

Peace.

Finally, for the first time in fucking forever, I feel a sense of peace between us.

That connection thrums through her body and into mine, binding us.

Kira shifts under me, snuggling closer, arms tightening around me.

I refuse to move, even though I know I must be suffocating her.

We just lay here, intertwined, our breaths slowing.

I don't know how much time passes. It could be minutes, hours, or just a few simple seconds, but it's heaven. A tiny sigh as she nuzzles into me almost breaks me with relief.

The small touch of her affection is a soothing balm. I didn't even understand how badly I missed it.

Exhaling softly, I let myself melt further into her, basking in the complete certainty of this moment.

I can fix this.

I will.

Nothing on earth is going to stop me from making it up to my girl.

It's going to take some more time, but finally, I see the light at the end of the tunnel.

I can heal her—heal us.

Fuck all the stepsister-stepbrother bullshit. We're going to be together, and I'll finally be able to give this girl everything I have.

TWENTY FOUR

Kira

August 7, 2015

"Kira, do you want popcorn?" Marilyn asks, drawing my attention from my phone.

I blink at her and nod before stuffing my phone back into my wristlet. There was a new message from Brayden after he texted me when he got home. I told him I'm with my friends, that we're seeing a movie, and he sent me a mad emoji.

A mad emoji. What the hell?

The damn thing grates on me as we get our food and drinks, ready to see *Trainwreck*. I've waited all week to see it, and I'll be damned if he ruins the good mood.

With all the things to get ready for this month, this is the first time we've been able to hang out in a week, besides trips to the gym. I've been looking forward to this movie and the downtime and the *not* thinking about Brayden time. The latter is a near impossibility.

He's all I think about.

We grab our snacks and drinks and head to the theater,

Jenna hogging the big-ass bucket of popcorn. Once up the ramp, I stop and turn.

"I have to go to the bathroom," I say, holding my soda out for Ash to take. "Be right back."

"Okay, we'll save you a spot." Jenna stuffs a handful of popcorn in her mouth as they head for theater nine.

The time away gives me a few minutes to shake him from my mind. While by myself, I take a few deep breaths and focus on anything but him. It's a good hair day, and I'm looking cute, and I'm going to have fun.

As I step out, I look both ways so I don't run into anyone, but my steps falter. My head snaps back toward the lobby, to the force making his way toward me.

Brayden.

He's vibrating with an almost violent energy. People make way for him, and I can't tear my gaze away.

He's still wearing the dark blue polo for his job, all the buttons undone and open. To make him even sexier, he's wearing his glasses, which have always been a soft spot for me. However, they do nothing to hide the deep furrow of his brow or the intensity of his near glowing green eyes. Even his jaw is locked in a tense bite.

I'm nothing but a deer in headlights. A gushing wet deer, because the sheer want he's directing at me hits straight at my clit. Heat rages through me in an avoidable ripple, setting off every nerve.

He's a determined man on a mission, and no one will stop him.

I'm that mission.

The intensity is so strong it forces me to step back, flight or fight kicking in. My chest burns as I blow out an unsteady breath. He's feet from me, forcing me to withdraw more until my back is against the wall, but unable to run because my body is begging to let him do what he's looking for.

"B-Brayden, what—"

His expression stops me. One of his strong arms swoops around my waist. He doesn't miss a step as he pulls me with him, down the hall.

We turn a corner and he pushes me against the wall, lips smashing against mine. His tongue laps my mouth open as his body presses into me. Desperate need and pent-up desire drive him.

Devouring me with his mouth, and I don't want him to stop.

Leaving me a panting, breathless mess when he pulls away. The edge is softer in his eyes, but the maddening desire is tenfold. It's been days, and I missed this. Need this, despite the protests I tell myself.

I'm a dumbstruck doll, letting him do things to me where people can see. People we know—friends, enemies—are all in the theater tonight. I've seen them.

But I don't stop him from forcing my legs open or his hands as they grab onto my thighs, pulling my skirt up. His fingers sink into my ass cheeks, pulling them apart and pushing them together as he picks me up.

I don't fight it.

Not even as his hard cock rocks against my pussy, digging in, grinding me into the wall.

His hips keep thrusting as he pulls back and rests his forehead against mine. Every one of his muscles is taut, desperate for a release. Everything about him is rough, dangerous, and has me so freaking lust high I'll let him fuck me right here if he asks.

"I fucking need you, Kira. Now."

The temptation to pull out his cock is only stifled by the giggle of a group of preteens as they walk by. It's the proverbial cold splash of water I need.

The reminder that it's not safe here, that anyone can see us right now. That if we're caught, everyone will know. Fuck the fact that he's my stepbrother, which is a bad enough bunch of gossip and ridicule, but I don't want to have to explain to my mom that I was thrown in jail for having sex in public.

"Not here," I manage to say. "Too many people."

He pulls back, but doesn't let go. "Come with me."

When he starts to walk, I pull back against him. "Brayden, my friends are waiting for me. I can't go back to your apartment right now."

He shakes his head and grabs my wrist as he drags me down the hall. "I can't wait that long."

"So where—"

He cuts me off. "I know the manager. Told him I needed to borrow the break room."

We step through a door with an Employees Only sign and into a nondescript cinder block hall.

As soon as the door closes, I wrench my arm from his grip. "And does he know what for?"

His jaw ticks, and he adjusts his glasses. "Yes." The word is gruff.

"Brayden."

"He doesn't know who, Kira. Just told him I needed time with a girl."

My jaw juts out, and I cross my arms in front of me. "A

girl? So, this is a habit of—"

I'm cut off again as he curses under his breath and lifts me up and over his shoulder in one smooth move, making me yelp.

It takes me a second to gain my bearings, but he's already storming down the hall. All I can see are the back of his legs and the floor. I crane my head up, noting the camera sitting above the door we walked through.

It's not the only one.

Shit.

Someone's been getting a show. Someone we may know is watching us.

Someone who may know what's coming, because he's probably done this before.

Blood pulses through my veins in a growing, heated fury.

"Answer me, asshole!" I slam my fists into his lower back. "Is this one of you and your buddies' designated spot where you fuck girls?"

There were such spots. Over the years, on more than one occasion, I watched guys take different girls down secret corridors, much like this.

How many girls has he fucked here? How many girls are dying and have died to be whisked away like this to some secret spot?

"Not here," is all he says.

Not here? Confirming that he has fuck spots around town, but saying he hasn't done it here. I don't believe it, believe him.

A door slams open and we move out of the corridor and into another one, passing yet another camera. I flip off whoever might be watching.

"Put me down!" I begin to struggle against him, trying to push off him, but his arm is wrapped against my leg, hand latched only inches from my pussy.

"Calm down! Kira, I wouldn't take you to any of those spots."

"But you have them!" My voice is high, even to my own ears, a stupid lump in my throat. All the girls before me. All the girls that weren't me and should have been.

I hate it *and* the tears clouding my vision.

He heaves a deep sigh, his pace slowing, and his fingers release their death grip. Instead of letting go, letting me get away from him, his thumb begins to caress along my inner thigh.

Small, teasing circles that make my clit twitch in anticipation each time he swipes millimeters from my panties.

"I need you, the girl I love, right here, right now. No one's going to stop me. Not even you."

"So, I'm the fuckdoll this time?"

"No, you're the woman I want to do dirty things with over and over and over until the end of time. And right now, I can't wait. Not even another fucking second."

The fight in me dissipates. What he said turns all my resistance off, leaving me relaxed, pliant. Words I've always wanted to hear strung together in sentences that make me relent.

I use him, but he wants me. Not just to get off. Somehow, I finally get it—he really does want me for more than a fuck. He wants more than sex, even when I can't give that to him.

"Okay."

He caresses my thigh, almost in praise for giving in, and

turns his head to kiss my hip. The pace picks back up and he slams open another door, kicking it shut with his foot. The world spins again as he flips me back over and onto a small table in what looks like the break room.

His eyes are dark, heavy with the lust that drove him to search me out. The black frames surrounding them only accentuating it all.

"What happened to your contacts?" I ask.

He reaches up to remove them. "Ran out, waiting for new ones."

I shoot my hand out to stop him. "Leave them on."

He gives me a smirk and a nod before grabbing onto my thighs and dragging me closer. We're inches apart, so close I begin shaking in anticipation.

"So fucking demanding."

"Me?" Seriously? My eyes narrow. "You're the one that stormed in here and—*uhn*!"

His lips are on mine, the force bending me backwards as I arch up. There's a soul-sucking desire that breaks every defense down until my body is molded to his, arms around his shoulders pulling him closer.

Needing him closer.

My teeth scrape against his bottom lip, biting it as he rocks against me.

"Baby, I need inside you so badly. Need to come. Fucking fill you with me."

"Fuck!" I hiss out.

He needs to shut that dirty mouth up or I'll come before he's even inside me.

Reaching between us, mouth still on mine, I hear the zipper a split second before the hot head of his cock hits my pussy.

He pushes my panties to the side and shoves his cock in.

My eyes pop open, meeting his, then pleasure, lightning filled shudders move through me. His hips don't even pause, pumping, pushing him deeper until there's nothing keeping him from bottoming out with each stroke.

Everything happens so fast that all I can do is hang on and take all the pleasure he's forcing on me.

And I love it.

I'm beginning to doubt there is anyone else who can ever make me feel this good. Nothing is better than this. Forceful, possessive, taking and giving. High off the pleasure from being loved and wanted so much that he can't stop himself from devouring me with a level of passion I never believed existed.

Each pussy-stretching thrust only makes me greedy for more. Every time he pulls out, I practically drag him back in.

The table below me screeches each time he slams into me, scratching its way across the floor. My head is tucked into the crook of his neck, sucking the skin, marking him as my legs lock around his waist. Every available inch of my body is glued to his. I want to get deeper, closer.

I move down to his jaw. "Brayden." Our mouths are open, hot and heavy breaths exchanging between our open lips.

His hips rotate, slowing the pace, more sensual, and I let out a whimpering groan.

"Kitty?"

"More. Please, baby, I need more."

A growl reverberates from his chest into mine before he pulls me somehow closer. His arms lock around me.

Faster, harder, deeper. Each thrust wiping my mind more and more until there's nothing but his cock filling me, burning me. My nails dig into his shoulders as he leans me down on the table. One hand grabs hold of the edge, the other still secured around my waist.

The pounding increases in force, making my eyes roll back while I fist his shirt and arch impossibly closer into him.

"Oh, fuck, baby!" I cry into his ear, one hand grabbing his hair as I lose all ability to form words. Only sounds come out as my pussy squeezes down on him and everything in me tenses, drawing muscles tight, contorting my body.

Then everything breaks, causing me to shake beneath him as my pussy pulses and floods around him.

He's cursing above me, but it's lost as my brain is blasted of all thought. Just the pleasurable agony each time he thrusts, drawing my orgasm out as he finds his.

A few strokes with me coming and they become jerky. I can feel each pulse of his cock firing off, his body convulsing from the strain.

He falls down on top of me, our panting breaths in sync.

Neither of us move for a minute, both spent.

I can't stop from caressing his back and shoulders with my fingers. Light strokes that pull contented moans from him as he kisses my neck.

When he pulls back, his lips are soft against mine, almost reverent. The madness is gone, his eyes clear, staring straight into me. Still inside me, he caresses my hair, forehead resting on mine.

"Did you drive?" he asks.

I shake my head. "Jenna picked me up."

His lips move lightly against mine. "Can I take you home?"

"To Columbus? No." His lower lip juts out, and I can't help but giggle at the cute expression on his face. "But, you can

287

take me to my home. I'll even let you sneak in the shower with me once the parents are asleep, if you're good."

His face lights up, and he bites his lower lip. "I'm always good, baby."

I roll my eyes and slap his chest.

"Just imagine when you move to Columbus. Sex, sex, sex all the time."

He pulls out and steps back, walking over to the small sink and grabbing some paper towels.

"We have to have some study sessions where there is actual studying, otherwise I'm going to flunk out of school," I say.

He wipes his cock off, licking his lips as he stares at my pussy. "Okay, sex first, then studying."

"Why first?"

He puts my panties back in place, giving a little pat, letting me know he wants his come to stay right where he put it. "All that sexual tension in the air. How are we supposed to get anything done with that looming over us?"

"Sexual tension? Please! Just an excuse to fuck me."

He nods. "Kitty, I would fuck you every minute of the day if I could."

I reach up and caress his cheek before pulling his lips down to mine. Soft, sensual, spine-tingling bliss, and something I would never stop doing, because kissing Brayden is becoming my favorite thing to do.

"I have to get back to the movie," I say. I'm no longer concerned with it really, and I'm sure it has already started, but I don't need my friends sending out a search party.

Grabbing onto my waist, he puts me back on my feet and threads his fingers with mine, pulling me to the door.

"I suppose, if you have to get back. I can go hunt down our

brother."

"Ew, don't say it like that after we just had sex!"

He laughs, getting what I'm sure is the response he's after. Making fun of our situation does help a little with the reality of it.

When we get back to the door leading to the lobby, he stops and releases my hand.

"Thanks for attacking me."

"Anytime," His lip twitches up. "Seriously. Anytime."

I pop an elbow into his side and find I'm having a hard time leaving him. "You're such a jerk."

Leaning down, he gives me a kiss on the temple, along with a slap on the ass. "Have fun. I'll see you after the movie."

I sneak out the door, leaving him to follow a minute later. The halls have emptied some, but there are still a lot of people milling around.

The couple hundred feet down to theater nine seem to last forever, my heart beating wildly against my chest. I'm caught between wildly excited about our public sex and extremely terrified that someone who knew us saw what was going on.

The movie is already going when I enter, spotting my friends in the second row. I duck down to slide in next to Ashley.

"Where have you been?" she asks as she points to my drink in the cup holder.

I give her a blank stare and from the other side of her, Jenna starts laughing, but not at the screen, earning a glare from the person in front of us.

"You totally had a movie theater rendezvous, didn't you?"

I purse my lips and glare at her as I grab a handful of popcorn and try to make sense of the movie that started fifteen minutes ago.

While it helps me to ignore the giggles of my friends, it does nothing for the feel of thick liquid slowly pooling in my cheekies.

TWENTY FIVE

BRAYDEN

Yeah, I just came at her like a beast. Manhandling her until my dick was pumping inside her like a male ruled by the basic need to fuck my seed into a female of the species.

Only, it was really a shit day with pent-up anger and blue balls after she fucking teased me this morning. Walking into the bathroom as I was getting ready for work, wearing almost nothing, smirking while she stripped off her clothes and got in the shower, knowing I didn't have time.

How the fuck was I supposed to stop the cock busting through my zipper or the madness that took over with each passing minute of the day without being inside her? Did she really think not being home when I got there was going to help her cause? That because she was in public I wouldn't come after her?

Hell, no. My dick couldn't wait.

I'm calmer now, the testosterone no longer pulsing through my veins like I was jacked up on steroids or some shit.

"Better?" Dana asks as I sit down at a table a few blocks

from where Kira is to wait.

My brow scrunches. "Better?"

"Ryan said you were having a rough day."

I turn to my best friend and cock my brow.

"Don't give me that look." He knocks back his half-gone beer. "You're the fucker who sent me a text going off about my 'cock tease' of a sister."

Fuck. I did do that when replying to his text about meeting at Fox and Hound.

"Yeah, well . . . Better."

"Good. Now can you do me a favor and stop fucking telling me anything that goes on between you two below the belt? That's my fucking baby sister."

I nod. "Sorry, man. So, where's Craig?"

"Should be here any minute."

"It's been a while."

"He was at the graduation party, wasn't he?"

"Yeah." But I hadn't seen him since I abruptly stood to follow Kira on her trek to the bathroom that led to us both leaving. "How're the Reds doing?"

"Losing."

And that was how the game ended just over an hour later. I'd timed it out, my exit, making sure to head back to the theater right as the movie let out.

"All right, I'm out," I say as I throw down thirty bucks for my beers and burger.

Craig throws his hands up. "Dude, you just got here."

"Sorry, man. I told Kira I'd pick her up from the movies so these two can have their date."

Lies. They're beginning to flow. Soon, they'll be the norm. An everyday occurrence to hide our relationship.

Ryan quirks his brow at me but says nothing while Dana smiles up at me and waves. "Thanks. And be safe!"

Craig grabs my hand in a firm shake. "See you in a couple weeks."

I nod. "It's about time, isn't it?" I step back, giving a last wave and "See you later" as I walk toward the door.

Spending the rest of the night with my girl is exactly what I need, so I'm happy she relented and let me pick her up. Just me and her. Maybe we'll go to the basement and cuddle.

Yeah, cuddle. She promised me shower sex, and after sex, my favorite thing is my girl curled up next to and on me.

My fingers drum on the steering wheel, excited to pick her up, to just be able to chill with her the rest of the night.

There's a horde of people streaming out of the theater doors, making the drive through to park a near impossibility and grating on me. I scan the crowd, but don't see her. About a hundred feet away I spot a group of girls, two with identical hair, walking toward the other side of the building. It's then I see my girl's gorgeous hair that I'm suddenly dying to fist as I fuck her.

Looks like chilling is going to happen after my cock pops in her again. I'm still a bit pumped up from earlier.

Three break off just as a tall blond walks toward them, and I crawl another twenty feet, getting more frustrated by the second. My fingers tighten around the wheel, turning my knuckles white, because the blond stops at her and I can finally make out who it is.

The second I see him, my blood begins to boil.

Austin.

The exact moment I see he's stopped, standing next to Kira, my insides implode. I'm unable to take that he's near her, no longer able to contain the anger coursing through me.

Everything is bathed in red.

He's giving her those puppy dog eyes again, touching her, trying again to take her from me.

They're getting way more comfy looking than I can stand, but I'm still stuck in the droves of idiots who won't get out of my fucking way.

A gap finally opens, and I manage to get a parking spot about five in on the farthest aisle.

I'm out of my car as soon as it stops, pulling the keys out and stalking my way over.

There's only twenty feet between us when I hear the advocacy of death by my hands.

"I want you, Kira, please, give me a chance. Be my girlfriend."

I don't know what he's said to her before I got in range, but his pleas have my fists balled up tight, ready to lay him out in front of everyone. Make an example of him for all fuckers to see. Mash his face until he's an unrecognizable, bloody, pulp of a human.

She's *mine*.

I don't know if she responds, but I stop in my tracks as he dips down and presses his lips to hers. She jerks, and tries to pull back, but he's got her arms in his grip.

"What the fuck are you doing?" I scream so loud, so harsh, it startles everyone in a fifty-foot radius.

Murder pumps through me, ready to finish this once and for all.

They both jump. Kira's eyes go wide, while Austin's harden. He stands straight, chest pumped up, fingers curling into fists as well.

Fucker wants to have it out.

Fine by me.

I finish the gap and we're here again, facing off, foreheads pressed together while every muscle in our bodies is tensed, waiting to blow.

"Are you really this stupid?" I ask between clenched teeth.

"Brayden, stop!" Kira tries to push us apart, but neither of us is budging.

"Butt the hell out, Hunt," he snarls. "This is between me and her."

No, there is nothing between them, and my rage and anger toward him snap, unable to be contained. Pushing against his chest I move him just enough to swing my arm back and fly it forward, connecting with his face.

He falls down to the ground, giving me enough time to step over to Kira, who's staring down at Austin, hand over her mouth.

"Are you okay?" I ask, drawing her attention back to me.

She nods, her beautiful hazel eyes wide. Another look to the bastard on the ground, one who's getting up, and she pushes against my stomach.

"Let's go," she says, almost frantic.

She's worried, and rightfully so. Austin glares up at me, stretching his jaw. I don't even notice the ache in my hand.

"Come on, Brayden." She's still trying to get me to move, but it's not happening.

I pull my car keys out of my pocket and place them in her hand.

"Wait in the car."

She glares up at me. "What the fu—"

The breath gets knocked out of my lungs as Austin's

football moves come into play, digging his shoulder into my abdomen, a solid hit, sending us both down to the ground.

It's fucking hard, concrete scraping against skin, knocking my head at least once. There's no pause as we pick ourselves up. I grab onto his shirt and jab my fist into his ribs.

"I fucking told you to stay the fuck away from her!"

I don't care that we've gained an audience. The sounds of surprise and shock, some egging on, are the soundtrack of my hits connecting, beating into him the ridiculousness of his grievances.

My head is flung to the side as he gets in a blow. I can taste the tang of blood in my mouth, probably from a split lip. Everything is a bit blurry as I turn back to him, my glasses missing.

"She's an adult. She can make her own decisions," he says as if that's some type of argument in his favor.

We're grappling, stuck in a hand-to-hand struggle, both straining to gain the upper hand.

"Yes, she can, but you can't seem to take no for a fucking answer."

He sneers at me. "She hasn't told me to leave her alone."

Fuck! My gaze snaps to her as my chest fucking clenches at the worst time. She's horror struck, but staring right at me, not him.

The words may not have passed her lips, but she doesn't talk to him, doesn't hang out with him, and most definitely doesn't have his come inside her.

A strike to my abdomen brings me back to the assclown whose arm I have pinned in place with my own. I grab onto his neck, pushing him away as he gets in another few hits.

"She doesn't want you."

With all my force, I swing my fist around and land a punch right at his cheekbone. It sends him stumbling to the ground again.

He spits on the ground, painting the concrete red, and looks up at me. "You're just a pathetic asshole who can't get it through his head that he can't have his stepsister."

Rage comes over me again and before he stands back up, I lay him out again.

"You're the pathetic one who can't tell when a girl doesn't want you!"

He bolts up and charges again, digging his shoulder into mine, slamming me into the brick wall. The impact knocks the wind from me and the disorientation gives him time to pummel my sides. It takes more than a few ticks to get my breath and focus back to retaliate.

I swing my elbow into the side of his head repeatedly until he lets go.

He falls back, and we're grappling for control again,

"You're in love with your stepsister," he hisses at me. "Do you understand how sick that is?"

"Shut your face!" I scream, folding his arm under mine, trying to punch at his ribs again until I can get to his head. I need to knock the fucker out.

The crowd is far enough away they might not hear the shit coming out of his mouth, but he needs to stop, and I'm determined to shut him the fuck up. He doesn't get how what he's saying affects Kira, too.

I don't give a fuck anymore if people know how I feel about her, but Kira does, and I'll be damned to let this asshole put her through that.

A siren goes off and suddenly I notice the blue and red

lights flashing, bouncing off everything around.

Shit.

Austin lands another hit to my face, setting a ringing off in my head and my vision to blur.

Damn.

I swing blindly back at him and connect with something, just as the booming authoritative voice ends it all.

"Break it up, boys."

Fuck all that is fucking fuck.

We're both breathing heavily, reluctantly breaking apart.

"Get on your knees, hands behind your head."

"Kira, catch." I pull my phone out of my back pocket and toss it to her before complying.

I get a dirty look from one of the two cops, who eyes Kira. She looks at me in confusion, but there's something else in her eyes I can't make out.

"Call my mom," I say to her. The last thing I need or want right now is my father finding out what happened, at least not first.

The theater manager is there now, talking to them.

We're only on our knees for a minute or two, a spectacle for all to see. Whispered words, gossip in the making, but it's all about the fall of Brayden Hunt and Austin Reed's friendship. A few talking about protecting my *stepsister*.

It's all people we went to school with and a few curious onlookers.

One cop walks around and pulls my hands behind me, linking, caging me with metal handcuffs before hauling me up to my feet. This is a moment I never expected to happen to me.

A hand on my head as I'm stuffed into the back of the

patrol car.

I look back to Kira. Her brow is furrowed, my phone clutched in her hand. I want to kiss the worry from her lips, but I have a feeling the next few days are going to be full of nothing but shit.

The cops enter the vehicle. Out of the corner of my eye, I see Austin being shoved into another car. Of course they wouldn't put us in the same patrol car together. We'd probably fucking kill each other, even cuffed.

I focus on Kira again. The tears in her eyes kill me.

Fill me with hope.

I pray she can see how much I love her right now. I love her for not looking away from me during that fight, not even once. Love her for showing me how much she still cares by simply standing there, all of her defenses gone.

The cops talk among themselves, but I pay them no mind. It takes them a few minutes to start driving; I stare at Kira the entire time, and she doesn't stop staring at me either.

Her heart's breaking for me. She hates seeing me in this like this and it's obvious in her expression.

Finally.

I'm finally getting the real her. The raw truth. It took this, but for the first time in a long time, I'm once again sure.

This girl still loves me.

She wouldn't look at me the way she's looking at me now if she didn't.

I feel warm liquid leak down into my eye.

Blood.

Kira flinches, her eyes filling with tears.

The car pulls away from the movie theater, heading to the precinct. I crane my neck to keep her in my sight for as long as I can, my heart pumping wildly.

She still loves me. *Fuck*, she loves me.

I'm on my way to jail, and it does nothing to diminish the relief in my veins. I exhale slowly and let my head fall back on the headrest, my mind churning.

I hope she knows there's no going back now. Not after what she just allowed me to see.

As soon as I'm a free man again, we're going to finish this.

As soon as they let me out, I'm making her my girl once and for all, and there's nothing that can stop me.

TWENTY SIX
Kira

I want to scream. Break things. I want to tear out my own motherfucking hair.

My body is motionless. Incapable of moving. Signals fire off in my brain, commands sent to limbs that have no plans of responding.

Austin's face was destroyed.

So was Brayden's.

They almost killed each other, and it's all my fault.

Most girls would be thrilled that two guys fought over them to that extent. I'm just sick to my stomach. On the verge of a panic attack. I'm worried for Austin.

But I'm fucking *terrified* for Brayden.

Is he okay? Oh God, he needs stitches. What if he gets a concussion? Austin had pounded into his ribs really bad. What if something was cracked? Are they taking him straight to the hospital for a checkup?

I can't think straight. Can't function.

"Kira!"

I recognize the voice calling out to me, but I don't respond to it.

This is going to go on Brayden's record. There's no way it's not. I don't know enough about the law to even begin guessing how this is going to affect his future.

A hand lands on my shoulder, and I'm urged to turn around. It's Ashley. She's panting, blue eyes worried. Distantly, I wonder where the other girls are. I lost sight of them when Austin approached me.

"Are you okay?" Ashley asks me.

A sob catches in my throat and I shake my head. "M-my fault."

She squeezes my shoulder. "What?"

"This is all my fault," I whisper, trying to hold back the tears. My attitude pushed Brayden to this point. I should've been more upfront with Austin, done an even better job of pushing him away. Had I done so, he wouldn't have come up to me today.

Had I been kinder to Brayden, he would've never felt threatened by Austin's presence.

I pushed both of them to this point because I was too mentally fucked up to do right by either of them.

"Come on. I lost Lyn and Jenna in the crowd. We need to find them so Jenna can drive us to the precinct." Ashley grabs my hand.

I'm thankful one of us has a clear head. Without her, I'd probably still be rooted to the same spot.

We walk a few feet through the crowd. I see Ashley looking around for the other girls; my mind still can't focus past the back of her head. Brayden's keys and phone are clutched tight in my hands, along with his broken glasses that

I picked up off the ground during the fight. My hands are braced against my broken heart.

"There they are!" Ashley points at her sister about thirty feet away from us, and we head in that direction.

Is it me, or are most of the people we pass turning to stare at me? I know a lot of them, too. People both Brayden and I went to school with. Austin hadn't been too discreet when hurling his accusations at Brayden. I wonder how much of that did these people hear.

Probably all of it.

Even more probable? By tomorrow afternoon, this entire town will be aflame with gossip about how I'm fucking my stepbrother.

I'm going to care about this tomorrow. I'll be furious with Austin. He loves me, but he practically ruined a good portion of my life because he couldn't keep one of my most important secrets to himself.

I've hurt that man. More than I had any right to. I will hurt him again the next time I see him because I'm finally going to make it clear to him that we're never going to happen. Ever.

But that doesn't erase what he's done.

Right now, though, I don't care about any of that. I can't. Getting to Brayden, making sure he's okay, is all that matters.

"Yo!" Ashley calls out.

Marilyn and Jenna's heads snap in our direction. They jog in our direction, both of them staring at me worriedly.

I don't even know what the fuck to say.

"Dude," Jenna says. "I want to crack a joke about how fucking lucky you are, but your expression tells me it's not the right time."

I roll my eyes at her.

"We need to get her to the precinct," Ashley tells her, letting go of my hand. And that's all it takes for the four of us to start pushing our way through the crowd. We make it to Jenna's car and she presses the button to unlock the doors.

I open one of the back doors.

"You're fucking disgusting."

All four of us freeze.

There's no need to turn around and see who that is. I know. An old, familiar anger burns through my veins.

"Do us a favor," Marilyn sneers, looking like she's ready to storm around the car and start throwing punches. "Leave her the fuck alone before we make you."

"Oh? Is the little girl incapable of defending herself?"

That's it.

I spin around, my free hand fisting. Jennifer's malicious, narrowed eyes focus on my other hand, the one holding Brayden's phone and keys, and they narrow even further.

She knows this is his phone.

She knows it because this bitch has the bad habit of paying way too much attention to *my* fucking man.

"Do you want me to break your face?" I ask her slowly, calmly.

"You mean like Austin had to do to poor Brayden because of your slutty ass?"

Her arms are crossed. Her posture is entirely defensive. This cunt is preparing herself for my attack and she's afraid of it, yet she has the nerve to still goad me.

"When are you going to stop being the pathetic bitch who sucks every dick you can find while waiting, praying, *hoping* that Brayden one day looks beyond how cheap you are and falls in love with you?"

Everyone around me gasps.

Jennifer's mouth falls open, her face paling.

I meant every word. At this point, nothing in the world could make me take them back. So I stand here, eyes on hers, waiting for whatever comes my way after that statement.

The last thing I want is to be delayed from going to Brayden.

But so help me God, if this bitch doesn't realize in this moment that it's in her best interest to back the fuck off away from what's mine, I think I'm going to kill her.

The next round of cop cars that arrive will have to bring an ambulance in tow.

Jennifer snaps her mouth closed, practically shaking with her fury. "You have so much fucking nerve, little girl. Who the hell do you think you are? You're fucking your *stepbrother,* and you think you have the right to believe you're better than me?"

I knew this was coming, but my stomach bottoms out regardless.

She knows now. Without a doubt, she knows.

If the whole town didn't know before, I give it a matter of hours before it's all over the grapevine.

"She could be fucking the pope and every crack-dealing pimp within a two state radius, and guess what, whore?" Ashley sneers. "She'd still be fucking better than you!"

Despite everything going on, that comment makes me want to laugh.

I love my girls.

Jennifer glares at Ashley, but it doesn't take her long to

redirect her venom back at me. "What are you going to do when everyone finds out about you and Brayden, huh?"

My first impulse is to tell her, *"It doesn't matter, bitch, because I'll still be the one fucking that cock."* I want to spite her. Lay a claim on what's mine.

Something holds me back. Jennifer is studying me just as hard as I'm studying her. As if . . .

She's unsure.

This bitch is probing. Looking for proof. She's not as certain of what's happening between me and Brayden as she's pretending to be.

It makes me sick to my stomach, but I have to deny it. Lie. What's happening to Brayden is bad enough. The last thing we need to handle right now is the social implosion this would cause us if Jennifer decided to spread her suspicions.

God, I hate this chick. Now more than ever.

"You should try learning your lesson and moving on, *Jenn*. Maybe then you wouldn't be jealous of every girl he spends time with instead of you." I turn to get into the car.

"You're the only girl he spends time with!"

Damn right. Because right now, his body is mine. His heart, too. I just don't know how long I'll own both.

Not that it's going to stop me from going to him.

"You think you know the truth about me and him, but you don't know shit." It's the last thing I tell her. I'm the first one to get into the car. My friends take a bit longer, and I know it's because they're staring Jennifer down, daring her to say something else about me.

Eventually, Jennifer turns to leave, and one by one my friends get into the car.

"What a fucking skank." Marilyn slams the front passenger

door closed.

Jenna gets into the driver's side. "I want to slice her face apart. I know that's probably wrong of me to say, but I'd love to disfigure the bitch for life."

"It's not wrong. She has it coming." Ashley gets in last. "I don't know how we're going to keep her from running her mouth."

I don't either, and I can't think on it. Jennifer's gone. My mind fixates on Brayden once more and how worried I am for him. I don't know what possesses me to try looking into his phone.

Jenna's driving as fast as she legally can. When I swipe my thumb across the screen, I almost gasp with shock. There's no passcode. It automatically takes me to the home page, and the first thing I see is my picture.

It's a picture of me sleeping in his bed, my arms curled around one of his pillows. He caught me with the sunlight illuminating my features, and goddamn it, there's a smile on my face.

I'd probably been dreaming about him. About all the things he'd done to me the night before.

Heart in my throat, I open up his gallery.

Me.

Nothing but my pictures as far as I can freaking see.

In a lot of them, I'm asleep. In others, I'm awake and he somehow managed to catch me unaware.

Others are from my Facebook. He must have downloaded close to a dozen of my pics.

"Oh, Brayden," I whisper, closing my eyes as two tears leak out. Yes, it's his fault he engaged Austin. Both their faults that they couldn't control themselves.

I can't get out of my head how vicious the fight was.

They'd been two men out to truly kill each other. Had the cops not arrived, God knows what would have happened to either one of them.

I don't know what's going to happen to Brayden now. His father still pays for his college tuition. He's going to kill Brayden when he finds out about this.

More tears leak out.

Afraid one of the girls will see, I try to surreptitiously wipe away the tears and turn my head to stare out the window. It takes me a while to even realize I'm hugging Brayden's phone to my chest tightly.

Ashley rubs my shoulder soothingly again—her go-to comfort move. "Kira?"

"Hm?" I don't look at her.

"I know there's a lot of bad feelings between you and Brayden, that he hurt you really bad in the past. Even if you don't tell us the details, it's obvious."

I have no idea where she's going with this, so I remain quiet.

"Have you ever entertained the idea that . . ." She pauses, and I hear her take a deep breath. "Girl," she says in a low tone. "I think it's obvious you're still in love with him."

It's like being stabbed in the chest, but it's something I had already admitted to myself deep, deep down.

I still love that crazy, stubborn asshole.

It's why I'm in this car heading to him. Why I, without responding to Ashley, beg Jenna to go faster.

It's the most frightening, uncertain moment of my life.

For all I know, by tonight, the entire town will be filled with the rumor that I'm sleeping with my stepbrother.

By tonight, Brayden's father might ruin his life further and decide to no longer help him with college.

This might go on Brayden's record and fuck up a lot of his employment opportunities in the future.

I have no clue if I can forgive him enough to be good to him. If I can fix myself enough to stop mistreating him.

All I do know for a fact is that, yes, I still love him. And nothing, absolutely nothing, is going to stop me from being by his side.